IMPACT VELOCITY

Leah Petersen

Praise for Fighting Gravity and Cascade Effect

"...a deep look at what love is, and that it doesn't really matter who or what the person you love is, or is not."
— Chris Jackson, award-winning author
of the *Scimitar Seas* series.

"Cascade Effect is a beautiful novel, a worthy sequel that's profound on multiple levels."
— #sffwrtcht YA Report
(Science Fiction and Fantasy Writer's Chat)

"*Fighting Gravity* is like if Ursula K. Le Guin and Orson Scott Card could co-author a book without exploding. On the one hand you have the liberal and social science aspects of Ursula K. Le Guin, and on the other hand you have a character-driven story that isn't afraid to be entertaining."
— author Bryan Thomas Schmidt

"...a unique perspective on the interaction of the public and private spheres and the experience of "Othered" individuals cautiously guarding their sexuality with what little social capital they might hold."
— Science Fiction Research Association's
SFRA Review, issue 304

"...a character study of one man's journey from crushing poverty to the rarest heights of scientific achievement, from obscurity to notoriety, but it also includes themes of love, passion, and dangerous/dysfunctional relationships that form the story of Jacob's life."
—Left Hand of Dorkness

"Would that I was only going to say one thing about this book, it would be to praise it for getting me, a wholly unromantic heterosexual male, invested in a narrative which convincingly puts the Prince and the Pauper in bed together."

–Adam Shaftoe, reviewer; PageOfReviews.com

"Ms. Petersen has penned a riveting story that will take you on an emotional roller coaster ride and leave you breathless at the end."

– Readers Roundtable (recommended read)

"The science fiction is merely a backdrop for a wonderful story that becomes a wonderful love story. Ms. Petersen introduced me to a new universe and left me wanting more."

– Dana Gunn, reviewer; Unleaded: Fuel for Writers

"IMPACT VELOCITY lives up to its title in the best way possible...turning what you think you knew from the previous books on edge before giving the characters a spin."

– K.D. McEntire, author of *Lightbringer*

"Fighting Gravity is a sweet...love story; a fantasy for science geeks rounded out by the preciousness of an honest attraction and a careful courtship, and stuffed with the thrill of illicit encounters, and the horror of a world where serious social missteps come with serious consequences."

–Lambda Literary Review

IMPACT VELOCITY

Leah Petersen

Copyright © 2014 by Leah Petersen

For information, contact Dragon Moon Press: www.dragonmoonpress.com.

ISBN 978-1-897492-78-9

Printed and bound in the United States

Acknowledgments:

I suppose someday I'll get to the point where writing is easy. Since I haven't yet, I have to thank all the people who have helped me get to this point, the third book in my first trilogy.

Many and much thanks to Adam Shaftoe who coached me through the beta read on this one. No, you may not have him. I found him first.

I must thank J.M. Frey, who preserves my sanity and keeps me grounded.

Thanks go to Gwen, who quietly and without fanfare makes it all happen.

Thank you too to all my faithful readers, who remind me why I'm doing this.

Thank you to my husband, Shane, for all his patience in brainstorming with me, and to my kids for keeping me humble by not being the least bit impressed.

Finally, thanks must go to Gabrielle who has not only been an incredible editor, but who has been my mentor, friend, and partner in crime since the beginning.

Dedicated to Gabrielle.

Her contributions to this series, my writing career, and my life are far too numerous for me to ever adequately thank her for.

6 December 303, 5:30 Imperial Standard Time, 7 lbs 9 oz, Marquilla Sophie Cho Ayana Helen Dawes-Killearn

Ummm, yes. I was there.

I know. I was just looking at the record again.

You're such a sap.

So are you.

Me?

You don't hide it as well as you think you do.

iv^1

I always was better at math than I was at life.

Yet, somewhere in the year or two following Blaine's conviction and "execution," for all he had done to Pete and me, I found a peace with my life that I'd never expected. A lot of that time fogs and runs together in my brain, but I have a vague sense of how it happened. Not just one moment or choice, but a cascade of the events of my life, toppling to their inevitable conclusion. Chance, circumstance, choice, and just plain dumb luck, good and bad. I might have understood it better if there were a formula I could have used to confirm the results.

She came to us on a crisp winter morning. For the empire, a princess had been born, an imperial heir, a figurehead and symbol, a future sovereign. But, cocooned in the nursery, Pete and I met our daughter for the first time. The empire knew her as Princess Marquilla Sophie Cho Ayana Helen Dawes-Killearn, Heir to the Imperial Throne. We called her Molly.

We'd had a year of practice at parenting. Owen Blaine was two years old when he became my ward and moved into the Family rooms. Two was not an easy age, and I'd thought I was prepared for Molly, but the reality of parenting a newborn made my head spin.

She was tired, yet she didn't sleep, she wanted to eat, then she didn't, instead she threw up, and pooped more than should be possible for such a tiny body. Then she did it all again. Those days hazed into long hours of sleeplessness and confusion, the keen edge of despair when you realized you were powerless to make her happy, the utter frustration of matching wits or engaging in a battle of wills with someone who was three days old, and losing.

But there was something magical in her tiny perfection, the astonishing phenomenon of her contented little sighs, the way her mouth screwed up and then opened in a wide yawn from that little mouth. The utter bliss of realizing you'd figured it out, or just gotten lucky, and she was sleeping in your arms, a tiny bundle of the most important atoms in the universe.

I remember Owen, sitting in Pete's lap, his chubby little arms still dimpled at the elbows, cradling "his baby." He would stare at her so seriously sometimes, as if trying to puzzle out this mystery the universe had thrown into his family.

There were nights I was beyond exhausted but sat up long after it was my turn to sleep, just to watch the way Pete would look at her as he held her, brushing a worshipful finger over her chin and nose, smoothing her little eyebrows when she'd scrunch up her face in sleep. I knew I made Pete happy, that he treasured our marriage. But Pete with his daughter was another thing entirely. I couldn't have been jealous if I tried.

And thus for a while I had a family, and happiness, and peace. I tried to remember the last time I'd felt so content, so hopeful. Besides snatches of time in between the crises that defined our lives, I could only compare it to the three years Pete and I had been together when we were teenagers. So stupidly confident, so invincible, before the disaster that was my treason and the years we both paid for it afterward. For those first years, though, Pete had been quietly happy, and I had too. I had also been determinedly blind to anything I didn't want to see, believing that was the same as Pete's clean, uncomplicated optimism and hope.

I was no longer a child to believe something simply because I wanted it to be true. I had children of my own, and I had to be better than that for them.

I tried.

Did you want anything from the store?

What?

Did you want anything from the store?

You're not going to a store. You've never been to a store in your life.

I know, but normal people ask each other stuff like that. I wanted to try it.

iv^2

"D addy?"

It took no more than Molly's soft whisper to wake me, as if I'd never been asleep. She stood by my side in her nightgown and little bare feet.

"Owen's crying again."

I nodded and slid out of bed as quietly as I could, so I wouldn't wake Pete. Pete and I shared parenting duties as equally as we could, but Owen's bad dreams were my purview. He and I shared a lot of the same nightmares.

Molly took my hand and steered me out of the huge imperial apartment to her own room. This was part of the ritual, just as much as the fact that it was Molly who listened for the sound of Owen's cries, and came to get me, rather than allowing a servant to do it.

She never failed to hear him.

We walked in silence through her room, our feet making no sound on the deep carpet. Molly's room and Owen's opened into a shared playroom, and it was through there that she led me.

Owen was still asleep, but tossing and fretful, whimpers escaping his lips, his face damp with sweat and tears. Molly slid into the bed beside him, wrapping her arms around him, watching his face anxiously. I sat down beside her and put my hand on Owen's shoulder, squeezing gently.

"Owen?"

He jerked awake, his eyes wide and frightened before he focused on Molly's face, then mine, the tension draining from his rigid frame in increments of recognition and awareness.

"What was it this time, buddy?" I asked, quiet in the solemn dark.

His eyes filled with tears. "He was trying to take me away."

My hand tightened on his shoulder. "Who?" But I knew who haunted his dreams.

"Duke Blaine," he whispered, as if afraid that speaking the name too loud would summon him, like a genie in a fairy tale. His eyes darted back and forth, studying my face, begging for reassurance that his father really was dead, even though he refused to call him that. My heart ached. I knew the feeling only too well.

I stroked his damp hair. "It's okay," I said. "You're safe here. No one can take you. You belong with us now, and we're not going to let anything happen to you."

"That's right," Molly insisted. "He's dead and he's not your father anymore." I winced, grateful that he was looking at her. Aliana once told me I was a terrible liar. I wondered sometimes if that was the reason Owen asked this question again and again. Did he see the lies on my face when I talked about Blaine?

Because Owen's father was no more dead than mine had been when I was his age. Unlike Owen, no one ever told me my father was dead, I simply assumed and believed and never questioned. Owen questioned all the time, in the face of "proof" and reassurances on all sides. His doubts were a weight of guilt in my gut.

I'd told Blaine I'd be a good father to his son, and at the time I said it to needle him, to take a petty jab at the man who had done so much to hurt me. But I *had* meant it. Owen was the son of my worst enemy, but he was also Hera's son. She had been one of the best people I'd ever known. Her son would have a family.

"You're safe, Owen," I said, rubbing his back gently. "Go back to sleep. No more dreams tonight." Molly stroked his cheek with her little hand.

His eyes were already drifting closed. A past he didn't remember may have haunted his dreams, but he was remarkably trusting. When Owen's breathing returned to the even cadence of sleep, I stood and gestured to Molly to follow. She shook her head.

"Come on, Mol," I whispered. "Back to bed."

"I can sleep here," she insisted.

"He's fine, sweetie."

She just shook her head, watching me. Finally she whispered, "Please?"

I sighed, tucking the covers around both of them. I stooped to kiss her, and then kissed Owen's cheek as well.

"Goodnight."

"He okay?" Pete mumbled sleepily when I slid back into bed beside him.

"Yeah."

"His father again?"

I lay still, looking up into the darkness. "Did we do the right thing?" Pete turned to face me.

"With Owen?"

"With Blaine. Maybe you should have just executed him. Maybe it's not fair to Owen for it to be like this. So...unsettled."

Pete was quiet. "Unsettled for him, or for you?"

"I think he knows. Why would he keep asking otherwise?"

"He's only seven. It's not like it was with your father. Owen's father is a shadow that follows him everywhere he goes. There is no one in the empire who doesn't know who he is and what his father did. Of course he keeps asking. The man is too much a part of his life, and he still would be, even if he was really dead."

"He's eight in a few days." That was an important distinction to me. I'd lost my own father at six, and had been happy to see him go, but at eight I'd lost the rest of my family. Pete had already pointed out that my losses at eight were what put me where I'd been at fifteen, when he'd met me. But, illogical or not, eight frightened me. And there was a lot of time between eight and fifteen. I had a bad track record with childhood in general.

He was right, and yet it took a while for me to sleep again. Years ago Pete had faked Blaine's execution and sent him to a secret labor camp. He did it for me, because I'd asked him to. I thought it was justice, sending Blaine to the same hell he'd once arranged for me. Sometimes I could acknowledge to myself that it probably wasn't justice, but revenge. And I discovered I wasn't proud of that at all.

Laudley should be here tomorrow.

I thought he wasn't coming until Thursday.

He's arriving earlier than planned.

Lovely. Can't wait.

iv 3

Among the many things Blaine's treason had accomplished was a sort of renewed breach disguised as a reconciliation between the Grand Duke Laudley and the emperor. Decades past, the Grand Duke, who was the most powerful man on Torrea other than its king, had fallen out with the then-emperor, Pete's grandfather, over the emperor's choice of wife for his only son.

Pete's father married a young duchess from one of the oldest noble lines on Earth rather than Grand Duke Laudley's sister. The Grand Duke had sworn not to speak to the emperor again, and so he hadn't. Not that emperor, or the next, or even Pete, until Blaine was convicted of treason and Owen was given to me.

Hera had been Laudley's daughter and Owen was his grandson. If he wanted a relationship with the boy, he had to deal with us. I resented his presence in our lives, but there was no good reason to restrict his access to Owen, other than our complicated history with his family. Laudley was a stubborn, spiteful bastard, but then, so was I.

It was sunny the morning Laudley arrived, ahead of Owen's eighth birthday. He was presented to Pete and the royal family in a private garden in our wing of the palace. The children had been chasing each other, squealing with laughter, but they went abruptly quiet when he entered, sidling up beside us and watching him with solemn eyes.

Laudley bowed to Pete. "Your Excellence." He faced Molly, her hand clutching Owen's as if the Grand Duke meant to take him from her. "Your Highness." He bowed and Your-Highnessed me as well, and then faced his grandson.

"Hello, Owen."

"He's Your Highness, too," Molly said.

I hid my smile. "Molly, this is Owen's grandfather. He doesn't have to do that."

"Well he has to do it for me, and I'm Owen's sister."

"Enough, Molly," Pete said, mild and calm but allowing no argument. She glared at Laudley.

The Grand Duke only laughed. "Suspicion serves her well, Your Excellence. In her position, it is valuable. It might protect her from cultivating unsuitable companions."

A long, stunned silence followed. "Perhaps she will learn to guard her tongue, as well," Pete said, "as some still have not."

No one moved. Owen was watching the faces, Pete then Laudley, back and forth.

I turned to Molly. "We're going to have a picnic in the woods today. Why don't you pick the path?"

She flashed me a grin and, with one last scowl at the Grand Duke, pulled Owen along with her into the hallway. We followed; the silence was deafening.

We took Molly's favorite path through the woods in a private preserve kept only for the nobility. Pete preferred to keep our outings with Laudley to semi-public areas, rather than in the exclusively Imperial sections of the palace and Imperial City. For him, I suppose, it was pragmatism and setting precedent. I was simply happy about the reminder that Grand Duke Laudley, for all his connection to Owen, was not part of our family.

Not counting our constant compliment of guards, Pete and Molly took the lead, Owen and Laudley behind, and I trailed at the end. I wanted to be able to watch Laudley and Owen. I told myself it wasn't jealousy, and that was probably somewhat true. I didn't feel like Laudley was competition for Owen's affection. Owen never seemed comfortable around his grandfather, but that too was its own burden of guilt. I didn't want to be the one to alienate him from what family he had. Most of Owen's relatives were dead because of me in one way or another.

When a pair of squirrels sped out of the trees and down the path ahead of us, Molly and Owen took off together at a run, paced by their guards. Pete sped up a bit, keeping them in view as much he could, and I would have too, but the trail here was narrow and Laudley was ahead of me. As Pete and the children drew farther away, Laudley slowed, until I was forced to slow down myself or come level with him.

That seemed to be his intent, because he paused. Unless I stopped, I'd run right into him. I approached as slowly as I could, hoping he wasn't trying to walk with me. I had no such luck.

"It is a lovely day," Laudley remarked.

"Yes. Perfect for a picnic." I picked up my pace. Maybe he only wanted to let me go ahead, so he could keep an eye on me.

"I understand you are going to have Owen tested on his eighth birthday," he said.

"Like all the other children, yes."

Laudley made a rude noise. "The common children."

"Noble children take the year-eight tests as well."

He waved that away. "The lesser nobles. Perhaps that is the misunderstanding. The truly noble families are not subjected to such—" he seemed to search for the word, "classification. The imperial family certainly is not. Nor any royal family. No one in my line has been tested in the three hundred years since the empire was established."

"That's probably for the best," I muttered, but not quietly enough. Laudley sniffed.

"Jacob, I understand that this is not your sphere and you still are not familiar with our ways. But it is simply insulting to subject a child like Owen to the common 'testing' that others require to place them in their positions in life. His position is clear."

"This is no attempt to belittle, or 'classify' him, Duke Laudley. It can be a valuable tool for understanding him. Cognitive and aptitude tests may show us an area of talent we haven't seen in him yet, and help him discover where he excels. It's no different than any other test he's given by his tutors."

"Grand Duke."

I cut him a sideways glance, surprised and amused that he should try to correct me on the use of his proper title when he'd made no attempt to use mine.

"Owen's education is none of your concern," I said.

Laudley stopped and faced me. "You truly do not understand, do you? Do you imagine you are really a prince, or even a duke? You are nothing. An unclass. Less—you are not even that anymore. You think he made you something but really he made you nothing at all. Do you think anyone believes otherwise? You have no right to even speak to my grandson, much less dictate his path in life."

I stared at him and almost laughed. "I've never taken you for a stupid man, Laudley. But I'm willing to reassess the conclusion. Do you really think you can insult me like this and get away with it? Do you imagine the emperor won't care?"

A smile quirked at his lips. "So you have learned to speak to him, then? I was wondering."

I flushed hot and cold. "I'll be the first to admit I've done some idiotic things in the past. I learn from my mistakes."

"So I see." He looked away as if unconcerned, nodding toward Owen. "He looks more like his father every day, do you think?"

I took a deep breath. One of the things I had learned from my mistakes was how to control my temper. Sometimes. The importance of doing so, at least. That time, I managed it. "I see more of Hera in him."

Laudley paused, and I got the impression that it was difficult for him to pass that comment by. That he was able to do it made me think less of him than I did already.

"He has his father's eyes," he said. "I wonder what his father would think to see him now? He would not have allowed the testing. Of that I am certain."

"Blaine is dead. I'm his father now."

Laudley turned to me with a wicked grin. "You really believe that?"

A cold chill washed over me.

"I mean I'm the one raising him," I rasped.

He huffed an indifferent noise. "It is odd that none of the family was there to witness his father's death. That is very strange, even for a private execution." He paused. "Perhaps Owen was there?"

"He was two. No, I didn't take him to see his father beheaded."

"Ah. Who did witness that, exactly? The records are so unclear. Were you there?"

"Of course."

"And did he die well?"

I turned to face him. "You saw the recording. That's all there was to see. He was executed. He is dead. Owen is all that matters now. This family, the emperor, Molly, Owen, and me. And none of it is any of your concern."

A wicked smile spread across his face. "Oh, Jacob. So much of what you believe you hold in your common, unclass hands is not what you think it is at all."

"I didn't give you permission to call me by name."

At the tone of my voice, one of the guards behind us stepped closer, her weapon held at an angle that wasn't threatening but suggested she was terribly interested in what was going on. Laudley didn't even look at her, or reply.

"I'll overlook the disrespect this time," I said. "See that it doesn't happen again."

Owen's decided he wants to learn the trumpet now.

I thought it was the violin?

This is in addition to, not instead of.

That's rather a lot for a child, don't you think? That would be three instruments at the same time.

What's the harm in letting him try?

I wonder where he gets this talent from.

I'd rather not think about that.

iv 4

I stepped up the pace after that, closing the distance between us and Pete. The children still ranged ahead but never completely out of sight, and never far from their guards. So it all seemed to go in horribly slow-motion when a too-loud "pop" rang out ahead of me and Owen recoiled, his face stunned and pale, his eyes finding mine as a red stain spread beneath his fingers where he clutched his arm.

I was thrown to the ground, startled exclamations ringing out around me, Pete's voice, Molly's.

"Owen!" There were heavy hands holding me down.

"Please, Your Highness." It was the voice of one of the servants. My head servant. The man whose name I suddenly couldn't remember at all. The one who wasn't Jonathan. "The guards are securing the area."

"Molly! Pete!"

"They appear to be fine," he said. Nef. That was his name. He was crouched over me, enough that he could see what was going on while still shielding me with his body as the guards were doing. I felt a ridiculous moment of relief that it wasn't Jonathan putting himself in danger for me. And then anger at myself both for feeling charitable toward the man who had betrayed me and for even thinking about him in this moment.

"What about Owen?"

Nef was scanning the area with sharp, efficient movements. "The medic is there. She doesn't appear to be overly concerned."

A hammerblow of memory kicked me in the stomach. Hiking in the woods around the IIC. The pop of a weapon discharge and the sensation of impact in my arm. The slow spread of fire in my body, the overwhelming pain.

"Are you sure? It could be izellium—"

"I'm sure that's the first thing she considered, Your Highness," one of the guards said.

Yes, of course she would. These were the empire's best. Maybe he'd never even feel it...

"Come," she said. "We're moving you all together."

We stayed low to the ground, with the guards clustered around us like a living wall, herding Pete, Molly, Laudley, and me together into a clump around Owen. I fell to my knees at his side. He was pale and trembling, but patiently enduring the medic's attentions. Even though I was looking for the worst, he only appeared to be scared, not hurt.

"Guardsman?" Pete said. She nodded.

"I've administered all the preventatives and antidotes, just to be safe. But—" She ripped away a piece of Owen's shirt. It was red, the color of fresh blood, and yet when Pete touched it, he frowned. I followed his example. It wasn't even wet. We looked at Owen's arm. It was whole and unharmed, only slightly pink where the shirt had been torn away.

"It doesn't hurt," Owen said, meeting my eye with a directness that I realized was meant to reassure me. He did the same to Pete. "I'm not hurt."

Sam, our guard captain, came crashing through the underbrush nearby, hauling with him a boy I vaguely recognized. He was a little older than Owen, ashen under his dark skin, tears tracking down his face. In Sam's other hand was an odd looking gun. Several of the guards made exclamations of relief, even startled amusement.

"All clear," Sam said. "Stand down, everyone."

Pete and I stood almost at the same time. Sam stopped in front of Pete, holding out the weapon.

"Paintguns."

We just stared at him for a moment. Pete glanced at the boy, back to the weapon, and then his eyes closed in relief. He exhaled a long sigh. "Paintguns." He put his hand on the boy's shoulder. "It's all right, Gannon. You're not in any trouble. Who were you playing with?"

Even as he said it guards were returning with other boys and girls in tow. Paintguns. They released a chemical that stained like blood but disappeared entirely when a tiny emitter was activated at the end of the game. Paintguns.

"Some of us," the boy was trembling so hard it was difficult to understand him. "Plu and Aaron and Indira and—"

Pete squeezed his shoulder and the boy's words cut off as if with a knife. Pete's voice was soft, reassuring. "You were just playing paintwar with your friends. You didn't even know anyone else was out here."

The boy shook his head hard, tears flying off his jaw.

Pete smiled at him. "Were you having fun?"

Gannon nodded uncertainly. "We were winning, I mean, until—" his voice choked off and he started to sob. "I'm sorry, Your Excellence. We weren't trying to—" The tears choked off anything more and Pete pulled him close, hugging him briefly.

"I know you weren't. It's just fine, Gannon. Everyone's fine and no one's in trouble." Pete looked up at Sam. "Will you see the children back to the palace? Make sure everyone understands that no one is at fault."

Sam gave him a crisp nod. I turned to find Owen standing beside me.

"I think I lost this time, Gan," he said to the other boy, grinning shakily. "First time you beat me." Gannon coughed out a strained laugh and gave him a weak smile in return as Sam steered him away.

Molly crashed into Owen, gripping him around the waist. "No one's allowed to hurt you!"

He hugged her back, petting her hair. "Yep. Nothing to worry about."

Have you had Laudley's gifts scanned and searched thoroughly?

Oh, Jake.

iv5

Owen still had dinner with his grandfather that night. It had been a scare, that was all. Still, Owen and Laudley dined alone. Pete, Molly, and I did as well.

While Pete and I lingered over coffee, Molly played in our room and I told Pete about the conversation with Laudley. Keeping things from Pete was something I'd learned to stop doing before it had completely destroyed our lives, though it had been a close call.

Pete sat in silence for a long time, staring out over the ocean, his face pensive. He shook his head. "It just doesn't make any sense. What can he think to accomplish by openly insulting you? Unless he thought you wouldn't tell me? But even that isn't the only thing that could hurt him. You're the one who has the final say in Owen's life, not me. You could practically cut him off from Owen without even mentioning it to me."

I cracked a smile. "Like you wouldn't have noticed."

He returned a grin. "I've always noticed. It's just that now I would ask you about it."

The events of our early marriage had taught him a few things too. He'd always known a lot more than I'd ever told him. But he tried to respect my choice about how much to share. Maybe that worked in other marriages, but he was the emperor, and that changed everything.

He'd essentially let me control the marriage all that time. That made sense on some level, considering the power differential between us and the fact that he literally could dictate my life in its entirety. But it wasn't safe for either of us for him to tiptoe around my feelings and—even I could admit—my temper and unreasonable reactions.

"Maybe he just wanted to get it out of his system," I said, "things he's wanted to say for years. Maybe he feels safe enough now. Owen's old enough to want to preserve the relationship for his own reasons and ask me to let him keep seeing Laudley, even if I try to keep them apart."

Pete cocked an eyebrow. "You think he would?"

"Not really." I spun my coffee cup slowly on the saucer, watching its revolutions. "Though I think that's more due to temperament than whether or not he cares for Laudley."

"Do you think he cares for him? He never talks about him."

I frowned at my cup. "That may be temperament too. He's smart enough to pick up on the undercurrents." I looked up at Pete. "He knows we don't like Laudley, no matter how much we might pretend otherwise. I think, no matter how he feels, he won't talk to us about Laudley because he doesn't want to hurt our feelings, any more than he would ask *not* to see Laudley, so as to not hurt *his* feelings."

Pete sighed. "I agree." He smiled sadly. "It's never going to be easy for Owen, is it?"

I shrugged. "Someday it might. Laudley can't live forever." I gave Pete a wry grin. "And when he's of age he'll have a place and power in his own right. A duke living independently is in quite a different position than the minor son of a convicted traitor living as the ward of the emperor's husband."

Pete took my hand. "Whatever happens, we'll deal with it. We'll do the best we can for both the children and that's a lot." He chuckled. "Whatever game Laudley's playing, it can hardly be worse than The Patriot was."

I shivered.

I couldn't sleep that night. Pete managed it just fine. He'd spent his whole life as a target and had learned the trick of tuning that out and moving on. When I thought about it, I'd spent most of my life as a target too, if for different reasons. The child in Abenez, the unclass at the IIC, the emperor's lover, the condemned traitor, and the pardoned prince and consort. I still didn't know how to sleep through the fear, though.

Molly stayed with Owen that night. She refused to let him out of her sight. Long after the rest of my family slept, I stole quietly into Owen's bedroom and sank into the armchair, watching the synchronized rise and fall of their breaths, Molly's little arm draped over Owen's neck.

Jonathan would have tried to give me one of Dr. Heinriksen's remedies, and then stood silent vigil with me when I refused.

But there was no Jonathan anymore. He'd been betraying me to Blaine, all the years I'd believed he was my friend. If I'd waited for imperial justice, Jonathan would have died a traitor's death. I exiled him instead, without even asking Pete. That was years ago now. For all I knew he was dead already. I shouldn't have cared anymore.

But it was a hole in my chest, an ache in my throat, the need to simply have him there in times like this, when he'd always been there before. When I'd trusted him.

It would have been easier if I could hate him.

I got up and stood by Owen's bed. I kissed his forehead, and Molly's cheek, the last of the babyfat still clinging to her face. I missed the simplicity of those days, when we were too busy with diapers and scraped knees to worry about their future.

It was coming fast now. Whether I was ready for it or not.

Did you ever give me that list of things you wanted from Prussia?

Jonathan should have it.

Nef. I meant Nef.

iv 6

One of the things that had suffered from the chaos of the early years of our marriage was my work. I felt at times like I was losing my identity, the man I had been slowly subsumed in the roles I had taken on. But what bothered me the most was when it distanced me from my work.

I have always been a physicist. It's something I knew about myself since before I knew what word to give it, before I knew it would ever mean anything more than that I saw the world in a way that no one else I knew did or could. And that I would never fit into Abenez, as if there were such a thing as "fitting" a slum and a life of abject poverty. As if anyone deserved or should reconcile themselves to such an existence.

But at eight, I'd been taken away from Abenez, to a place where they knew what it meant to see the world as I did, and where they gave it not only a name but a purpose, a dignity, a freedom of sorts. Had I been anything but unclass, things there would have been so different.

I had a feeling Laudley's objection to Owen taking the year-eight tests was as much about the changes Pete and I had been making over the years, and how the tests had figured into them, as it was about Owen himself. We'd taken it slow, both of us having learned caution, but in the five years since The Patriot had been brought down, we'd made subtle but meaningful changes in the social structure of the empire.

As a child I'd never questioned the structure of the empire. I'd barely known of life outside the all-consuming confines of poverty and hunger. We were what we were, we didn't have the time or even a reason to question it. As if it could ever be different.

Even when my life changed and I was in a position to study the politics and economics, I'd alternated between pretending the class structure didn't matter and railing blindly against it.

Eventually I'd set about to make changes, but I delegated to my oldest friend Kirti the understanding and analyzing of it. Somewhere in the time after her death and the destruction of Abenez, I'd realized I couldn't remain as ignorant or as distant as I wanted to be.

When I set out to finally understand why such poverty and suffering could exist in the face of so much wealth, power, stability, and technology, I discovered nothing that the experts didn't already know.

It was deliberate. The premise of our society was built on enforced stratification by wealth and class, the two having become practically synonymous. The unclass lived in cold and hunger and suffering because they were intended to. Stability was built on the back of predictable and entrenched social and civic interactions. Ambition and opportunity led to conflict and confusion. The empire didn't allow such things outside of clearly defined parameters.

It had been designed and put in place in a time when the people were too scattered and war-weary to object, when in fact they clung to the promise of peace by any means. Once that was accomplished, it was too well engrained, the propaganda too well swallowed and internalized to be changed.

And Pete had always known that.

It was the beginning of the worst time of our marriage, the time when the danger wasn't attacks from outside but strife at home. I was angry, he was defensive. We fought, a lot.

We survived it, we were stronger for it, and things in the empire began to change.

Twice already the parameters of the classes had been changed so that the low and middle classes were broadened, and the unclass reduced. At the same time, job classifications had been restructured so that many more jobs were available to the lower classes, with higher pay. The restrictions on newly up-classed families had been reduced. We hadn't touched the nobility, and the high class only fractionally, but it was a start. A very, very good start. Especially because the backlash over the first changes had been manageable.

The popular reaction to the second round was more severe, but brief. People in general were already forgetting that things hadn't always been the way they were. Though I doubted those who had been moved out of the unclass would ever forget.

I was between projects at the moment, or so I told myself. In truth, I was puttering around with some tangents to my earliest theorems. I'd had Owen in the lab with me, showing him the work that had produced the Dawes Laser before I was nine.

He was at other lessons that day, and I was well into my work when Molly entered the lab. She climbed up onto the stool beside me.

"What are you doing here, Mol?"

She propped her elbows on the table. "Papa said I could come see you."

That was odd. Pete respected my work hours the way I did his. He normally would have asked.

"Why did you want to see me?"

She sighed, as if the weight of the world was on her shoulders. It made my chest tighten to realize that, in some ways, it already was. "Are you going to let them take Owen?"

I blinked. "Am I going to let who take Owen?"

"Owen's grandaddy said when he turned eight you were going to make him take a test and maybe people would take him away then."

I clenched my jaw against the first reply that came to mind. There were words in it I didn't want my daughter to learn yet. "Owen's grandaddy misunderstood. No one's taking Owen anywhere. No matter what tests he takes or doesn't take."

"So Owen's grandaddy lied?"

"He misunderstood, that's all." There was a different answer I wanted to make to that.

"So no one is going to take Owen?"

It wasn't like Molly to need the sort of reassurance Owen did. She usually took you at your word and was content.

"What's the matter, honey?"

"Owen's grandaddy said since you weren't born here you didn't always understand how things work." Her voice got quiet. "They came and got you."

Ah. She'd known that already, but maybe Laudley had connected the dots for her. I put my arm around her.

"I wasn't born in the palace, so things were different for me as a little boy. When I was eight and they chose me for the IIC, my mommy didn't get to say yes or no. But it's not like that for you and Owen. No one can do anything to either one of you without getting permission from me or Papa, and they're not going to get it. No one's going anywhere. This is our family and that's not going to change, ever." I squeezed her close. "Why don't you go see what Papa says about that?"

She gave me a satisfied nod. "I already did. That's what he said. I just wanted to make sure you understood too."

I snorted, amused, and kissed her on the top of the head before she scrambled off the stool and out of the room. I shook my head. Owen was such a wonderful part of our lives. Why did his relatives have to be among our greatest trials?

Do you really have to meet with Naganika today?

Why?

Molly's just come up with some crazy scheme for a scavenger hunt and she wants us to come.

Later? I've put Naganika off twice now because of Molly's crazy schemes.

So he should understand. I'll apologize to him for you.

Because I can't?

Because it's more my fault than yours. And I like him. I'm glad you picked him.

iv.7

T he next day was Owen's birthday. Pete's and Molly's birthdays were imperial holidays, but the celebration at the palace held for Owen's birthday was hardly any less spectacular. The children spent the morning on the palace lawn, with every noble child who could manage to be there. They rode exotic animals and ate tiny little creature-shaped cakes so intricately crafted they almost looked real.

Lunch was to be a formal affair. The family and those privileged to eat at the head table with the emperor gathered together in one of the sitting rooms just outside the great dining hall. There was always a fair amount of simply waiting for these things, though others called it socializing or politicking. I occupied myself with the kids. I supposed someday I would get good at this part of the life of the emperor's consort, but seven years of marriage had only taught me to tolerate it and to play nice.

When we entered, Laudley was already there. He'd cornered Pete's Head Minister. Lord Naganika had held the position for almost a year already, following Lord Sifer's retirement.

"But clearly it is unsustainable," Laudley said. "You have seen that yourself."

"I don't agree," Naganika replied, clearly trying to maintain the pretense that he was only chatting with Laudley while giving his attention to the frail Lord Sifer.

Laudley cast a look over his shoulder and saw me. He gave me a malicious grin. "Ah," he said to Naganika. "Naturally you support the emperor's policies. Loyalty is admirable. But do not forget you are also his advisor. Considering other points of view is not disloyal and may make you more valuable to him."

"I think, in this instance," Naganika said, his voice level, "the emperor's position is quite clear and not up for debate."

Naganika caught my eye and smiled.

I liked Naganika. Lord Sifer had handpicked and trained him. I'd first met Sifer at the IIC, right after I had condemned Director Kagawa to Resettlement with a few careless words. I'd been afraid of him then, but over time I realized that his forbidding manner was a natural reserve refined by long practice at disguising his reactions. He'd served Pete's grandfather, and father, and now Pete for more than two decades. By the time he'd pronounced my sentence at my execution-turned-beating-and-exile, I was almost sorry I wouldn't be seeing him again.

He no longer lived at the palace, but he had come for Owen's birthday, as he did for all the important events. Naganika was his protégé and was rarely far from him when Lord Sifer was visiting.

Naganika nodded politely to Laudley and left Lord Sifer's side to greet us. After the proper bow to Pete and Molly, he ruffled Owen's hair. "Heard you caused quite a stir yesterday," he said with a grin. "No injuries, I see. Not even a paint smear."

Owen gave him a shy smile. Naganika turned to Pete. "I spent a good bit of my morning reassuring Lady Efe that Gannon wasn't in any trouble with you."

"And was she reassured?" Pete asked.

"I think so."

"Keep an eye on that, please."

"Of course, Your Excellence."

Pete gave him a nod of approval before he stepped away to speak to Lord Sifer. Molly slipped her hand into mine. "Daddy—"

It was the sharp intake of breath and odd grunt that made me turn. I looked at Pete. He had the most peculiar expression on his face. Surprise, and a slight grimace. A guard stood close behind him, his gaze on Pete intense, focused. Pete jerked forward, his eyes going wider, his mouth open. His gaze came up and met mine. He looked more confused than anything else.

His knees gave out and he slumped against the guard. As he slid to the floor, suddenly I understood. I flew across the room in time to catch his head before it hit the floor, just as other guards were tackling the man behind him.

With Pete's body angled across my lap, I could feel the cold horror of the blade sticking out of his back, and the liquid warmth against my leg. "Pete?" I breathed, afraid to move, to even speak too loud.

His eyes rolled up to meet mine. He drew in one painfully ragged breath and was still.

Hands were tearing at me. "Your Highness!" rang, echoed, and rattled about in my ears even as my head spun with the sudden movement as I was hauled to my feet.

"No!" I shoved and fought against my captors. "Pete!"

"Please, Your Highness." Sam's deep voice rumbled in my ear as he clapped a hand over my mouth and others crowded me on all sides.

"No." The word was stuck behind Sam's hand and I tried to jerk away, struggling against his hold, fighting him, this, something. Wanting that simple denial to do something more, mean something more. To take back what was happening.

"I'm sorry," Sam said. Blinding pain stabbed through my side and my vision went black as the world slipped away from me.

I love you.

I know.

The familiar sights of the emperor's sitting room whirled past and away, giving way to the simpler lines behind the door to the servants' corridor.

"Here's Owen," a voice said. I struggled to right myself. I was moving but not under my own power.

"Daddy!"

I jerked hard against the hold on me at the sound of Molly's voice.

"She's fine, Your Highness," Sam's voice vibrated within my head. He was carrying me like a baby.

"Put me down."

"One more minute," he said, not slowing or changing his hold at all.

"What's going on?"

"We made it look like you were attacked too, so we could get you away. We've got the children. You're all safe now, and you'll be out of anyone's reach very soon."

I tried to focus bleary eyes and looked down to see that my shirt was soaked with something the color of blood. It was drying, itchy on my neck.

"All safe?" I said. "But not Pete."

He took several long, uncompromising steps before he answered.

"No. Not the Emperor." I wanted to bury my face in his chest like a child. "I'm sorry, Your Highness, they caught us by surprise."

36

"But you got me."

"They went for him first."

Of course they had. The days of someone trying to kill me before Pete were in the past. When had things changed so much that someone was willing to assassinate the emperor?

Pete was dead.

I was set roughly on my feet, jarring the thought away for all of half a second. The room spun around me as I got my balance. My head hurt a lot.

"I used a stunner to knock you out," Sam said. "I'm sorry, they're not designed to be gentle. You'll likely have a headache for a bit unless the doctor's got something for you."

"I've always got something," Dr. Heinriksen's voice cut in. I focused on her with a rush of relief.

"Doctor," I breathed, grabbing her arms. "Pete?"

She lowered her eyes as if looking for something in her bag, though I could see she already held the patch in her hand. She avoided my gaze again as she pressed the pain patch to my neck below the ear. I grabbed both of her hands, thin and bony now, the skin sagging and soft.

"Doctor!" I squeezed. "Pete?"

With a sigh she met my eyes. There were tears in hers.

"I'm sorry, Jacob," she whispered. "The knife was infused with acid. There was nothing left for me to repair."

The room spun around me and I felt Sam's thick hands on my arms again, holding me upright when my knees would have given out.

"Daddy!" Molly rushed at me, burying her face in my leg. Owen was right behind her. He went pale at the sight of me. I searched the eyes all around me, frantic to know why.

"Here we go," Sam said, producing a small silver object. He activated it and there was a faint buzz, my skin going up in goosebumps. I looked down to see the blood smeared all over me shimmer and disappear. I stared at Sam. "Paintguns," he said.

Owen's face melted with relief and he rushed over, throwing his arms around Molly and me together.

"What's happening?"

My throat closed around the words. *They killed Papa. Pete's dead. Pete's dead.*

My stomach heaved but somehow I didn't throw up. Dr. Heinriksen's voice was soft. "The patch should prevent nausea as well as pain. There's also something there to help keep you calm, for now."

I looked at her, wide-eyed. *Calm?*

"Until we get you out of here."

I stared at Sam.

"They were trying for you too," he said, uncompromising, "and if two of my guards were assassins then you're not safe here at all." Bitterness was icy and sharp in his voice. "You have to get away from here. At least for now."

"How are we going to do that? Someone just killed the emperor! You think someone who can do that can't keep me and the kids from getting out of the palace?"

Dr. Heinriksen's voice was calm and matter-of-fact. "Yes. The arrangements for getting the Imperial Family to safety in case of emergency are independent and separate from day to day security measures."

I blinked at her. Somewhere in my head I knew she'd just said something simple, but my head felt thick and sluggish. I looked around. It wasn't a room, but a garage. There were no windows, no decorations, only an odd transport. Plain, simple, unremarkable, and small, it looked nothing like any of the imperial family's large and luxurious vehicles.

"It's the emergency escape plan," Sam said. I stared at it.

Sam stood by the transport. "It's locked against entry; only you and the children can open it or get in."

"But—"

Sam's hand closed around my upper arm, gentle but firm, steering me into the transport. "Please, Your Highness, there's no time for discussion."

Owen gripped my hand the moment I was on board.

"Wait—" But the door closed and I met Dr. Heinriken's eyes for the last time. The lines of worry on her face were my last glimpse of that life.

I was in the toilet when I heard that the emperor had been assassinated.

iv ⁹

My face slammed into the unyielding poly. Warm blood trickled into my eye. One of them shoved me against the wall and jerked at my pants. I pressed my face to the cold surface and closed my eyes. The opened cut on my brow stung. I concentrated on that, not on what he was doing.

I wasn't even sure which one of them it was. Not that it mattered. When he was finished he grabbed a fistful of my hair and slammed my face into the wall again for good measure.

You don't care. I fell into the mantra. *It doesn't matter.*

A second one planted his hand in my back, pushing me into the wall so hard I could barely breathe.

You don't care. It doesn't matter.

"That's enough."

I cringed at the voice even as my knees went weak with relief. They'd stop. Did it matter who rescued me? I still hated that it was her.

"Yeah, yeah." That voice was Bait, which was a ridiculous name for a man his size. The man at my back didn't stop. "When we're finished."

"I think now would be better," Kafe replied, level and deceptively calm. The man behind me stuttered. The pressure eased up.

"We just started," he snapped.

"And now you're finished. You've had enough fun with this one for a while." A dangerous edge was in her voice and the man pinning me moved away. I snatched at my pants and fastened them quickly. There was nowhere to go except past Bait and his friends or Kafe and the men flanking her. I put my back to the wall and watched.

Bait and Kafe faced each other like wrestlers. She was less than half his size but more than a match for him in all the ways that counted around here.

"Find a new toy," she said. "You've been playing with this one a little too often. We've noticed."

They stared each other down for a long, tense moment before Bait jerked his head at his men. "Come on. We're through here."

Kafe watched him go before she turned to me, a predatory grin on her face. "You've been popular lately."

My jaw tightened. "Jealous?"

She laughed. "You're welcome, by the way."

I scowled at the floor, wanting so much to ignore that and walk away. It was bad enough that she'd seen and had to save me. It just made it worse, having to be grateful to her, though it wasn't as if I had a choice. Here there were no choices, just compromises and lesser indignities. Antagonizing her wasn't worth what little satisfaction I might get out of it.

"Thank you."

She smirked. "Try to stay out of trouble, Eight." She drew out the name they'd given me as if she thought I still had the energy to care about that anymore, much less hate it the way I once had. "I won't always be around to protect you." She laughed to herself as she walked away, followed by her goons.

The moment they were gone I bolted for my cell, not quite running. Running drew attention. She was right; I'd been a popular target lately, and I wasn't going to rely on her assurances. I wanted a wall between me and the rest of them.

I found my cell and triggered the transparent door. That was one protection Dead End allowed us. We could lock out other inmates, if not the guards. I sank to my cot, laying back and staring at the ceiling.

Four cells down, a woman lay on her bed, crying into her blanket. She was new. I shoved the thin pillow over my head, trying to block out the noise.

"You're Eight, right?" Her voice was clogged and hitched from crying. I tried to ignore her. "You're that duke, aren't you?"

"No."

She made some sound that might have been a choked laugh or genuine choking. I didn't care.

"They're calling me Lore." I didn't move or reply. "Hey, I know you can hear me," she snapped.

I threw my pillow blindly in her direction. It made no sound against the invisible force field wall. "You'd better learn to shut up," I said. "If they think we're banding together they get mean about it."

"What?"

"Us. The targets. There's an order to it, believe it or not. A rotation. But things don't go so well if you try to make friends with any of the others. Keep to yourself. You're safer that way." I turned my back to her. "And you'd better learn not to cry. That really pisses them off."

I'd been five years at Dead End. When I'd arrived, I stupidly believed my rank would still protect me. Instead it made things worse. Everyone wanted their turn putting the former noble in his place. I thought I was going to die. That I'd be beaten and raped until finally someone went too far. But after a couple of months, inexplicably it stopped.

Someone explained to me later that the inmates had their own set of unwritten rules. We were stuck out here, discarded and forgotten, consigned to manual labor until the day we were spaced. This same group of people would be together for a long time. They maintained a sort of equilibrium.

There were three people who were untouchable. The three gang leaders, and their chosen favorites, ruled with a dedication and consistency to rival any palace official. Everyone else beat or got beaten, took or got taken as they could, or couldn't avoid. But no one bully or gang was allowed to get too strong or too greedy. Those of us firmly at the bottom of the hierarchy were protected to some extent. We could be targeted only so often and for so long before someone would step in and put a stop to it. For a while.

But even without the violence, the other inmates still made my life a living hell in every way they could, small and large. I was afraid all the time, I hid in my cell every chance I got, and I barely slept.

At some point it began to taper off, a year, maybe more. I wasn't a novelty anymore. I fell into my place among the small fish and the victims and went on with what passed for my life, always dreading when it would be my turn again.

We were being supervised in the showers. I was taking the opportunity to use the toilet while there were guards on watch, and was just about to leave when Hix came running in.

"He's dead!" he shouted. "The emperor. They killed him!"

I stopped, shocked rigid. The emperor? Impossible. With all of the ambitious, empire-changing schemes The Patriot's other followers and I had come up with, assassinating the emperor was never even discussed. Who could? Who *would*?

One of the guards cut a glance at me, his face set and hard. I threw up my hands in front of me, falling back a step.

"I had nothing to do with it." He didn't look terribly convinced, advancing on me. My voice came out in a squeak. "Do you think I'd still be here, like *this*, if I could even *communicate* with the people who could do something like that?"

"How did it happen?" Enten asked. He was a sickly color, his face bleak, and I wondered why he cared. The emperor wasn't exactly popular around here.

"Don't know," Hix said. "Just overheard it in the captain's office."

One of the guards shook him. "You've got no business spreading tales. You probably didn't even hear it right. No one could—"

He was cut off by the shriek of the emergency alarm. The guards snapped back into cold efficiency like trained animals.

"Back to your cells. Go! Move!"

I felt heavy and nauseated. Hix had overheard no idle speculation. Spreading unofficial word of the assassination of any of the Imperial Family was treason punishable by death. If the captain had received word of it, then Rikhart IV was truly dead.

My knees were weak. "What about the rest of the family?"

A guard slammed the butt of his weapon into my back. I pitched forward with a pained grunt, only just keeping on my feet.

"Shut up."

The growled warning thrummed with barely checked violence. Did they think I asked because of Dawes? In a vague, ever-present way I hoped to hear that he was dead as well, but the question had been driven by concern for someone else entirely.

My son was counted among the emperor's family.

The need to know burned within me, but I wasn't stupid enough to ask again. I concentrated on remaining upright as I was herded back to the barracks with the rest of the prisoners, lightheaded with a whole new fear.

Kafe sidled up beside me. "Interesting news," she said with a casual, almost bored expression. A guard snapped at her to shut her up. She glared at him—she had enough power to get away with that much—but didn't say any more.

I walked faster. No doubt she had little care for who ruled the empire. Perhaps she even enjoyed the thought of this emperor being brought down—a line of rulers stretching back centuries, my own line tangled through it a dozen times. I entered my cell, watching the force field snap back into place. It was a moment of zen I usually clung to. This time I flinched.

The alert signal sounded and projections appeared on each wall. The Imperial crest filled the screen in front of a rippling black backdrop. The mournful sound of bagpipes filled the room.

Citizens of the Empire. Today the greatest of tragedies has befallen us. Emperor Rikhart IV is dead.

The silence was absolute and shocking, as if no one breathed. Across the room, someone barked a laugh.

"Live forever, my ass!"

The other inmates joined in, laughing, flipping up middle fingers at the screen where a picture of Rikhart IV was displayed so that the entire empire could observe ten minutes of silence at the passing of our emperor. Apparently Dead End didn't count. Even though the guards stalked about, threatening and shouting, the prisoners just escalated.

"Too bad he died before I could get a piece of that!" Bait yelled, grabbing his crotch and laughing.

I fell back on my cot, staring at the gray ceiling that was so familiar now, fighting back tears I hadn't given in to in years. The emperor was dead, and this was their tribute to him. For years these thugs had erased from me any trace of nobility or connection with that world. Despite all the horrors I'd survived, all the indignities I'd suffered, the way they desecrated and defiled the most important symbol of the system in which I had been great was somehow the most unbearable.

I wrapped my arms around my head and tried to hear the silence everywhere else in the empire. The skirl of bagpipes signaled the end of the period of silence. The last note faded and with it the mockery, as if it had been only for show, and there was no heart to sustain it.

"What does that mean?" someone down the line asked.

"They didn't say anything."

"I don't understand."

My neighbor pivoted on his cot, speaking to me for what must have been the first time since I arrived. "They didn't say anything about the next ruler. What does it mean, Eight?"

I fought to keep my voice steady. "It means nothing."

"They always say 'Long live' and the name of the next one. Always."

"You're an expert on Imperial transitions?" I snapped, too

dizzy with emotion to be prudent.

"You know what I mean." Any other day he would have insulted me, threatened me for talking to him that way. Now he didn't seem to notice. "Last time, when Charles XVII died, they said 'Long live Emperor Rikhart IV.' You know they did."

I scowled. "Of course. We knew Charles XVII was dying. This must have happened suddenly."

"Min says he'd been murdered," a woman down the row added.

"Yeah, and Min's dumb as shit."

"But what if he was?"

A cold knot of fear lodged in my chest. They were right. There should have been something. Princess Marquilla was the heir, even if she would need a regent. There was no question about the line of succession.

"Maybe the little princess died, too," a voice several rows away added.

"Shut up, Gore!"

Others joined in. Some stood, as if they would have thrown things at Gore, or worse, if the walls had permitted it. The way that just the suggestion of the Crown Princess' death sent them into a quivering rage was shocking, since they had just profaned the moment of silence for the emperor. It was raw emotion; a mask for the fear that thrummed with violence in the air.

If she was dead—bile rose in the back of my throat—then the succession passed to Rikhart's cousin, Aliana. No. She'd become the Queen of Torrea and was no longer in line. Torrea's rules of succession were complicated to outsiders, but I knew them very well. My late wife, Hera, would have been in line after her.

That put Hera's son in line after the princess. Our son.

Owen.

I put my hands over my face and tried to think about it in a way that didn't lock my lungs in a vise. If the emperor and the crown princess were both dead, Owen could be dead too. I ground the heels of my hands into my eyes, as if I could force the thought out the back of my head.

The shriek of a different alarm sliced through the air, startling exclamations and cries out of many of the others. The guards looked as shocked as the rest of us when every force field in the room blinked an angry red, humming audibly. Pained yelps echoed around me as prisoners came into contact with cell walls that were no longer passive.

"Lockdown in progress." The announcement rang loud through the room. "Full lockdown in progress. All guards report to Bay 1."

Guards snapped to attention, filing out from the barracks to the common area without sparing the prisoners a glance. When the last guard cleared the entryway, a pulsing red force field flashed into place, sealing off the barracks entirely.

The anxious babble of voices grew louder, swelling into a wave of near-panic. We were well and truly locked in. If no one returned, we would all die here, slowly. We had water but no food. On Dead End, being stranded, helpless, locked into the cage you would die in was a fear we carried with us always.

We were stuck separately and together in our eight-by-eight cages. The prisoners rapidly and noisily succumbing to fear were pockets of spiraling panic in the midst of a crowd that could do nothing about them. Long minutes melted into an hour, more. Screeches morphed into ragged sobs, tension ratcheting up or ebbing cell by cell.

I judged that less than two hours had passed before the field isolating the barracks blinked and disappeared and our walls were suddenly colorless and passive again. A company of guards entered the room. They broke into three groups, one lingering at the entrance, two others making separate paths down the rows of cells. One group stopped in front of my cell.

"E28. Up. Let's go."

The guards weren't known for their patience. One simply stepped into my cell and grabbed my arm, hauling me upright.

Half-panicked myself, I jerked out of his grip as soon as I was standing.

"What's going on?"

His gun slammed hard into my side with a crack. I doubled over my ribs, hoping nothing was broken. Stupid. Careless. I panted against the pain.

He grabbed my arm and jerked me up again. I bit back a yelp and did my best to appear as if I weren't half-leaning into him, and that the quick shuffle out of my cell was my own idea.

After decades of playing the most sophisticated games of politics and intrigue—on a scale no smaller than the empire itself, with stakes that were quite literally life-and-death—sometimes it appalled me to realize what I'd been reduced to.

I was steered out of the barracks and into the hall. Across the room, the second group of guards approached with Kafe in their middle.

"If you think I had anything to do with this, you're crazy," she protested to no one who was listening. In wordless precision they marched us through the prison common areas and on. We passed into corridors I hadn't seen since I'd been processed, and passed through into the prison proper. The surreal feeling of reliving that experience crawled up my spine and prickled as goosebumps on my arms.

We came to a stop in front of the wide metal doors to one of the receiving bays and for a brief, panicky moment, I wondered if Kafe and I were about to be spaced. But the doors opened to bright lights and slightly stale air and a sight that nearly bowled me over with shock.

"Blaine. So good to see you again."

It was the Grand Duke Laudley. My father-in-law.

I was ordered to write this account of that period in imperial history, and the events I was privy to. I do not think it was intended as a punishment, but writing of those days on Dead End feels like one.

iv 10

"Who's this?" Kafe said.

It took no effort to ignore her. My satisfaction grew as Laudley did the same.

"I assume you intend to have this conversation in private?" I said, astonished at the way his mere presence brought back a certain amount of calm assurance to my voice. He nodded, a smile creasing his face. He turned to Captain Saubers.

"Your loyalty to the empire is to be trusted, as before?"

"Of course," the captain said. "The automated safeguards are already in place. I will be speaking to the guards immediately. None shall hear of your visit, Your Grace."

Laudley nodded, perfectly imperious and controlled. The captain bowed.

"May the empero—" The captain blanched. "May the empire stand forever."

Laudley wore an expression of grave sympathy. "May the empire stand forever."

The guards followed the captain out. I tried not to watch, but the temptation was oddly compelling, an almost-fear at watching them leave. I didn't even understand why. Wasn't this what I'd longed for every day since I'd arrived?

Or had I? At some point, years ago, I'd lost hope. I hadn't longed for this because I hadn't even considered it. Rescue from this hell seemed its own new and frightening thing.

I turned back to Laudley. A quirk of amusement twisted the corner of his mouth and ice clamped over my heart. I could not afford to show weakness. Not now. Not again.

The Grand Duke gestured toward his ship. "Shall we?"

I straightened, ignoring the stab of pain in my ribs, and walked out of that storage bay, that facility, and I meant it to be forever.

Kafe, still unacknowledged, trailed in our wake. As soon as we passed the doors to Laudley's ship, two of his guards flanked her.

"This way."

"What's going on?" she demanded, but the Grand Duke and I were already walking away, and if she was given any answer, I didn't hear it.

Laudley led me into a sumptuous lounge, the lavish furnishings and tastefully exquisite decorations set against the backdrop of space beyond the great windows in the outer wall. I looked away with a jerk. I had become quite familiar with that view in the last few years.

If Laudley noticed my discomfort, he gave no sign of it. I chose the nearest settee and sank into it with a grunt of pain I tried to turn into a sigh. The seat was soft and decadent, and it had been far, far too long.

"I suppose you will appreciate that more than most, just now?" Laudley said, as if reading my thoughts.

"What took you so long to get here?" I replied.

His expressions were always subdued, guarded, and he betrayed no reaction to the question. "I had to kill the emperor first. That is not as easy as it sounds."

The casual flippancy took my breath away. That he could admit to having done such a thing was unnerving. That he sounded so blasé about it was horrifying.

"That was a surprising move on your part," I said, forcing my voice steady, emotionless. "Even when you invented The Patriot I never realized your ambitions were so grand."

His eyebrow quirked. "Oh, I think you did."

Did I? I scanned my memory for any hint, any clue. I found none. And yet, I had a horrible suspicion that I'd never known of his plans not because he'd never hinted at them, but because I hadn't wanted to see. In any case, that wasn't a path of conversation I was willing to go down just yet.

"How long have you known I was here?"

He scoffed. "Since the beginning."

I couldn't move, couldn't think. "You—" Horror was thick and choking. "You knew all this time?"

"Of course. You think I fell for that farce of an execution? Ridiculous."

"I've been out here—" I spluttered. "At any time you could have come and—"

"The time wasn't right. I had other considerations, Enryn."

I surged to my feet, clenching my fists to keep my hands away from his neck. "Do you have any idea the hell I've lived?"

His expression was bland, mildly surprised at my reaction, but his eyes were knowing. Of course he knew. If he could assassinate an emperor and break me out of a secret labor camp, of course he could access security feeds. He would have seen.

He watched the realization spread through me. "Naturally I had to make sure you weren't...damaged beyond usefulness."

My hand was trembling with fury and I realized I was rubbing the just-healing cut above my eyebrow. It would leave a scar. There'd been a scar there already. I couldn't even remember which time I'd gotten that first one. I squeezed my eyes closed— it tugged at the cut—and forced myself to calmness. *You don't care. It doesn't matter.*

A huge shudder gripped me when I realized I'd fallen back on the mantra. No. Never again. I sat down.

"Where is Owen?" I said, my voice hoarse.

The briefest flicker of frustration crossed his face. "He is well, and quite safe, I imagine. In some sense of the word."

"You imagine? Don't you know?"

He shot me a look of contempt. "I do not have him in my custody, if you require clarification. The unclass was supposed to die as well, but he managed to escape, and the children with him. I do not doubt that if he is alive, they are as well. The creature seemed to actually believe Owen was his son."

He shook his head in disgust. "At least he will let no harm come to the boy. Owen is safe, and will be even safer when I have located Dawes and killed him." As if an afterthought he added, "I will see to it Owen is not there when that is taken care of. The boy is too young to understand, and Dawes has taught him to be soft."

It still burned that Dawes had my child, but it was an old pain, buried deep. "What happens now?"

He sat back with a smile. "I must return to the palace. I am not officially away. It would look very bad for me to do anything that would give the appearance of running. But I wanted to rescue you myself."

"My hero."

He only smiled. "In any case, it is too early for you to be seen just yet, so rather than going back to the palace, I thought you would prefer to go home for a while."

I sat back to disguise my sudden lightheadedness. "Home?"

Like the other nobles of my station, I'd spent most of each year at the palace. Besides that I had countless houses, cottages, estates, even a small moon. But there was only one place I could properly call home: the estate of Appalachia. I waited until I could be more certain of my voice.

"None of that belongs to me anymore. Or so I was told at my execution."

"It belongs to you again." Laudley made a dismissive gesture. "It will soon. In the meantime, I made sure it would be accessible to you even during this time of turmoil."

I gave him a wry sneer. "No one will be looking for me at my family's oldest holdings?"

He scoffed. "You are dead. No one will be looking for you at all." And yet he couldn't be the only one who had considered I might still be alive.

"What about her?" I said, jerking my head in the direction I'd last seen Kafe. It felt like I could track with each cell in my body the distance that grew between me and Dead End. But she was here with us, like a rash I couldn't ignore. Her presence tingled at the back of my neck like a premonition of danger.

"The woman?"

"Yes, what do you plan to do with her?"

He shrugged. "I leave that entirely up to you. I have no use for her, yet she knows too much. I am certainly not going to leave her out there alive. I would kill her, personally. But perhaps you have some use for her?"

Kafe. How many times over the years had I wanted her dead, had imagined doing it myself? Fantasized about it. But now that it came down to it, I was oddly conflicted. Still, I shrugged. "Do whatever you want with her. I don't care."

Laudley's smile held an edge of malice that unnerved me. He nodded to a servant who then departed the room.

"Here," he said, turning back to me, "have some wine." As another servant poured, Laudley watched me, the ghost of a smirk on his face. I took the glass without a word, studying and sniffing it as if I hadn't just spent years with access to nothing but prison slop. The wine sang on my tongue and I closed my eyes, barely biting back a groan of pleasure.

He settled himself across from me, a faint smile on his face as he took in the view. For several moments we sat in silence, as if we had nothing more important to contemplate than the vintage. My head was reeling but I didn't think it had anything to do with the wine.

A servant entered the room and approached Laudley. "They're ready, Your Grace," he said quietly.

Laudley nodded, turning to me with a smile. "Come see." He stood and gestured for me to accompany him to the window. I couldn't let him see how very much I didn't want to be any closer to it than I was. I forced myself to join him. "Ah," he said, pointing to something just coming into view. "There she is."

The sight of Kafe's lifeless body spinning away into the void kicked me in the gut. The reaction was visceral and completely unexpected. I hated her, but this—being spaced—was bigger than her or me. It was every Dead End inmate's fear. Both because we were afraid of it and because we wanted it. I pressed my lips together and concentrated only on staying upright, showing Laudley nothing.

Laudley cocked an eyebrow, but when I didn't react, he turned away as if bored. "So now there is nothing to do but return you to Earth. I hope you take this opportunity to relax and refresh yourself and re-acclimate to life as a free man. You will have little enough time, soon."

"Why is that?"

His grin became something sharp and predatory. "I have not tried it myself, but I hear that ruling the empire is a difficult job, Your Excellence."

What time will you be back?

Late. If I get back tonight at all.

The kids want to stay up for you.

Better not, I don't know how long I'll be.

They miss you.

Just them?

I always miss you.

You'd better.

iv 11

The shuttle sped through a simple underground tunnel and we slipped out into the ocean, like a newborn sea monster. Water whooshed by the thick windows in momentary flashes of colorful sea life staggered through long stretches of water. I kept expecting that we would surface and take flight. Surely we were leaving the planet? But our course remained unvaried.

The children at first were fascinated, quickly forgetting things like fear and loss in the face of something so grand and new and amazing. But when the abundant life nearer the shore gave way to long, uninterrupted stretches of ocean, they began to lose interest. Molly slowly inspected the transport, but Owen settled into the seat beside me, slipping his hand into mine.

"Where's Papa?" he asked quietly. My throat closed around the answer and I looked away from him, fighting hard to force back tears. I wanted to scream in frustration. How many times had I wanted to escape this life? Clean and complete and untraceable. But not like this. Not like this at all.

Pete was supposed to be here.

Owen's hand spasmed. I pulled him close, burying my face in his hair.

"I'm sorry, Owen," I said, choking on even the vague acknowledgment. He wrapped his arms around me, squeezing hard.

"Did they kill him?" he whispered.

I nodded against him. He hiccoughed a loud sob. Molly turned at the sound and wrapped her arms around him. "Are you having a bad dream?" She turned her face up to mine. "Where's Papa?"

Owen's shoulders jerked and Molly buried her face in his back. "What's wrong?" Her body grew taut with tension as it became obvious that something really was not right. Her jaw set and she glared at me, demanding that I fix it, refusing to be weak.

She'd have made a good empress. I started at the thought. She was empress now. Or should be. Should have been? The thought pulled a strange sound out of me, some combination of grim amusement and grief. We were speeding through the ocean, running as fast as we could from the palace, the throne, to some place no one in the empire knew how to find. Would we ever even go back? *Could* we? What were we now?

Pete was dead.

I gathered the children close, sharp elbows and chins and knobby knees clashing and shoving themselves into some conglomeration of family I meant to have now. So that I could never lose one again.

I cried into Molly's hair as I explained simply and without detail that Papa was gone, that he wasn't coming back. That we were three where we had been four. Whatever else we were or weren't, I left alone.

I didn't know.

The children fell asleep because they were tired, as only children can do. More than an hour of unrelenting ocean passed by the windows. I gently disengaged them from around me, laying them together in a tumble of arms and legs and made my way to the front of the ship. I didn't like our chances much, and I wanted to know what I could of this series of secure protocols that were literally hurtling us through the depths of the ocean.

The readouts were fascinating. Half of the technology the transport bore didn't officially exist. There were so many camouflage and deflection, defense and protective measures that I began to wonder at the fact that *I* could see and touch it. From inside.

I'd seen some of this tech before because I had access no other scientist in the empire had, but there was plenty I didn't recognize at all. The scientist in me could have lost himself in it for days.

Somewhere in my absorption I noticed the ship slowing. Before long, the underside of a manmade structure came into view and we slowed further, making an approach to an underwater garage. The water was lighter in color here, nearer the surface. The doors opened and swallowed the transport, closing behind us. Water drained slowly from the bay and we were once again sitting in a visually unremarkable ship in a nondescript room no one in the empire knew about.

With dread heavy in my gut, I triggered the door to the transport and stepped out into the garage. Water dripped from the ship and the ceiling, running along the edges of the room in a soothing trickle, disappearing through drains in the floor. A door into the garage opened and a man stepped through.

It was Jonathan.

So how do you like your new rooms?

You mean your rooms?

Ours.

Jonathan corrects me every time I say that.

You leave Jonathan to me. He's wrong. They're yours too. I plan on keeping you, you know.

Same goes, Emperor.

iv 12

For a long time we stood there, just staring at each other, as if neither of us had the brains to use to open our mouths and say anything.

Or that either of us had any idea what to say.

"What are you doing here?" I managed to croak.

His answer was slow in coming. "I live here. I am the caretaker of the safehouse."

"In what universe?" I sputtered. "You were—you were exiled! I was there. I *did* it!"

His reply was slow and careful, as if confronting a skittish animal. "When you banished me I came here."

I shook my head, running a hand through my hair, looking around the garage as if there was something here that could make sense of this.

"You were banished from the empire and *this* counts?"

"Like you were banished to the IIC?"

"That's not the same thing."

He didn't bother to argue. I just felt tired. I didn't want to talk about it anymore. I didn't want to remember. Anything.

I heaved a huge, shaky sigh, turning back to the transport. He came to stand beside me, looking at the sleeping children. "Shall I carry one of them?"

"Stay away from me. Stay away from my family."

He stood still and silent. Waiting. Because he was the servant and that's what they did. It infuriated me years ago, when I wanted him to stop pretending to be a robot and admit we were really friends. Now it infuriated me for a whole different reason.

"Stop that!" I cast a quick glance at the children to make sure I hadn't woken them. "Stop," I said again, but more quietly. "Stop playing 'good servant.' It's a lie and we both know it."

I turned my back on him, sick with fury and loss and emotions I couldn't even name.

I picked up Molly. She shifted to put her arms around my neck and her head on my shoulder without opening her eyes. I shook Owen gently.

"Owen. Buddy. We're here. Come on, let's get you to bed." He blinked sleepily, standing, leaning into me, heavy lidded. I turned to the garage again, trying to figure out this place.

"I can show you to their rooms," Jonathan said quietly.

I blinked away ridiculous tears shaking my head and, exiting the garage through the only door there. I couldn't see him, but the back of my neck crawled with the awareness of Jonathan following behind.

What do you want for your birthday this year?

I don't know, ask Jonathan.

Ask Jonathan what you want for your birthday?

Sure. If you don't know, I'm sure he will.

Because you don't?

I live with the emperor. I already have everything. Wait, how about a lot of sex?

That I can definitely manage.

iv 13

The garage opened into, of all things, a kitchen. I stood there for a strange moment, wondering when I'd last been in a kitchen. Abenez? It was so...normal, and yet so completely abnormal to me, considering the life I'd led. I sputtered a laugh. I took the first open doorway out of the kitchen into a wide, window-walled living area. One large hallway led away from it and I turned down there, hoping it was the bedrooms, because I didn't think I could handle needing Jonathan.

I stopped in front of the first door and stared at the room inside. The walls all around were painted with one continuous mural of an outdoor scene, complete with animals, both real and fantastic, that tracked from sunrise at one corner through the progression of the day and night until it met itself again with the sun rising. Overhead were the stars, laid out precisely as they would be seen from Earth, probably from this vantage point. It was breathtaking.

"I didn't know if Princess Marquilla had developed any particular interests so I went with a more general theme I thought she might like. I can change it, over time. I'm not very fast, though."

"You did this?" I breathed.

"I'm not a painter, but I found enough pictures of what I needed and traced it when I could." Out of the corner of my eye I could see him watching my face. "It's my job here. I make sure the house is always ready for you, should it be needed."

I entered the room, setting Molly down on the bed. I tugged off her shoes and clothes, tucking her gently under the covers, Owen sleepily did the same for himself, crawling into the bed on the other side, asleep again instantly. I'd have to figure out nightclothes, I supposed. There was an odd moment when I stood there, wondering when I'd become the man who thought about such things.

Jonathan was there when I came out and I pretended I didn't notice, continuing down the hallway. I peeked into the next open door and stopped in shock. The lights were low but it was still easy to see the stark contrast of white walls covered in the black accents of musical symbols, instruments, notes, even a three-foot high set of rows, just waiting to be filled with the dots and stems of a music score.

Stunned to find a room so perfectly tailored to Owen, I crossed to the closet in a daze, opened it and walked into the space filled with clothes and shoes, all Owen's size. Jonathan was waiting for me in the hallway. Just like old times.

"How did you know?" I blurted. "How did you know he loves music? How did you know his shoe size!"

His answer was measured and impersonal. He was respecting and adapting to my mood. I hated it. "My entire purpose here is to keep the house maintained should the Family need it. I'm kept informed by the Family's servants as to your tastes, preferences, the children's sizes."

"Don't tell me you sewed their clothes."

He huffed a small laugh, so unlike the proper Jonathan from when I'd known him. "Things are sent, and I am able to requisition as needed."

"I thought you couldn't communicate with anyone?"

"I don't, directly. There are many people in the web of procedures set up to maintain this place and most have no idea what the orders really mean or what they're for. What messages I'm allowed to send are all filtered through automated systems. I am only placing orders that eventually show up here."

I shook my head at the enormity of it all, and how it could still surprise me after living with the emperor so long.

Pete.

"Shall I show you to your room?"

I turned away, sick from remembering and dangerously close to forgetting all Jonathan had done; how careful I needed to be now that it was just me. I clenched my jaw against a surge of nausea and nodded curtly. He pointed me toward another room at the end of the hall, its door at the very center. I cautiously stepped inside.

The light was soft and golden, the perfect counterpoint to the darkness of the windows set throughout. The sitting room was separated from the bedroom only by a set of French doors with raised curtains. It looked exactly like any room for the emperor you would find on one of his transports or any other place where something grander wasn't possible.

Except, it didn't look anything like that. The colors were quiet and simple, the furnishings and decoration probably priceless and unique yet they weren't ostentatious or even regal. They were...comfortable, homey. It was the sort of thing I would have chosen for myself, if I'd ever been allowed. Other than my lab, I'd never had something so completely refreshing, completely... normal as this looked.

Stupefied, I wandered into the bedroom. There was an open veranda that I couldn't make much of in the dark, but it spanned the length of the room, hints of greenery at the edges. The bathroom was exactly where I expected it to be. I only made it one step into the room before my knees gave out and I fell to the floor, stricken and shaking.

The emperor's bathroom at the palace was an elaborate, costly affair, studded with jewels and priceless murals and sculptures. This wasn't anything like that.

It was our nebula.

Somehow, with painted walls and colored tiles, Jonathan had created the illusion that we stood right inside of the Dawes-Killearn nebula. The place that meant everything to Pete and me, that was the most basic and true piece of anything we could claim in the universe, that was ours, and us. I clutched my arms around myself as if I could hold myself together, as if there truly were forces of nature in here too great for puny humans, forces to which I was nothing at all, that would rip me apart and make use of me and never even know they did it.

Pete.

A sob wracked through me with the force of a gravity well, a black hole. I huddled over my knees, crying in great heaves as if I could retch up the past twenty-four hours, everything that was rank and horrible and rotten inside me. Someone touched me and, for a disoriented moment, I believed it was Pete and I reached for him, only to find I was clutching Jonathan's shoulders instead. But his grip was hard and sure and grounding.

"I'm sorry," he rasped. "I didn't mean—You must understand, I've spent years preparing this place for you, hoping with everything in me that you would never come, that I would never see you again, because of what it would mean. But this is—"

I wanted to stop him. I wanted to beg him not to say any more. And yet I'd spent all the years we were together begging him to do this very thing. To talk to me, to acknowledge that we were friends, not just master and servant. He looked at me, raw emotion on his face as I'd never seen it. Begging me in return to ask him to stop, to not have to say any more.

I couldn't have spoken if my life depended on it.

A spasm of pain crossed his face and he dropped my gaze. "It's lonely here. And—and I have many regrets, and a lot of time to think about them. This," he said, gesturing around us, "was an expiation of sorts, an apology. It was a way to have the spirit of you here. A way to know your daughter somehow. This was—" He sighed, shaking his head at himself. "This was as much for me as for you. Probably more so, since I didn't think you'd ever see it."

To my horror I heard myself say, "Pete would have loved it."

He shivered once, all over. And then I saw him do it, pull the cloak of servant over himself, the careful and proper distance. "I had hoped so. And not. Your Highness."

"Don't call me that," I said, scrambling to my feet, backing away as if running from the words. "That's not what I am anymore." I shook my head. "I'm not sure I ever was."

He answered, very soft, still on his knees in front of me. "I think you're wrong about that." When I had no reply he continued. "What would you have me call you?"

It was incredibly hard to say, and not for the reason I would have thought. "Jake."

He paled. For a long moment he just stared at me. "I can't. Only your friends call you that."

I laughed, so harsh and unexpected. "And who are they now? Am I even alive outside this place?" My throat tightened. When I could find my voice again I said, "You asked, and that's my answer."

His lips tightened and he looked away.

"Think of it as a punishment," I said, rough and strained. "You'll hate it every time you have to say it." He didn't acknowledge that. I sighed.

"Call me Jake. There are few enough people left who do. And, anyway, you're—" I looked around, pain stabbing through my middle, the ache of loss as massive as the nebula. I wasn't even sure what I was thinking, much less how to say it. I shrugged.

"You're you."

What time did you get up this morning?

I never went to bed.

You know, your work will still be there in the morning.

The secrets of the universe wait for no man.

iv14

The bright light from the windows woke me. I glanced at the time and realized I'd slept half the morning away. I jumped up, snatching at the patch Dr. Heinriksen had put on me and jerking it off. I'd forgotten about that. Dr. Heinriksen and her stupid medicines.

Pain tightened my throat. Would I ever see her again? She was the second person I'd met at the palace. She'd been kind to me from the moment we met, back when I thought everyone would always hate me on sight.

The first person I'd met had been Jonathan, of course.

Jonathan. Here. Which explained how I'd slept so long without the children waking me. Jonathan would have seen to that. Confusion and conflict swelled within me. The children didn't know they shouldn't trust him.

Except that they should. Shouldn't they? Shouldn't I? *Could* I? I rubbed hard at my forehead. I couldn't deal with this now. It was too much.

I made my way out of the bedroom, following the soft noises of activity and found myself in the kitchen.

Owen and Molly were perched on tall stools at one of the counters, eating something that smelled very good. My stomach rumbled. Molly slid from her chair and barreled into me, squeezing me around the waist, which was about as far as she could reach. I lifted her up so she could wrap her legs around me and drop her head on my shoulder.

"Jonathan said you were just sleeping. He let me look but we had to be quiet. He said we shouldn't wake you."

I petted her hair, kissing the top of her head absently, avoiding looking at Jonathan as I took in the ridiculously homey sight. "Are you OK?" I asked. She nodded, popping her head back up.

"He cooks too," she said, scrambling down and back up onto her chair. "It's really good."

Owen was watching me with an oddly mature intensity. I ruffled his hair, hugging him where he sat. "How are you, buddy?"

He just nodded, glancing at Jonathan, who was pretending to ignore us, before he turned wide, frightened eyes up at me. "I think it's my fault," he whispered.

I blinked, unsure what we were talking about for a moment until I saw the tears begin to well in his eyes and I understood. "No," I said firmly. "No, it's not your fault. Not ever, in any way."

He shook his head. "I think it was my grandfather," he insisted. I went very still, glancing at Jonathan. He too was motionless, waiting.

"Why do you think that?"

Molly interjected without looking away from her food. "Because he's a mean man," she mumbled around scrambled eggs. Owen wouldn't look away from me, as if doing so was dangerous.

"Molly, he's..." I couldn't defend him. He probably *was* behind it. He *was* a mean man. But how could I say that in front of Owen who already carried the burden of a father who had committed terrible crimes against the emperor Owen had called Papa?

Owen glanced once more at Jonathan and I took his hand. "Let's talk somewhere else, OK? Are you finished with your food?"

He nodded, though whether he had eaten enough or was just too frightened to eat anymore I didn't ask. His hand was sweaty in mine as we found a small sun room off the kitchen. I sat down, pulling Owen around to stand in front of me so I could hold both of his hands and meet his eye.

"No matter who did this, it was not your fault."

"He said I should be emperor," he forced out in a whisper I almost couldn't hear. "He said that Molly shouldn't be, because something was wrong with her, because of you, and that I should be emperor, not her." Tears ran down his cheeks. "I didn't tell you because I didn't want to say those awful things to you, and I didn't tell Papa and I should have. If I'd told Papa maybe he would have been safe and then—"

I grabbed his arms and shook him once to stop the hysterical rush of words, pulling him into a hug so tight he could probably barely breathe, certainly not spew self-condemnation anymore.

"No," I said again, this time soft against his cheek. "No. Papa knew to be careful, and he was as safe as we could make him. No one's at fault except the person who did this. Do you understand?"

He nodded reluctantly against my head. "Did my grandfather do it?" He was trembling.

I sighed. "I don't know, Owen. I don't know, but it has nothing to do with you. Papa loved you and I love you and Molly loves you and I'm keeping you with me and not letting anything happen to you."

At first I thought he was nodding before I realized he was shaking with quiet sobs. I pulled him into my lap and held him like I hadn't since he was much smaller, and let him cry until he couldn't cry anymore.

With breakfast forgotten, Jonathan showed Owen and me to a sunny playroom with a view of the wide-leaved trees shading the lawn. Molly stood at an easel, glopping wide streaks of paint on what appeared to be actual canvas. When she saw me, she ran over to Owen and squeezed him tight, glaring at me as if it were my fault he was upset.

He hugged her back, kissing her cheek just like Pete would, and smoothly redirected her attention. "What are you painting?" he said, his voice raw, breathing hitched, but doing his best to sound level and calm for Molly. My heart hurt a little to see it.

Jonathan stepped up to my side. "You have a message waiting," he said low enough not to distract the children. I frowned at him, puzzled, following his gaze to one of the comm units the servants always carried. The indicator showed new mail in my inbox.

"I'm still getting my mails?"

He shook his head slowly. "Not from outside. This must be a message that was stored here and has been triggered by your arrival."

"Oh," I said quietly, turning away, my stomach heavy and giddy all at once. Back in my room I sank into the chair at the desk, staring at the blinking light in the corner that promised a message I wasn't sure I could handle. I opened it.

"Hi, Jake."

He looked younger. I glanced at the time stamp. Five years ago, before Molly was born.

"So, if this is the message you got, then I'm dead," Pete said, "but you've made it to the safe house. I hope I got to say goodbye." He glanced down, as if the words were difficult for him. I couldn't breathe.

"You'll already know by now that Jonathan is the caretaker. I just wanted to explain. I arranged for him to be sent there. He doesn't know that, and you can tell him or not, however you want. I couldn't just let him go, the way you said. Sam knew he was a security concern and he came to me. He was prepared to quietly execute Jonathan if I gave the order, though he was clearly relieved when I didn't.

"I hoped there would never be any need for you to know he was there, and I hope, now that you've found him, it hasn't upset you. I know isolation is a painful issue for you."

I honestly hadn't thought of that yet, how Jonathan had essentially been in permanent solitary confinement. Trust Pete to remember why that might be hard for me.

"I don't know how much time has passed since I recorded this, if you've had enough time to deal with how you feel about him and what he did. But I'm not the only one bad at holding grudges. You get too angry to really stay mad at people you love. You burn out fast and then you just feel guilty. So I hope seeing Jonathan again will be some healing and comfort for you both."

He sighed. "If you're at the safehouse that means things have gone badly for us. I hope—" he hesitated. "The surrogate's pregnant right now, and I think finally it's going to work, and we'll have a child soon. But maybe Aliana is still my heir." He looked frustrated. "I have no way of knowing what's happened to put you here. It's a last-resort measure, and that means something has gone terribly wrong. If there's a way to put things right, a way back for you—and our child, if we have one—Jonathan is the one who could find it." He grimaced. "Don't take that the wrong way."

I huffed a laugh then remembered he couldn't hear me and my gut bottomed out .

"Listen to him," he said, "please. You don't have a lot of options now, though I know you're going to do everything you can to see that whatever happened to me is dealt with, and that my heir takes the throne. But please, Jake, please be careful. You're safe now, as safe as you can be anywhere in the empire." He smiled sadly. "I know you won't accept that as the final word on anything, but be careful. If I've been captured or killed, you're in as much danger as you think you are, probably more. Listen to Jonathan. Even if you can't forgive him yet. He'll keep you safe, and I want you to be safe."

His expression twisted. "I'm sorry I'm not there for you anymore. But I love you, I always did. Don't ever doubt that. You were the best part of my life and I'll never be sorry I fell in love with you, no matter how it ended for me." He reached forward and pressed his palm to the screen. Without conscious thought I placed mine against it. "Goodbye, my love. Thank you for marrying me. Thank you for everything."

There's been a measurable increase in the density of the central cloud of the nebula. You picked a good one, Emperor.

Well, I had to find something that would impress you.

iv15

It was quite some time before I could compose myself and rejoin Jonathan and the children. I found the three of them as I'd left them, the children conferring over their art and Jonathan standing aside. He made no attempt to hide the fact that he was watching them, something like hunger in his expression. Suddenly I realized why.

"Where is your daughter?" I blurted.

He looked up at me, an expression of mild surprise on his face. "The last I heard, she and her mother were still on your estate in Mexico."

That shocked all the words right out of me. "*My* estate?"

A puzzled line appeared between his eyes. "Were you not aware of that?"

"I—No. No one saw fit to tell me," I grumbled, feeling both wounded and sad that they'd been there all that time and I hadn't known. Why not tell me? Did they think I would mind? Why put them there in the first place? And yet it was so like Pete, to put them under my protection but wait to tell me, when it would hurt less.

I looked at my children helplessly, watching Owen at his own easel beside Molly and wondering what in the galaxy I was going to do.

As if reading my mind Jonathan gestured to the sun room where I'd sat with Owen. "If you like, I can update you on what I know." I gave the children another long look, realizing with a sort of startled surprise that I was hesitating about leaving them alone. I didn't think they had ever been alone. "We'll be in the next room; we can hear them."

I scowled at myself, feeling stupid for worrying. I'd spent most of my early years without much supervision, taking care of my sister and mother while I was still younger than Owen. Sometimes it struck me how incomparably *different* these children's lives were from mine. From anyone's, really. I wondered what would become of them now.

I shook my head and followed Jonathan. Like every other room I'd seen in this place, the windows were wide and plentiful, offering expansive views of what I guessed was tropical rain forest. On a table set between two chairs, a tray held tea and coffee and a plate of the food the children had been eating.

"Do you really cook?" I said.

"I do now."

I huffed in amusement, startled to realize that between the message from Pete, and the simple familiarity of Jonathan's presence, I'd lost my wariness of him somewhere. It was probably stupid of me. Except that I didn't have the strength to maintain it anymore. And Pete had put him here. Pete, who always knew better than I did and who would never have done anything to hurt me. I dropped into the chair and picked up a cup of tea, the weight of despair settling over me again.

"Oh, Jonathan. What am I going to do?"

"Right now you're going to eat something."

The practical, straightforward answer startled a laugh out of me and I found myself reaching for the plate without even thinking about it. The moment died quickly. The food may have been good, but it felt like sawdust in my mouth.

"Do we even know what's going on? What are the news broadcasts saying?"

71

"What the news broadcasts are saying and what's actually going on are two different questions."

I grimaced. "Yes, I know that. But we're not getting status reports here or anything."

"Of course we are."

I sat up, startled. "But I thought..." I trailed off, trying to piece together what Pete's message had said with what I knew of this place—which was nothing. "Well aren't we stuck here now? Even if we did know what was going on, it's not like we can do anything."

His smile held a hint of amusement. "With all the planning that's gone into this place, do you think it's just a fancy retirement facility? It's a defensive position. Now we work on getting you back where you belong. Princess Marquilla can hardly inherit the throne if she's stuck out here."

"Molly," I corrected absently. "How are we going to do that? You said you can't contact anyone except for requisitions or whatever."

"I said no provisions were made, not that I couldn't do it. There aren't many who know as much as I do about these things."

"Not all of it obtained honestly."

He didn't look away or flinch. "No. Not all of it. Maybe not even most."

I couldn't face his raw honesty. How was it possible that he could do this to me after all this time? That after all he'd done, I could look him in the face and still feel like the lesser man.

I scrubbed my face hard with my hands. "I'm sorry, I didn't mean that. I don't even know where this is coming from."

He gave me a faint smile. "Don't be too hard on yourself. You're going through a lot right now. I'd be surprised if anyone could handle it well. You especially."

I looked up at him in shock. His smile was faint but teasing. It drew a startled laugh out of me. A long moment passed in which we just stared at each other, and it felt like something changed, though I didn't know what. I had to look away.

"Anyway," he continued, as if we hadn't deviated from the

conversation at all, "it's an entirely different matter now that you are here. There are automatic processes that have already begun that are designed to help me coordinate with whatever allies we have now. I've also separately established contact with the head of the Resistance. I know him as TG."

"The Resistance?"

Jonathan nodded. "They've been in place for some time, as an official A49372 organization for the promotion of imperially sanctioned causes. UpClass, is what they're called."

I frowned. "Why would they need a secret organization for that? We were doing that openly."

He shook his head. "UpClass worked within the system your husband was creating. But, knowing this to be a radical and often unpopular agenda, behind the public face of UpClass they created a contingency organization. One that could quickly and easily organize a resistance for such situations as this."

"As this?"

"In case the empire's interest in improving the situation of the lower classes ever changed. They already have a solid base to work from. As of yesterday they've gone underground—though that's known only to a very few. For now."

"How did they know there needed to be any sort of 'resistance' at all? Do people really know what happened already?" I scowled. "I don't even know what's going on yet."

He gave me a funny half-smile. "They have at least one highly placed informant, probably someone in their organization is within the imperial power structure as well. Or Laudley's. I don't know yet."

I mulled over that in silence. "So they're like Blaine as The Patriot?"

"Well, like The Patriot, though we know that wasn't Blaine, don't we?"

"We do?"

Jonathan gave me a look that only mostly disguised his disappointment. "I told you that before. And even if you didn't believe me then—which wouldn't have been surprising—I would think that would be obvious even to you now."

"But everything stopped happening as soon as Blaine was sent— executed. As soon as he was executed. This is something new."

His mouth quirked. "In case you were under the impression that you were going to hide from me the fact that Blaine was never executed, let's set that straight now. I know where he is. Or, at least, where he was."

My breath stopped in my throat. "Was?"

Jonathan frowned. "There are indications that Blaine is no longer on Dead End."

My heart pounded loud in my throat. "Are you sure?"

"He was taken from Dead End shortly after the emperor was killed. I have that from both my authorized sources and from the unauthorized ones."

"You know, what you're doing is probably completely illegal. And unbelievably inappropriate for someone who was convicted of treason."

He gave me a funny smile. "It always has been."

It was so oddly familiar, Jonathan patiently guiding me through something I hadn't wanted to understand but that he wouldn't let me avoid. It was like when I was young and suddenly with the emperor and had no idea what to do. He'd held my hand through it. Back before I knew he was betraying me. Back when I had Pete.

A heavy dread fell over me, choking me with possibilities, fear for the children, the overwhelming weight of loss. Pete was dead. I groaned, my face falling into my hands.

"Anyway," he continued, "it's funny that *you* would criticize anyone for treason."

My face grew hot. "Mine was different."

"How, exactly?"

"Mine wasn't deliberate."

"No?"

"No! How dare you even suggest that!" "

He shrugged. "I've wanted to ask, I just couldn't before. I always believed you precipitated that crisis in hopes of convincing the emperor to give the unclass more than he was ready to, but that it got out of hand."

"What? No. I wouldn't do that!"

"No?"

"What's wrong with you? Why are you even saying this? You can't believe that?"

"I probably don't."

I gaped at him. "Then why are we fighting?"

"Because anger distracts you, and when you're yelling at me you stop thinking about other things."

Other things hung in the air for a moment as I tracked backward and realized he'd started making the ridiculous accusations as soon as I started thinking about Pete. My breath caught. "Have you always done that?"

"Yes." His calm, which used to both amaze and infuriate me, felt so odd in such a moment. And so achingly familiar and safe.

"You did better by me than you think," I said.

"How do you know what I think?"

"I don't. I mean, I didn't realize how much you did for me. It might have helped to know that. When I found out what you did for Blaine..." The flash of betrayal heated my face, but faded quickly. "Well, I thought all of it had been lies, that I'd misunderstood everything."

"I know," he answered quietly. "There wasn't much I could do to make you believe I'd had good intentions. Or good among the bad, I suppose."

"I wouldn't have asked you to choose me over your daughter." I gasped in sudden horror, catapulting out of the chair. "Your daughter! Revan! They'll go after my daughter. Or yours. Maybe someone knows you're still helping me and they're going to try to use them as hostages." Panic seized my throat. "Of course they're going to do that with Revan. Of course." I rounded on him. "We have to do something!"

That he could still sit there so calmly in the face of that was definitely on the infuriating side.

"They are safe," he said.

My knees gave out as I sank into my chair. "They are? All of them?"

"Yes. My daughter's mother and Revan's adopted parents as well. TG has secured them somewhere. I don't know where yet, but I will."

"Are *we* even safe? We didn't even leave the planet. How could they *not* find us here eventually?"

Jonathan pursed his lips. "Most are going to assume, as you did, that the safehouse wouldn't be here on Earth. And when your transport left the palace it sent a false signal that could be interpreted as a cloaked ship leaving the planet. No cloaking system is perfect, after all."

"But they're not going to ignore the planet entirely, even if they don't focus on it. And we're *right here*."

He tilted his head in acknowledgement. "This island is easy enough to find on the map. There was an imperial research facility here long ago that handled research of the highest sensitivity and sometimes dangerous materials. According to the records, there was an accident here long ago and the facility was shut down and used as a dumping ground for hazardous waste."

"It doesn't look much like a research facility, if you do a flyover."

He grinned. "It doesn't look anything like a research facility from here inside the camouflage field."

I sat back. "Oh. Makes sense." I stared down at my hands, trying to think past the immediate worries that I apparently shouldn't be worrying about. "So what happens now? What do we do?"

"We wait."

"Wait? While whoever did this consolidates power and destroys evidence?"

"We have to wait because we don't know who did this, and watching to see who consolidates power will help us figure it out, or at least give us a place to start."

"I know who did this," I grumbled, but I shook my head at myself. "What's the official word? What are they saying about what happened and who did it?"

"Nothing. They've said nothing at all other than to acknowledge the emperor is dead. Not one official word on how that came about or even anything about the succession. They can't help the implication that there is some trouble regarding the princess as well, but no one will comment on it one way or the other."

"Who's controlling the messages? Who is actually in charge now?"

"The council, supposedly. Lord Naganika is the official spokesman."

My stomach twisted. "He's working with them." I choked on the words. "I liked him." Bitter deja vu washed over me. "I trusted him."

Jonathan's reply was soft. "He was already the official spokesman for the palace. Everyone involved will want that maintained, both those for us and against us. Where he personally stands and how much he does or doesn't know is impossible to tell from that simple fact." He paused. "Don't forget, Lord Sifer chose him as his replacement. There aren't many people I trust more than Sifer."

I blew out a breath, biting back some comment about the irony in him talking about trust. "You're right." I frowned.

"Give me a week," he said. "Let me gather as much information as I can before you do anything, please. If it were just us, I'd follow you as you bumbled into the middle of it all, screaming defiance and losing your temper as you're wont to do and getting yourself killed, if that's what you really want. I owe you that much." He paused, glancing in the direction of the room where the children played. "But I don't think that's what you want to do this time."

I deflated. "A week. How can I sit here, waiting, like the whole world hasn't just fallen apart." I sighed. "My world, at least."

"It might be good for all of you to have some time to grieve. I thought you might also want to plan some sort of ceremony to say goodbye."

I closed my eyes against the pain. Pete. They were going to bury him in great pomp and splendor, locking him away in the imperial mausoleum, without me. All of it, without me. Pete hadn't wanted to be put in that stuffy old edifice, and I'd never wanted him interred forever in the place that had held us captive and controlled us and finally killed him. He wanted what physical remains he left behind to be joined with the Dawes-Killearn Nebula. Our nebula. He'd said he'd do it for me.

I buried my face in hands that were trembling and breathed out a shaky sigh.

"Yes, of course. Goodbye."

My biggest fears in these days after I was freed from Dead End weren't about the danger of what we were doing, the potential for disaster, the number of things that rested on the reactions of others that I couldn't control, the people I was forced to blindly depend on and who controlled me as much as they controlled the empire.

More than all of those things, I was afraid of myself, of what I had become, that perhaps I was truly broken and couldn't find my way back.

iv 16

I stared at Laudley in astonishment. "Your Excellence?"

He didn't stop smiling, though the expression took on a funny cast before he waved away my question. "Time enough to discuss the details when you are at the palace."

I sat up straighter. "No, I think there's plenty of time now. You can hardly expect me to let that go with no explanation."

He examined me. "Of course you want an explanation, but I am not ready to give it to you just yet."

I made some odd, startled noise of disbelief. "You can't be serious."

His smile was vicious. "I have a great many things going on at present, and much of it benefits you. Which I think you might thank me for."

"I might, when I know what it is you are planning."

"I think you will better project the air of innocence and of just being rescued from years of unjust imprisonment if you remain ignorant for now."

"You expect me to play emperor, or something like, but you don't think I can maintain the proper pretense?"

He raised an eyebrow. "I think that you have spent the last five years locked up with the offal of the empire and I am not sure what to expect from you just yet."

I sat back slowly. As much as I hated it, he had a valid point. Did I even know what to expect from myself?

"Do not worry," he said, making another careless dismissive gesture. "It is one of the reasons I do not plan to return you to the palace just yet."

"And the other reasons?"

He gave me a long considering look, and I bristled at the reminder that he held all the information and was doling it out to me as he wished.

"For one, we must make it seem as if your whereabouts were only discovered in the chaos following the assassination of the emperor. That you remain entirely unconnected to the tragedy is a vital part of my plan. To be honest," he said, with a casual shrug, "it would have been more prudent to leave you out there a few more days, but I wasn't sure what the announcement of the emperor's death would do to your situation."

He smiled maliciously. "So, you see, you've caused me trouble already and forced me to make less than optimal decisions. I will need you to be very careful to play your part correctly."

I considered punching him. I had some experience with punching now, though I'd learned early at Dead End that I always came out the worse for it, and hadn't tried it in some time. But what did Laudley know of such crude measures? I wondered how many good punches I'd get in before he even realized what was happening. I turned away, picking up my wine glass again, gulping until I coughed.

"Also," Laudley continued, as if he hadn't noticed, "I must return to the palace and see where things stand. I have made many plans, and this is a crucial juncture. Much will be decided based on what others do now. I must arrange your return carefully, and with present circumstances in mind."

I hated how relieved I was that he was taking it all in hand, that nothing was expected of me now. I wouldn't have admitted it, but I felt completely lost and out of my element, doing this, at which I had once been one of the best, one of the most successful.

Our return to Earth was brief. The ship was new and impressive, and not Laudley's. It had been acquired for him by some associate who took care of things at the palace for him. He refused to tell me who that was.

We landed at an anonymous waystation and parted ways, he in a shuttle to the palace, and me toward the last place I'd expected to see again.

I had no idea what I would find at my oldest estate, and tried to prepare myself for anything. The gathering of servants waiting to welcome me was nonetheless a surprise. I disembarked, trying to hide my hesitation and suspicion.

The meaning of the welcoming committee became clear when the assembled reacted to the sight of me with startled gasps, exclamations of shock, even disgust, and a hard glare from Lady Chou.

Hers wasn't the only face I recognized, though she was the only one I knew by name. She had grown up on the estate. Her father, a minor noble too poor to have his own holdings, had served as the steward of the estate since before I had been born. He had been ancient the last time I'd seen him. She must have inherited the position by now.

I affected a casual pose that was by no means genuine but came easier than I'd feared. "I take it from this lack of joy at my return that you were not expecting me?"

Servants whispered behind her but Lady Chou's answer was immediate, each word bitten off. "That would be correct. We were not expecting to have to endure your presence ever again."

I stiffened. She was a servant. My servant. "Then who were you expecting to welcome here?"

"We were only informed to expect a noble guest. And then all communications out of the estate were blocked." Her posture softened a bit but it was defeat, not forgiveness. "From the obvious need for secrecy and concealment, I had hoped to find Owen, even the Prince Consort and the Crown Princess."

The thought of Owen, here, sent a hard shiver of longing through me. "Well, I can't blame you for being disappointed to find me if you were expecting Owen."

"Disappointed isn't the word that comes to mind."

I should have reprimanded her, punished her even. My own steward shouldn't speak to me like that. But I was so badly out of practice, and who was I now, to them or to anyone? To me? I took a deep breath.

"How unfortunate for you." I looked at one of the younger men. "Is my room prepared?"

"You don't have a room here," Lady Chou snapped. I turned very slowly to face her.

"Why don't we clarify a few things so we all know where we stand?" My voice was level and cold. "Yesterday, you thought I was dead. Now I am here. You have already figured out that I have friends who continue to assist me, ergo the communications blackout that prevents you from contacting anyone and telling what you know about who is or isn't here. No matter who officially owns this estate, it is safe to assume that it is in my control now and you would be advised to obey me as your duke."

"And yesterday the emperor was alive," she said. "I suppose you're 'in control' of that situation too?" Her voice wobbled but she stood as stiff and forgiving as a granite cliff. "You killed the emperor."

Murmurs of anger and grief passed through the group, and I almost sympathized with them.

"You can suppose whatever you choose. But you *will* do your job or leave."

Lady Chou scoffed. "Leave? How far would we get, Enryn? All things considered, there's no way any one of us will get off this estate alive."

She had named one of my own, newborn fears. My fists clenched and I stepped very close to her. To her credit, she didn't back away. "You will not address me that way again. Use my proper title or be silent."

"What title would that be? Traitor?"

I slapped her. The sting in my palm was like a balm after so many years wanting nothing more than to hurt the people who were hurting me and being powerless to do so. The moment stretched as she stood there, my handprint pinking on her cheek.

She spat in my face and, before I could react, turned on her heel and stormed away.

Lady Chou retreated to a small hunting lodge on the outskirts of the estate. I let her go. It wasn't something I would have done before, but before was a long time ago, and a different life I'd lived. In truth, I felt too uncertain, too disoriented to deal with her, as if properly chastising a high ranking servant was some old skill I'd taken for granted but forgotten how to do, so long without practice.

I isolated the cabin even from the rest of the estate and told the other servants I'd sent her away. If they didn't believe me, they didn't show it.

The estate is the same as it has been for as long as I can remember. I'm the one who is different.

iv 17

I inherited the duchy when I was eighteen. My mother called me into her sitting room, the day after my birthday. My father had died only weeks before, and the loss was still unfathomable and raw. That day, my mother sat across from me, reclining on a divan like Cleopatra herself, a priceless goblet of wine in one hand. She sipped from it, gracefully and artfully, as she spoke.

"I wish I could put this off, my love," she said, "so it would not ruin your celebrations, but I have delayed as long as I have been permitted."

I presented the impassive, noble expression and posture she required, though I was hung over and unsettled by the atmosphere in the room.

She sighed, setting down her goblet, but her eyes followed it, flinching almost imperceptibly when it clinked against the glass of the side table. She picked it up again, sipping from it with a nervousness I'd never seen in her. "Your father did not kill himself."

I sucked in a startled breath. The emperor had already ruled on the cause of death. Poison. Self-administered.

She swirled the wine in the glass, watching it intently. "He was murdered," she said. Her head came up and she met my eye. "By me."

I had been raised to be the example of noble mien and composure, but I might as well have been a spawn of the slums for all I was capable of concealing at that moment. "What do you mean?"

She sighed, giving me a sad smile. "It was necessary, Enryn, for your future. Your father had become too liberal. He was threatening your inheritance, the established order of things, and your place in that order. I couldn't permit it to go on."

I sat in a daze. I'd thought my parents were happy with each other, or at least content. Theirs had been a political marriage, but that was hardly unusual. Twenty-five years they had been together, and it had seemed peaceful and without much strife.

"I believed I had done it well enough," she said, "and that I had gotten away with it. But the emperor knew better, and he has offered me an option. A quiet, dignified death at my own hand, in order to avoid the scandal and public execution that would result from exposing my crime."

"Mother—"

She held up a hand and I stopped. "You and I both know that there is no choice in the matter at all. Scandal and exposure must be avoided at all costs. For the family name, and for you, my son."

I stood, unable to remain still, and yet I didn't go to her, because that wasn't how it was done in our family. I didn't move, trembling with emotions of every kind, rigid with anger and fear and loss. "You don't have to do this," I said. "We will find some way to hide you, fake your death. Don't do this, Mother."

She nodded toward my chair and I sat down, obedient as ever to the one person in the universe I deferred to completely. She swirled the wine in her glass once more before finishing it off, draining the dregs, and setting it down on the table with a trembling hand.

"I already have."

I was home again and I had no idea what to do with myself. My body was weak; Earth gravity felt like the weight of a mountain on me with every step. I was tired all the time.

But there were other sensations, things that I never realized I missed until I had them back. The brush of the breeze in my hair, the warmth of the sun on my hands and face, the clear and complex smells of life, not just a human stench covered by the sting of sanitizers. The world, in all its colors and sounds; the beauty I had once struggled to capture on paint and canvas, laid out before me like a banquet.

These things I noticed, but as if they were happening to someone else. I could detect, even understand the perfume of flowers, but it was as if I existed here as only an actor playing a part from within the cocoon that surrounded me.

I spent what energy I had wandering the estate, and when I grew too tired, I simply sat outside. When I had to be indoors, all the windows and doors were open. Many times, I drowsed off in the peace and comfort of it, only to find myself back on Dead End. Each time, I woke in panic and cold sweat, wondering if that was the reality and this was the dream.

In spite of Lady Chou's dramatic exit, the servants warmed to me again rather quickly. I had no doubt it was because I told them to come to me at any time if they had a story of Owen to tell. It didn't surprise me that most had an anecdote or two. What servant didn't have many and varied observations of his master?

What I didn't expect was that so many involved some conversation or interaction with my son. When I was a boy, my mother had always discouraged any familiarity with the servants, but apparently my son was being taught differently. While I wanted to hate that, it yielded little treasures of him, glimpses, insights into the person my son was becoming. Stories of him at play, laughing and smiling, full of delight and moments of childish unconcern about the world around him. He had a gentle temperament, like his mother.

They also told me that he came to the estate twice a year with Dawes and the young princess. The emperor came as well, though he usually didn't stay as long as they did. It was the same amount of time they spent each year in Dawes' own duchy. It was little less than I would have brought him here, if things hadn't fallen out the way they did. That Dawes would take care to see that my son knew his home estate was unexpected and baffling.

I was grateful for the time I had to wait before being dumped back into the most dangerous game in the empire. In that wretched prison, I had never let down my guard, lived every day using the words, looks, and expressions necessary to keep myself safe. But on Dead End, the worst they could do was hurt or kill me. The stakes at the palace were much, much bigger.

And there was no denying I was no longer the man who had lived that life, been that person of power, sure in his place and his purpose, so earnestly idealistic. That man had believed himself invincible. How naive he had been.

I was afraid of the man I had been, and the man I had become. I was almost more afraid of the devious and insular world of imperial politics than I was of Dead End. There is more than one way to destroy a man.

I need your help.

Are you all right?

Sure. Except I think Molly's going to drive me crazy.

Oh. I'll be right there.

iv 18

We ate dinner on the veranda, in the cool breeze and with the remnants of sunset. The view of the ocean was blocked from this vantage point and I was glad. The associations were too strong, and I felt so fragile that even such a little thing could break me. We were a subdued group; even Molly's easy chatter was missing for long intervals, and from time to time she examined all the other faces at the table, frowning.

Jonathan's was one of them. He'd tried to fall back into the servant's position and I barely had to growl one complaint before he gave in and sat with us. For a disorienting moment, it felt like a skewed and distorted version of the family I'd had only yesterday, with Pete sitting where Jonathan was now. My stomach roiled but when I looked up, Jonathan was watching Molly, almost entranced, and the feeling passed.

In the middle of one of the long silences, Molly threw down her fork with a clatter.

"Where's Papa?" she demanded angrily. Jonathan and I looked at each other in shock. Owen had gone pale. I reached for Molly's hand. "We talked about this, sweetheart, yesterday. Don't you remember?"

She frowned. "But I'm tired of this game. I don't want to play it anymore."

My stomach dropped. "Mol, baby, this isn't a game. Why do you think it is?"

She glared at me. "Because we've played it before. It's the Being Safe game. It's usually just me and Owen, or just me, but this is how it goes, except we never got in the little ship before. I'm tired of the game now. I want to go home and see Papa."

I closed my eyes against the pain.

"Oh sweetheart." I pulled her into my lap. "I'm so sorry. I didn't know. But this isn't a game, it's real. We can't go home. And Papa's not waiting for us there."

"Why?" Her voice was still sharp, a demand, but her hard determination sounded brittle.

"Because someone killed Papa. We're not going to see him again. It's just us now."

"No!" she yelled into my face. "Papa said that if he was gone I'd be empress. So he can't be gone." Her hands fisted in my shirt. "He's not gone. Don't say that!"

Owen touched her hand. "Molly."

She shook him off, refusing to look at him. I think she knew as well as I did that she'd believe Owen if he told her it was true.

"Molly—"

She scrambled off my lap and ran into the house as fast as she could go.

It took a long time trying to reason with a hysterical four year old before Molly finally cried herself to sleep, furious, her back to me, but holding my hand so tight in her sweaty fist that it hurt. Pete was better with her. She was too much like me.

But Pete was gone. I watched Molly's sleeping form with a knot of dread tightening in my belly. She needed him, not me. He could handle us, that was how it worked. He knew how to temper the ragged edges. What would we do now?

I sat with her longer than I realized. When I finally went to look for Owen he was asleep in his bed. I wasn't sure how I felt about the way he trusted Jonathan enough to have fallen asleep without needing me. Owen was incredibly perceptive. I sometimes trusted his opinions more than my own. With a sigh, I sought my own bed.

Two hours after I'd gone to bed, as I lay there wide-awake, Jonathan entered the room. He didn't knock, or ask, because that was how it went with servants, and I'd lived that life for years. I wondered why it felt strange now. I sat up as he crept quietly into the bedroom.

"Don't you knock?"

"Never."

For some reason that made me smile. The motion felt odd on my face.

"Did you always creep into my room at night?"

"No. There were nighttime servants for that. I did make sure they came for me if you truly weren't sleeping well." I thought about it, how there had always been a servant nearby if I asked, but how it had only ever been Jonathan who would try to bully me into using sleep meds or just annoy me enough that I stopped brooding in bed and started walking around the palace. And it was always him quietly following when I did.

"Did you ever consider me a friend?" I asked.

He settled into a chair, something he never would have done before.

"No. Not because I didn't want to be, but because I knew that I was being everything *but* a friend to you behind your back."

I sighed. "I was never very good at friendship anyway. I'm a dangerous friend to have. Who's left? Chuck. Dr. Okoro. Aliana." I shook my head. "Are they safe now?"

"Yes."

I scowled at him. "That was too quick. You don't even know, do you?"

He gave me a small shake of his head as his mouth cocked in a faint smile. "Of course I do. They're all in very secure positions, and I've checked on them. They're fine."

"You always have everything taken care of and under control, don't you? Do you ever *not* know what you're doing?"

There was no trace of a smile on his face anymore. He stared at his hands in his lap. "All the time, Your Highness. All the time."

"Jake," I corrected quietly.

He didn't look up, and he didn't reply.

I stood on the surface of the asteroid that was home to Dead End. I was alone, in silence under the pitiless, hungry expanse of space. A noise crackled on my com, which should have been dead because once again I was on solitary for something I hadn't even done. Solitary that was slowly driving me to madness and the siren song of death.

"Jake!"

The com noise was faint but the panic in the voice was all too clear. Pete's voice. I spun, too fast, because gravity was more idea than reality here. And I saw Pete, drifting, drifting. Too far away, too high off the ground. The void had already claimed him. There was no getting him back. I could only join him. And I was going to join him. There was no question about that.

"Daddy?"

Molly's sweet voice was like a stab of ice through my heart. I looked down and saw her. She held her arms up to me. "Daddy?"

I cast a look of longing and despair at Pete, already so far away. "I'm sorry," I choked. He reached toward me in desperation, his eyes wide with panic. I couldn't bear it. I bent to pick up Molly, tears fogging my vision and clogging my throat. I lost my grip, shoving at her instead, sending her spinning off in the opposite direction. She screamed.

I bolted upright in a tangle of panic-soaked sheets, my throat raw from screaming. I scrambled from the bed, stumbling blindly toward the closet. It had been the only refuge from the dreams when I was at the IIC. When I didn't have Pete.

The closet was too big, of course. Even away from the palace, everything in this life had always been too big, too much. I wanted to weep in despair. But then I saw a door, set within the closet, just beside the shoes. I opened it.

It was a small closet, big enough for me to lie in if not stretch out. There were clothes hanging in it, things that might have been for Owen, or me, or Pete. Little dresses Molly was too big for now. A tattered sheet. And on the floor was a pillow and folded blanket. I curled up on the floor, closing the door behind me, reaching out to touch the illusory cover and protection of the things hanging above me. I pulled the blanket over my head and gave in to tears for all I had lost, and everything I hadn't.

I crave their stories of my son as I crave air and sunshine. And yet they hurt, sometimes more than any beating I ever endured. So many years lost. He doesn't know me at all.

iv 19

I **wasn't sure what to expect**, and Laudley sent me no message. But on the fourth morning after my return, a standard transport for official palace business arrived. A man stepped casually out of the transport. His posture was open and easy, sure. He was young, no more than his late twenties, and walked with a confidence only a man raised with power could affect. Though he was vaguely familiar, I couldn't place him.

"Your Grace," he said, his voice oddly lyrical.

No, I'd never met him before, but I'd seen him on the broadcasts. This was the new Head Minister, Lord Naganika. He gave me a friendly smile and a slight bow, the formal greeting between equals, but he held it a little longer than I did, dropping his eyes before straightening. I wondered what it meant.

No matter what his rank otherwise, as Head Minister he did not have to show deference to a duke. That he did so now, even with so minor a gesture, carried a great deal of meaning. But what that meaning was, I didn't know. When he straightened, he gestured toward the door of the house.

"Shall we have a chat, Duke Blaine? I have quite a lot to tell you, and I'm sure you have many questions for me."

"This way."

I led him into my study with its expansive view of the lake and the stream cascading into it in a delicate waterfall. When the door was shut, he sank into a chair in front of my desk and nodded toward the corner of it.

"I understand you have something there that we might want to use right now."

Embedded in that side of the desk was a spy filter, and activating it would make our conversation as private as it was possible to be. If the empire had methods capable of penetrating the web of defenses that device activated, I didn't know about them. This office was one of the few places my father-in-law had ever been willing to have detailed conversations. And if he'd sent Lord Naganika here for a chat, the anti-eavesdropping and recording measures must still be up to date and reliable. I triggered the device. Lord Naganika sat back with a smile.

"Have you enjoyed your holiday here? I'm sorry it must be so short."

I settled into my chair with nonchalance I had been practicing for days. "I have. What news from the palace?"

His smile quirked a bit, as if I'd passed a test. "The news is, at present, that Grand Duke Laudley has taken control of the council. With all appearance of benevolence and concern for the former Imperial Family, of course, and they believe him. Or, if they don't, they're afraid to cross him." He shrugged. "Either way works for now."

"Indeed. And what does he tell them?"

"What they need to hear. He's securing the palace against whoever was behind the assassination, he's searching for the children, he's determined to see justice done for Rikhart IV, and he will personally ensure a safe and peaceful transition to the rightful heir."

"So he's ruling the empire until such time as the rightful heir is produced?"

"Correct." He grinned wryly. "Though that's not exactly how we've been phrasing it."

I made a dignified sound of dismissal. "And to what 'rightful heir' is he referring?"

Lord Naganika sat forward, elbows on knees, eager. For a moment I thought less of him for giving himself away so easily. But then I wondered if he'd done it on purpose, and I decided not to let my guard down. "Well that's the question, isn't it? He's certainly implying that it's Princess Marquilla."

"Is it?"

He grinned. "Of course. If she's alive."

"Is she? Does he intend for her to be?" I hated the words even as they left my mouth, but I was proud of the way they did. Calm and steady as if I wasn't discussing the murder of the imperial heir, a child.

Lord Naganika may have felt the same, or at least he pretended he did, because he sobered. "We don't know one way or the other, at present. But there's been no immediate discussion of killing the princess." I allowed myself to raise an eyebrow but I said nothing.

My own ignorance frustrated me. If I knew anything more than any inmate on Dead End, it was information five years old or more. I tried to remember how long this man had held his position and I was appalled to realize I wasn't sure. Not only that I hadn't known already, even a guess from the first time he appeared on the broadcasts we were shown on Dead End, but also that I hadn't thought to look it up yet. I was badly out of practice.

I sat back, considering the man. The revelation that his loyalties hadn't been with Rikhart was disconcerting. It wasn't a question of virtue or duty so much as a reminder of my own failures. For all my lying, scheming, plotting, and acts of treason, I realized only later that I'd been terribly naive.

I had one purpose: to eliminate the dangerous stain on the empire that was an unclass in the emperor's bed, whispering in his ear. I'd been focused on that, and I hadn't even considered playing a double game against my co-conspirators. I might have been the only one among us who hadn't. I certainly felt the impact when I was caught, and discovered that some of the very people who worked at the emperor's side to condemn me were the ones who had helped me work against him.

Not that I'd betrayed any of them, or even felt they'd betrayed me. It had always been a part of the arrangement that we worked separately and if any of us were stupid or unlucky enough to get caught, we would go down alone and protect the others as much as possible. The extent of the others' duplicity had surprised me, though, and I was ashamed of that now.

"So where do I come in? Laudley clearly has plans for me."

Lord Naganika smiled. "Yes. Indeed. In fact, don't tell him I said this, but much of his plan at this point depends on you. More than he intended it to, I think."

I raised a brow. "How is that?"

"Well, he expected to have the children in his possession. Dawes being gone isn't a terrible problem. Laudley intended for him to be dead, but that can be arranged easily enough. He will be found, eventually, and all his protections have been stripped away. He is of little concern. The fact that he has the children, and that we currently don't know where they are, is the trouble. It's what makes you more important than you were intended to be."

"What was I intended to be?"

"The Regent," he said, with enviable nonchalance. "Laudley intends to set Owen up as the next emperor."

My heart beat faster. "So he does intend to kill the princess?"

Lord Naganika tilted his head. "I think he hopes that will not be necessary."

"Because she'll already be dead?"

"Yes," he said, "that would be ideal. But there are ways around even that. Much can happen before she is old enough to rule alone."

"But he doesn't intend for her to rule."

"She's the child of an unclass."

So simple, so direct. I'd felt the same way. At least, before talk of murdering a child had come into the picture.

"Does my status not present a problem for him? I'm not only a convicted traitor, I'm supposed to be dead."

Naganika cocked a grin. "But don't you see? That's the beauty of the situation. When the empire learns what Dawes did to you, a duke of your standing, behind the emperor's back, they'll be quite upset, don't you think? And what better way to see justice done than to compensate you for the Prince Consort's despicable and illegal treatment of you?"

"It wasn't behind the emperor's back."

"With both of them gone, I think we can direct the story as we see fit. What we say is what is true, now. You'll be hailed as a returning hero—you're a symbol of all the things Dawes was doing to destroy the empire, now restored to your proper place in the grand scheme of things. And with your son still missing, your role as a grieving father will build sympathy and perhaps help us find Dawes—and Owen—as well."

"Do we have any idea where Dawes is?"

"He went to the safehouse."

"And where is that?"

"We have people working on finding it. I'm not optimistic that we will. Almost all of the information about it is emperor-level clearance only. We don't even know which planet it's on, if it's even in the empire. But once you are certified as the legal Regent, you should have access to information that we do not have at present. If only more clues for our team to work with."

I put my elbow on the armrest of my chair, propping my chin in my hand, feeling transparently obvious, even though it was a gesture that had come naturally to me once. "Then I imagine we have some work to do, Minister. And not here."

He smiled slyly. "No, not here at all." His grin broadened. "Would you like to return to the palace, Your Grace?"

Stop by the lab before you go so I can give you a proper goodbye.

The lab?

I've got that new couch in here if you're not up to anything more adventurous, old man.

I'll show you who's old.

I wish you weren't going away again so soon.

I know. Me too.

iv20

We spent the morning questing about the island, looking for the perfect branches, twigs, and leaves. The children and I built a small canoe and in the light of a brilliant sunset, three days after Pete's murder, we stood on the beach and placed our offerings in it.

Molly went first. Hers was a sheet of real paper, which I didn't even bother to wonder how or why Jonathan had laying around. "Papa," she had written, in her careful, blocky handwriting, "I promise I'll take care of the empire as good as you did." I looked away, my throat tight.

Owen's was on paper too, but his was folded and sealed. He hadn't shown anyone what was on it, and I hadn't asked. That was between him and Pete.

It wasn't until my turn that I realized I was twisting the ring on my finger so hard it had left a mark. It was a simple ring with only one black stone in the setting. For the first three years we were together, up until the day of my sentencing and exile, I'd never seen Pete without the ring on his littlest finger. That last horrible day, he'd put it on mine.

It was an heirloom belonging to the rulers of the empire. He'd had no business giving it to me especially since, at the time, we both believed I was never coming back. I'd protested but he said, "It's fitting it should go with you. Another thing I thought I'd never part with."

It was almost painful to pull the ring from my finger, as if I were tearing away a piece of myself. I looked down at it, cupped in my palm, fighting the urge to close my hand around it and keep it. But it wasn't really mine. He'd sent it away with me when he believed I was never coming back. Now it was my turn. He was never coming back.

I laid it in the little boat with the other things.

I looked back at Jonathan. He met my gaze and held it for a long time, waiting, until realization began to dawn on his face, his brows rising as the carefully controlled body language dissolved into something closer to shock, and defeat.

"I don't think it's appropriate—" he started.

"Shut up, Jonathan," I rasped past the pain in my throat, "and put yours in there. I know you have one."

He stared at the boat, conflict warring in his features. Temptation battled his everlasting stubbornness and a guilt I understood far too well. Finally he reached into his shirt and pulled from around his neck a simple chain from which hung an odd-shaped pendant. When he laid it reverently in the boat I realized it was a lock of dark brown hair. I sighed, my eyes closing against the understanding.

"It's your daughter's, isn't it?"

"Yes."

"You don't have to do that. Pete wouldn't have wanted you to—"

"Shut up, Jake," he said gently. I froze. The times in my life when he'd called me by name were less than a handful, and some of those I wasn't sure I hadn't imagined. The only one I knew was real was the time in his cell in the palace prison. He'd turned his back on me, razor edged contempt in his voice that I now understood had been for himself not me. "Go away, Jacob." But, no matter what I'd said all those years ago or on arriving here, he had never, ever called me Jake.

I shivered.

Ignoring the reaction he no doubt meant to provoke, Jonathan crouched and laid the lock of hair in the boat with the other offerings. He stepped back and I took a deep breath.

"Is that everything?"

Molly rushed forward. "No, wait." She placed a bright green feather in the boat. Looking up at me she said, "I wanted to show it to him."

My eyes burned with tears I was saving for a better time. And then I realized there was no better time. I let them fall as I took two vials from my pocket and crouched by the boat. I snapped the vials together and placed them in the tinder at the bottom. The acid would eat through the membrane between them in minutes and ignite the kindling. I pushed the boat into the water, out past the low, rolling breakers, until it bobbed alone on gentle waves, waiting.

I held Molly's and Owen's hands as we watched in silence.

The first lick of flame appeared above the hull, growing until it was a full blaze that consumed the boat, the offerings, and finally doused with a sizzle as the boat broke apart, whatever was left of the items in it sinking into the ocean. I imagined the ring, all that I had in the way of my husband's remains to release into the universe, dropping slowly through the clear blue water, coming to rest on the ocean floor. Would anyone ever find it? Or would it lay there until the sun died and the earth was consumed in its funeral pyre?

I supposed it didn't matter. He was gone either way.

We returned to the house, dragging and wrung out. I carried Molly directly to her room and put her to sleep, trying to soothe away her little sniffles but not trying too hard. She should be allowed to cry because her father was dead. I sat with Owen for a long time after I'd tucked him under the covers. We talked quietly about Pete. I don't remember what we said, but I don't think the particulars mattered.

My return to the palace was as furtive, illegal, and inconceivable as my departure had been.

iv21

Naganika had with him a suit of clothes, new and cut in the current style. I no longer had anything appropriate. I examined the cut on my forehead in the mirror. A servant had tended it for me, bandaged and sealed it, but there was still a visible scar, ragged and ugly, the newer scar cutting through the old one.

"I hope you will not take offense," Naganika said, as he'd overseen a man handing over the new clothes to my own servant, "but Grand Duke Laudley believes it would be beneficial to leave the scar as it is and make no attempt to eliminate or disguise it."

My jaw tightened. He noticed and dropped his eyes.

"I understand that you might find it undesirable, and I would certainly expect you would deal with it in time, but for now it gives credence to your story and is a powerful symbol of what you suffered at the hands of the real traitors."

I studied him, wondering if I was impressed or disgusted that he managed the lie so easily and so consistently.

I pondered the scar. On the one hand, I couldn't be rid of it fast enough. It was a reminder of things I hoped to forget as quickly as I could. It was a reminder of the man I had to become to survive, of a set of priorities and beliefs that had been so foreign to me five years ago. I bore scars now—not just that one, and not all of them visible—because at Dead End, unless you were at risk of infection or too injured to work, the medic didn't want to bother with you. Bandages could be obtained with the other supplies we were allowed access to, like soap and toothpaste.

But inmates didn't use them. A bandage carried connotations that were dangerous, and made impressions you couldn't afford to make. On Dead End, you suffered and bled in silence or you suffered and bled more. There was more shame in patching up than in needing to.

I had a feeling it was a lesson I needed to carry with me into whatever happened now.

The ocean was bigger than I remembered. I caught my breath when it came into view, a great expanse of life and endless shades of color whooshing past the great windows of the transport, the strip of sand like the threshold leading into the great throne room at the palace.

"Surely it can't be this easy," I said. Naganika gave me his full attention with an air of respect that looked genuine, even if I didn't trust it.

"I beg your pardon, Your Grace?"

"My return. I am still a convicted traitor, the last time I checked. And I am dead, too. I'm simply going to walk into the palace and no one will object?"

Naganika smiled as if at a joke. "I do wish I could be there to see their faces when you arrive." But he sobered quickly. "You are not expected, but the Grand Duke has secured the cooperation of the palace security forces. I don't believe they know who they're expecting, but they will obey Laudley."

"Just like that? The same men and women who would have given their lives for Rikhart only days ago?"

Naganika's nod was slower, considered. "The ones who wouldn't cooperate have already been...weeded out. Most remembered that their oaths were given to the empire, not to a specific emperor."

At some point I realized Lord Naganika had left me alone. Perhaps it was only because he had work to do, but I had the strangest feeling it was because he was trying to respect my privacy. I was glad that I was alone when the palace came into view. I wasn't able to stifle a gasp at the sight. It wasn't as precious or dear to me as my own estate, but it was monumentally more important, and more meaningful. This place at the center of the empire, the seat of everything that was great and powerful and wondrous and dangerous. It was a place to make or destroy a man, and it had done both to me already.

The transport gliding to a stop at a private arrival platform felt like a rebirth, and I was afraid I was just as prepared for and capable of managing this world as any other newborn.

Laudley was waiting for us on the platform, dressed formally. He'd always dressed as a man of his station, importance and rank written into every stitch, but there was something about him now that exuded power as well, and I knew Naganika was correct. Grand Duke Laudley was running things at the palace now.

He gave me a superficial embrace and a smile.

"This must be quite the day for you," he said. "It has been a long time since you have seen this place, has it not?"

As if the truly important thing to me right now was being in the palace. I didn't bother to answer such an obvious question, and it annoyed me more than I wanted him to see. Laudley wasn't the only one who understood the importance of appearances.

Laudley may have been the architect of this little charade— from which I would benefit immensely—but whatever gratitude I had toward Laudley was a weakness, and wasn't even terribly grateful. What he'd done hadn't been for me.

I looked around and froze as I locked eyes with the guard captain. My mind raced, immediately cataloguing how big he was, how he vibrated with barely checked violence. Cold sweat broke out on my back and palms.

And then I remembered. This wasn't Dead End. This man answered to me now. A rush of anger filled me and I clung to it, taking a deep breath, stoking it. It felt strong and vital. I needed this; I needed to be angry.

I held his gaze, the hard, hot acknowledgement between us that he had been the one to load me onto a transport to Dead End as the rest of the empire watched my "execution." Fury set my shoulders and locked my spine. He looked away first.

When I looked at Laudley he was watching me with an eyebrow cocked, assessment and even amusement in the set of his mouth. I wiped all expression from my face, choking off the mantra that had reflexively started its auto-play in my head. No. Not that. I didn't need that anymore. I was strong. I was powerful.

Never again.

Laudley turned to the guard captain. "As you can see, Duke Blaine is not only alive and well, but is to be treated with all due respect and deference. I trust that your men not only know this and will act accordingly, but that there will be no unpleasant reactions among the civilians at the palace."

The captain—Sam—answered slowly. "Yes, Your Grace."

He nodded to one of his guards and she accepted the order, bowing briefly before departing, though she didn't look at me.

"But wouldn't it be better, Your Grace," Sam continued, "to make an announcement to inform the occupants of the palace of this...change? It would make for much less disruption and help prevent unfortunate surprises."

Laudley looked entertained. "No. I think I can trust your people to maintain order. I don't wish to make announcements yet."

I looked away from Laudley in disgust, holding on to my anger. Standing behind Laudley were two servants I didn't recognize, and another off to the side that I did.

"Sabria?"

The woman who had been my wife's head servant dropped into a perfect bow. "Your Grace."

I studied her face. It was hard to discern what she was thinking. I felt the weight of Laudley's gaze on us and I turned to him. He wore an enigmatic smile.

"Sabria has been Owen's head servant since he moved in with the Imperial Family," he said.

I froze, taking a moment to process that. Days ago it might have surprised me more. Now I only felt the stirrings of vague bemusement that was becoming the default reaction to any news of my son's life as the ward of Jacob Dawes.

Sabria was a tangible and real connection to Hera. I didn't wonder so much that Dawes would want to preserve that influence in Owen's life. Dawes had loved Hera, in his way, though I felt the familiar tightening of anger at the thought.

But Sabria had worked in my household all the time I'd been scheming against Dawes. He could have arranged for her to tell Owen of his mother without keeping her so close. The head servant's influence on a child can be enormous. How could he have trusted her? Why would he?

"I thought that you might like to have her as your head servant as well," Laudley continued. "At least until you find someone who suits you better."

I watched her, noting with approval the way she didn't shy from my gaze.

"She will do for now."

I didn't love Hera when I married her. I didn't even know her. But the time it took to transition from indifference to something more was so short I barely remember it. She was such a genuinely good person. I didn't understand her, but I did love her.

iv22

We walked openly into the halls of the noble section. Startled, frightened gasps and exclamations rippled around us as we passed. A servant screamed, dropping the laden tray she carried. Laudley nodded to one of the guards and I noted with little amusement that the woman would probably lose her position at the palace now. It simply wasn't appropriate behavior for a palace servant, even if she had just seen a dead man roaming the halls.

"Where now?" I said.

"To the council chambers."

I stopped. "And you think we'll have privacy there?" Anger fueled my sarcasm.

His self-satisfied expression infuriated me. "No. In fact, I've already requested a meeting with the council, as well as all the dukes in residence."

He hadn't stopped when I did, but he was forced to, now—I still hadn't moved from my spot. He gave me a disappointed look. "Surprise is the best offense, I think."

It didn't escape me that the council and dukes weren't the only ones he was surprising. I gave him a cold look. "If you expect me to be the public face for your schemes, you will at least keep me informed. This isn't a game."

He smiled maliciously. "Oh, Enryn, it is always a game." When I didn't reply he shrugged. "When you need to know something, you can be sure I will inform you."

"I refuse to do this until you answer my questions."

"You refuse?" He took an obvious look around at the astonished, even hostile expressions of the passersby, the growing crowd of gawkers, and the guards who were the only wall between me and them. "And what do you think that will accomplish for you."

Fury boiled within me. He grinned when I had no answer. "You don't have many choices here, Eight." The world went black and red at the edges. "Only one, really. You can walk into that council room with me. Because I don't think you want to go back into the only other place you can go if you defy me."

I couldn't suppress the cold shiver and his grin widened. "Come, Blaine," he said, "there's no need to make a scene. We have another one to make now that will be much more satisfying, I assure you."

I joined him, stunned, trembling with anger and ice-cold terror. I didn't look at him. He chuckled to himself as we walked on.

The men and women in the council room gasped and startled just as the others had, no more noble than the commoners in the corridor. It was ridiculous that I'd never noticed before.

Everyone was standing, so I took the seat at the head of the table, pulled it a little away, and sat down. I drew on knowledge and years of practice and positioned myself so that my body language projected confidence, even boredom, hoping it would hide the thudding of my heart and the trembling of my knees.

Laudley made his explanations, told his story of my tragedy and suffering. They watched me surreptitiously, eyes darting up to the scars on my face and quickly away again. I said and did nothing. It occurred to me that once upon a time that would have been a deliberate effort. Now, it was the default.

On Dead End the one place I could find some sanctuary was within my cell, but our walls were merely force fields, no visible separation from the others. I imagined them now, the walls between me and this group of entitled, naive nobles. I watched them, watched Laudley play them as I might have watched Kafe or one of the other gang leaders manipulate those who followed them. There was so little difference between the politics there and here—just the stakes, and the methods. These people were amateurs.

I sat silently as Laudley laid out his plan for the imperial rule.

"Emperor?" Duke Annis said, watching me sideways.

"Regent," Laudley clarified. Annis still watched me, as if he needed my reaction, but he wasn't going to get it. Both because there was power in silence and because Laudley hadn't told me his plans. I felt as if I floundered in deep waters. I knew how to swim, but I was weak, and tired.

"Regent for whom?"

I affected a small smile for Annis, holding his gaze until he looked away. The relief was overwhelming.

"For the child, of course," Laudley answered. I watched carefully, noting who did and didn't take that answer as enough.

"We don't know where Prince Owen is yet," Duchess Xian said.

I held my breath. So easily he had turned their minds to Owen. The princess was Rikhart's child, but she was contaminated. Half unclass. The nobles would not fail to take note, and no doubt he had been reminding them. Owen was the perfect solution for them. So long as Princess Marquilla didn't return.

A hole grew in my chest at the way I so easily thought of the death of a child, even as I longed for my own.

"And if Prince Owen does not materialize, how do we transition power away from a man who has been installed in front of the entire empire?" the duchess pressed. I deliberately didn't look at her, as if her objections weren't worth my time.

"Transition to whom?" Laudley said, a dangerous hush in his voice. "If the worst happens and Prince Owen is truly gone, who would you have in power then?"

"That's an important consideration," Naganika replied. "But who has more claim to the throne than the Blaines and the Laudleys? Prince Owen is the last of the Laudley line. If he does not return, Duke Blaine inherits those rights."

"The Xian family—"

"Oh come on," Duke Shanks snapped. This one was young and impulsive. I had worked closely with his father in the days before my exile, but the old duke had apparently died since then. "As if we need more upheaval now. You know Naganika is right." He sneered at her. "Besides, if you truly want to debate the point, the Shanks family has a better claim to the succession than the Xians will ever have."

Duchess Xian drew in a sharp breath. "What a completely absurd assertion—"

"Enough," I said, and I suppressed a smile when both immediately fell silent and turned to me. Did they not see the way they already acknowledged me as the superior of them all?

"The decision has been made. The technicalities of interim versus permanent power, and whatever adjustments will be necessary when the children are recovered, will be lost on the common people. They need surety and decisiveness now, and clarity. There will be an announcement and a coronation, the details and legalities will be worked out by the council before anything is sealed. This quibbling is only a delay and a distraction. It ignores the most important issue of all, the recovery of my son."

"And the traitor as well," Duke Shanks said. I nodded.

"The traitor as well. Though I consider those goals one and the same, since Owen will be with him." Several of the nobles nodded in agreement. "Now, I want reports on the progress of the investigation from those of you overseeing the efforts and I want the rest of the council working on drawing up the necessary documents. I'd like to speak to the Grand Duke now. The rest of you are dismissed."

How easily they fell into my hand. I trembled, with both anxiety and excitement.

When the others had departed, Laudley took a seat at an angle to me, a pleased smirk on his face he would normally have hidden. It galled me, this intimacy he pretended, even while he doled out information to me as he saw fit.

"I see you had things well in hand before my arrival."

He smiled. "I would not have brought you here otherwise."

I kept my face blank, stoking the anger that gave me strength. "You make it look so easy. Within scant days you've brought the entire power structure of the empire to heel."

He affected a casual pose. "If by easy you mean the cumulative effect of years of planning and preparation, then yes, pulling the trigger—at last—went nearly as smoothly as I planned."

"You subverted the nobles right under Rikhart's nose?"

"I exploited cracks Rikhart opened himself with his marriage to the unclass."

"I thought they had gotten used to Dawes?"

"Being used to something and agreeing with it are different things. They were not brave enough to do anything about it themselves, but many of your peers were only too happy to support someone else who had the courage to act."

"And the common people will accept this so easily? Dawes is something of a hero to them now."

He scoffed. "He *was*. But that is of no concern. The people will believe what they are told. Do you think the empire would have lasted this long if they thought for themselves?"

I stared at him in astonishment. He watched me, chuckling. "You know, Enryn, this is why I chose you to marry my daughter. You are not stupid, but you are so dreadfully sincere. Hera would have seen right through a more astute conspirator, but you truly believe all the propaganda. Smart and ruthless enough to do what needs to be done, but so naive about what we were actually doing and why."

I looked away from Laudley. He fairly radiated satisfaction. That was good. I could let him enjoy his victory. But not for too long, lest he get the idea that gratitude or weakness would put me under his control. The crown would sit on my head, not his.

Can you come to the lab? You have to see this.

Will it wait half an hour?

What have I told you about the secrets of the universe?

OK, they wait for no man. But could they wait just a little bit, for the emperor?

iv23

I didn't even try to sleep that night. I wandered the house alone in the dark, and that was when I found the lab.

It was a physicists' lab, to rival any of the small labs at the IIC. I stood there for a long time, just staring at it. It wasn't generic or for light use. It wasn't a jumble of the proper equipment with no understanding of function. It had been set up by someone who had taken care to make it efficient and logical. Of course Jonathan would do that.

I spent the rest of the night in and out of the garage, cannibalizing the transport, taking parts of it with me to the lab. Jonathan had explained that the transport had been deactivated the moment we arrived, and could no longer be used. That sounded like a challenge to me.

I broke it down, dissecting the things I was passingly familiar with, figuring out how the theories and concepts I knew well were constructed into useful applications. Sometimes I almost reached for the comm, meaning to tell Pete about something fascinating I'd learned, only to remember he wasn't there anymore.

I buried myself and my grief in physics. It wasn't a comfort, but it helped me forget for the night and it gave me a purpose. I worked into the next day, stopping only for breakfast with the children. Jonathan was doing his planning and plotting, all the stuff at which I was so useless. But I could do this.

Jonathan would come up with plans, plans that would work, backup plans for the backup plans. It would probably all be foolproof and look as easy as breathing when it was anything but. All my efforts in the lab might be redundant or fruitless, but at least they were something. Things could happen to the people you were depending on, who you believed were capable of anything, who were invincible. That wasn't a lesson I was going to forget again.

So while Jonathan worked on all the intelligent and meaningful ways we could act now, I worked on adapting the science and technology that had gotten us away from the assassins when we shouldn't have been able to. I would use it to keep us safe. The house may be well hidden, the empire's most protected secret, but with the resources of the entire empire and enough time, I didn't believe it would be impossible for a determined man to figure out.

The people who had killed an emperor had proven themselves determined, and they had too much interest in finding us—even if it wasn't for simple spite, or revenge, or to clean up the mess. I had the heir and Prince Owen. So I focused on a way to get us off this island under our own power. Not that we had anywhere to go now, and maybe not ever. But I didn't plan on being a sitting duck when or if they ever found us. And I knew better than to discount the possibility.

When I explained my project to Jonathan, his eyebrows climbed slowly as a small smile touched his mouth.

"It's a very good idea," he said. "That is one of the greatest weaknesses of the safehouse. The only way off the island is in a transport that must be triggered from the palace." At my expression of surprise he frowned at me. "There's little chance that it would be safe for you to leave here if your allies weren't already in control of the palace. I never even considered that we might be able to leave here in any other way. Transporting ourselves off the island expands our options considerably."

It was high praise from Jonathan, and I accepted it for what it was worth.

I considered trying to hotwire the return transport somehow, but that was hardly my area of expertise. Even though the propulsion system on the first transport had essentially self-destructed once we entered the garage, I still understood its principles better and had more confidence I could make that work.

Propulsion was physics and physics was what I did. I applied myself furiously. Owen joined me often but Molly, in general, ignored us. She had her other father's brilliance in the humanities, and gave our scientific endeavors all the attention she thought they deserved, which was very little of hers.

For all his interest in helping me, Owen rarely left Molly for long. I wondered if he realized that it was as much for himself as for her. They shared a grief that was different than mine. And there's some sense of control, even if it's false, in protecting the ones you have left.

Jonathan sat at my side when the children were otherwise occupied. The familiarity of his presence was easy to take for granted and hard to ignore. Sometimes we talked, and it was the exact opposite of what I expected. I thought we would stick to safe subjects, shy away from the rawness of pain, the wounds that had been re-opened with our unexpected reunion. But Jonathan avoided nothing.

"I don't think there was a worse punishment you could have come up with for me."

I frowned. "What do you mean? Back at the palace? Letting you go?"

He gave me a weak smile. "Yes. You made lies of all my excuses. I'd told myself that I couldn't stop spying on you for Blaine because you'd never understand, and the consequences would be too dire. And yet, when you found out, all you did was let me go.

I'd told myself that it was best for it to be me, that I made a buffer between you and Blaine because you trusted me. But I only made it that much easier for him to hurt you because you *did* trust me. Anyone else you'd have suspected, or at least considered, once you were being attacked in so many personal and intimate ways. But you never even questioned whether I could be behind any of it." The lift of his lips looked more like nausea than amusement.

"You took away all my defenses. I couldn't pretend that I was anything but a cowardly traitor, that I'd done anything short of absolute betrayal. I couldn't believe my own lie that anyone else would have shielded you from damage better than I did. Or even that anyone trying to hurt you could have done better than I did with no more than my silence."

I sighed. "We both made mistakes," I said. "Even with the best of intentions."

"Mine weren't always the best of intentions."

I shrugged. "Neither were mine." I turned to face him. "You were good for me, Jonathan, more than you were bad." I couldn't help a small smile. "I'm sorry you had to see you weren't as perfect as you thought you were."

His expression was hard and unforgiving. "I never thought I was perfect at all."

I gave him a wry grin. "Well, I did. That has to count for something."

He looked away. "More than you'll ever know."

It's 4:00am on Tuesday morning, 175 days since I sent you into exile. How can I still miss you so badly? I've been lying here for hours wondering what you're doing now that you're back at the IIC.

That first night we worked together in the lab on the ship, you told me that even science can be boring sometimes. I'd give anything for us to be bored together right now.

I really should stop writing these. I don't think they're helping. And I'm afraid I'll break down and send one to you eventually.

iv.24

I put the children to bed that night, exhausted beyond belief, but still not certain I could sleep, or if I wanted to. At least in the lab I was *doing* something. But Jonathan was waiting in the hall.

"There's been an official broadcast." My stomach tightened and I just nodded. I followed him into the sitting room and watched him turn on the vid with dread heavy in my gut.

Lord Naganika's calm, familiar tones were almost soothing, if I didn't listen to the words.

The empire has issued an order for the capture and arrest of the former Prince Consort Jacob Dawes in connection with the assassination of Emperor Rikhart IV and the kidnapping of Crown Princess Marquilla and Prince Owen Blaine. He is to be considered extremely dangerous and in possession of hostages. Do not attempt to apprehend him yourselves. Contact the ISS or any local imperial officer if you see him or have information as to his whereabouts.

Naganika looked appropriately indignant.

But there is happy news among the bad. The empire need not know uncertainty and chaos in the wake of our emperor's death and the heir's disappearance. One of our own has been returned to us. Among the many crimes for which the former Prince Jacob will be made to pay are the ridiculous and entirely false accusations against Duke Enryn Blaine which led the emperor to condemn him to death for treason. Prince Jacob then defied the emperor's will and had Duke Blaine sent, in secret, to a hidden labor camp. We have found and recovered the duke and he is recuperating at the palace.

I stared at Naganika's face, his perfect air of relief tempered with a somber note of loss.

Duke Blaine is an example of what is good and great: the son of a house as old as the empire itself, he worked tirelessly to protect the unclass in cooperation with our late emperor. He was treasonously betrayed by the prince consort, just as our emperor was. His son, our beloved Prince Owen, is second in line for the throne. For these reasons and many others, the council has decided that it is in the best interests of the empire to appoint him Emperor Regent. With the diligence of no other, he will work for the healing of the empire, will defend us from enemies both within and without, and will strengthen and hold the throne for the heir's return.

Long live the emperor!

And that was how I found out that they were blaming Pete's death on me. That they claimed I had *murdered* him.

Fury stole my breath and for a long moment, I thought perhaps I would just explode, or dissolve and cease to exist.

"How?" I croaked.

"I'll find out," Jonathan replied, his voice gentle, all trace of distance gone. I stared through him, unable to see anything but the horrid images of Pete's murder, fighting nausea at the idea that I could have had *anything* to do with that.

"Jake." Jonathan laid his hand over mine and squeezed until it hurt. I focused on him.

"I will find out more. We *will* do something. We will fight back."

I nodded, trying to stand but falling back into the chair when my knees gave out. Jonathan was at my side, his hand under my arm, helping me up. "I need to sleep," I choked.

He nodded. "I'll get you something."

It had once been so foreign to me to feel uncertain or off-balance. But returning to the palace had the same feeling of triumph and assurance as being processed into Dead End.

iv25

A day later, Lord Naganika stood before my desk, waiting.

"Where are we on the search for the children?" I asked.

His expression became somber. "It is unchanged. We are still pursuing it diligently, but we have no new leads. We continue to work on the old ones."

"What leads?"

"Quite honestly, mostly rumor and suspicion. The location of the safehouse, even its existence, is one of the most sacred secrets in the empire. Searching official channels and records is of course being done, but in my opinion it's pointless. The security and secrecy wrapped around its location and maintenance are unfathomable."

He looked grave. "What leads we have are servants' gossip. There are some who are knowingly or unknowingly involved in the maintenance of the safehouse, and many more who think they are. We are following up on every supposition put forward, no matter how unlikely, but none have been useful yet. Even those who know they are part of the process have no more information than necessary. There is no direct link to the location or to any method of getting anyone or anything out there. Of that I'm certain. And many of those who do know anything, however unhelpful, have been—" he paused and smiled. "They have been as unhelpful as possible."

I frowned. "And this unhelpfulness amuses you?"

He dimmed his smile very deliberately, but did not wipe it away entirely. "Amused is not the correct descriptor, I think. I'm proud of them. They are highly placed and highly trusted. They understand that the directive to keep this secret at all costs supersedes that of any current ruler, no matter who he is or how he got here. For all that they loved him so universally, I think they would have been just as unforthcoming to Rikhart IV on this subject as they are being with us now."

I digested that. "I can appreciate the sense of it, but you understand that it is hard for me to appreciate anyone who is keeping me from my son."

Naganika went still. "May I speak frankly, Your Grace?"

"Always."

His expression was neutral. "I know your history with him is complicated at best, and I know you want to be reunited with your son simply because you want to be reunited with your son, but there is no one who will cherish Owen's safety and wellbeing more than Prince Jacob will." He paused. "The former Prince Jacob, I mean."

I stiffened. Perhaps I could admit to myself that Dawes had been good to Owen, but I couldn't bear the reminder that he was still keeping my son from me. "I appreciate you mean well," I said, each word clipped off in angry snips, "but I do not want to hear of that man's usurpation of my son in a positive light ever again. Is that quite clear, Lord Naganika?"

He bowed deeply to me. "Perfectly clear, Your Grace. Forgive me for offending you."

I reined in my temper with effort. "I am not offended. I simply mean to make my stance on this matter clear."

"Thank you, Your Grace." He waited. When I said nothing more he continued. "There is one more matter, Your Grace." I nodded for him to continue. "We have received a message that is of some concern."

I went still. "Who is it from?"

"Perhaps it will explain itself if I read it to you."

I gestured for him to continue. He glanced at his tablet, though he didn't appear to need it to recite the message, as if he'd read this many times already.

"*We know you killed him and we won't let you get away with it. Your pawn will never be king.*" He glanced up at me. "It is signed 'the Resistance.'"

"The Resistance?"

He nodded. "This is the first we've heard of them. But this message came yesterday. Before I had a chance to bring it to you, we received another." I nodded, my skin crawling. "This one reads *The heir will return. And the other. But not for you.*"

My voice was hard to find. "And this is also from the 'Resistance'? It appears they know a great deal about what is going on here."

"Or they've made the obvious guess."

I examined him but he didn't flinch from my scrutiny. "I don't think it's ever been a question of whether or not people might suspect the Grand Duke, but whether or not we can deflect suspicion well enough until it doesn't matter anymore."

"To whom were these messages sent?"

His mouth cocked in a bit of a smile. "In that we were fortunate. They came into a shared inbox that can be accessed by the councilors' aides and myself. I happened to be the first to access the inbox the day the initial message arrived. Since then, I have set up a filter so that all such messages come directly to me."

"You're sure the others didn't see this?"

"As sure as I can be."

I pursed my lips. "And Laudley has not seen these?"

"No, Your Grace."

I watched him, considering. "Thank you for bringing this to me first."

He nodded a small bow. "You are to be Regent, Your Grace. You are the one I report and answer to."

I held back a smile but nodded once in approval.

"You may go."

He bowed deeply and left.

Molly has to have grown an inch last night.

Dr. Heinriksen should be able to confirm that.

Oh Jake, you're so unromantic.

What's that supposed to mean?

I talk about how fast our daughter is growing up and you want empirical data.

Don't you?

iv26

In spite of the sleeping medicine, I woke well before dawn. Jonathan was already up, or perhaps he'd never gone to bed. In either case, he already had a great deal of information for me.

"The official explanation is that you were unwilling to allow your daughter to play any role in the governance of the empire if the emperor didn't accede to your demand to eliminate the class system entirely, and redistribute the wealth from the upper classes to the lower. The emperor supposedly not only stated he would do no such thing, but began to put into place measures that would prevent that ever happening, not just for him but for Molly as well. When you discovered he had well and truly thwarted you—and because you had only pretended to love and marry him for that very purpose—you arranged to have him killed so Molly would rule and you would have yourself declared Regent for her. You expected to be able to accomplish your ends that way."

I stared as Jonathan dispassionately laid out complete and utter nonsense. It could have been a plausible story, if I'd never loved Pete. If he hadn't been everything that was good about me. I slumped back in my chair with a heavy sigh.

"So why would I be here, then?"

"For nearly the same reason that you actually are. The assassin got him, but someone realized you were behind it and tried to apprehend you, so you took the princess and ran. Owen was insurance. And a backup plan."

I huffed out a long breath. "OK, so I screwed up their plans by getting away with the children. But how does Blaine fit into this, then? Whoever killed Pete must have wanted power after he was gone. Presumably, it's someone already in the line of succession. But they'd have to kill everyone ahead of them." I scowled. "Who's in line after Molly? It's not Aliana anymore, is it?"

Jonathan gave me a long look of barely concealed irritation. "No, it isn't. You should already know who is next, Prince Jacob."

I gave him a long, furious look. "Should I? Do you think I care who rules the empire if my husband and daughter are dead?"

"Owen."

"Well of course I care about Owen. But he and I wouldn't be anywhere near that snake pit if they were both gone."

"No, I mean Owen is in line for the throne after Molly."

I fell back into my chair, stunned. "He is? How?" I stared at him. "Wouldn't it be a relative of Aliana's?"

"Like a first cousin?"

"Yes."

"Like Hera Blaine?"

A rush of breath left me as if I'd been kicked in the gut. "Oh." My head jerked up and I met Jonathan's gaze, furious. "Then it *is* Laudley. Owen was right. He said it point blank."

Jonathan sighed. "I did hear that. And I came to the same conclusion."

"So Blaine orchestrated all of it somehow."

Jonathan's brows drew down. "How do you figure that?"

"Laudley's his father-in-law. Obviously Blaine was using him to scheme to get his son on the throne."

Jonathan shook his head. "Not even considering the immense difficulty of masterminding something like that from Dead End, I know it wasn't Blaine."

I glared at him. "How?"

He considered his answer. "Blaine was ruthless in his way, and very smart, but he was an idealist. He saw himself as a defender of an empire that was being attacked from within. He believed himself a crusader, doing what he must, even if it was treason, in order to protect the empire—and by association, all the people in it. He truly believed you were a disease infecting the empire, starting with the emperor himself. He was zealous in his goal to get rid of you, but that was his goal in its entirety. To him, that fixed everything."

"Well, Sam said the assassins tried to kill me, too."

"Yes, but they prioritized the emperor. Blaine wouldn't have been behind that. Laudley, on the other hand, is not an idealist. He is more interested in power for its own sake. And he has no love or respect for the imperial family. He established that long ago."

I absorbed that, wondering why I didn't have the urge to argue with him.

"So what do we do now? Do we even have any powerful allies besides Aliana?"

"The Queen is not in a position to help you right now."

The words were thick and heavy in my throat. "Is she not on my side?"

"She was always on your side. She's just in a very difficult position. Apparently several credible and serious reports recently caused her to send the bulk of her military forces into different areas of Torrean space. That was only sensible while the empire was at peace and ruled by her cousin. Now, it puts her in a position to have no organized force to oppose Laudley militarily, and she is not physically near enough to oppose Laudley among the powerful at the palace."

"You've talked to her?"

"No."

"Then how do you know?"

"The same way I know all the rest." He gave me a funny look. "Spying, logic, and faith."

I frowned at him. "So, in other words, you don't know where she stands at all, and anything's possible?"

"Anything is always possible. But Queen Aliana is one of the best people I know. I would stake my life on her trustworthiness, and I don't say that about many people."

My heart hurt. Aliana had been one of the first people to accept me when Pete and I went public with our relationship, back when we were stupid kids living on optimism and invincibility. I couldn't doubt her. And yet, in that moment, I doubted everything I'd ever known or believed. I doubted myself.

"We already know a great deal more than we did, and I will have a workable plan for you soon. Just give me a little more time, Your Highness."

"Jake."

He hesitated. "Jake." He said the word as if tasting it on his tongue, as if he'd truly never said it before, as if it were in some foreign language he didn't speak.

The world had turned upside down in a matter of days. I didn't blame him.

I had many times imagined my own coronation. What boy of my station didn't?

iv27

Rikhart IV lay in state for five days, and then he was buried in all imperial pomp and glory.

There was much debate, most of which I ignored, about what part I was to play in the ceremonies. I had no desire to be visible yet. Not now. Not for this. Queen Aliana, his closest relative outside his own household, would be the empire's public face. I merely wore the crown of the heir to the throne and ceded to her all honorary duties for the funeral. This was not my place or time, and I felt heavy with trepidation and a grief I couldn't entirely explain.

It was a day-long observance that began with a funeral breakfast at which the most important among us were given opportunity to recount some anecdote or memory of the late emperor. The speakers had been chosen ahead of time, and went in reverse order of importance. And so we endured a nasal speech from Lord Vandercook of how the emperor always chose him for his own team when they played soccer, and how the emperor had complimented him on his skill. We sat through Duchess Chaudhuri telling of childhood flirtations between Rikhart and her son, Umang, and how he had spoken to her son of someday taking him as his consort, before her son died. I remembered homely little Umang Chaudhuri and I doubted that very much.

Lord Sifer stood next.

"I remember the first time Rikhart met Jacob Dawes." A chorus of gasps followed the words, and I could hardly keep my own to myself. The old man was either very brave or very stupid. "I will tell the rest of this story calling our emperor, not Rikhart, but the name he asked me to call him, Peter, though I had served him several years before he granted me such an honor." Queen Aliana's face was hard to read. I stifled a sigh, reflecting with a sort of wry sorrow that there had been a time when I thought someday he would grant me the honor as well. "Peter had been emperor for only half a year, and had not even made a tour of the imperial worlds yet, but he wanted very much to visit the Imperial Intellectual Complex, and so it was arranged. During his tour and the presentation of the works of his scientists and great intellectuals, he recognized one item, the Dawes Laser, and noted also that he had seen the name of its creator on another project which had fascinated him. He asked to meet the man."

Sifer smiled fondly. "He was not expecting a boy of his own age, but once he got over the surprise, he was very pleased. After they had spoken of the project and Mr. Dawes had been dismissed, Peter turned to me with a great smile and said, 'Did you see how he kept forgetting who I was?' It was not censure or disapproval, rather a thing wondrous and pleasing to him. 'What must it be like,' he said, 'to live a life where nothing mattered as much as a job you were passionate about? Not even an emperor.'"

I was close enough to see that Lord Sifer was stiff and tense with emotion. "All here know how the story continued. He invited Jacob Dawes to tour the empire with him, and in the course of the journey they became friends. 'I don't think he even remembers I'm emperor anymore,' Peter said to me one day, weeks into the tour. 'It's not like at the IIC, where he would forget from time to time. I think he's forgotten altogether.' And he smiled so happily. 'I think he only tolerates me so long as I don't interfere with his science.'" Sifer spread his hands, as if to indicate such a thing explained all there was to understand.

"Though I doubted the wisdom of it, and I never changed that opinion, it was a gift to see my emperor, such a serious and responsible boy, grow to love someone deeply, and have that love returned by someone who did not love the emperor, but the man." He was almost shaking with emotion. "And if any of you still begrudges your emperor the joy and love he found in his husband, then you are a fool, and you should know it."

He all but fell into his seat, scowling at his hands which he crossed in front of him in a white-knuckled grip.

I don't think I even heard what Duchess Bosi or Duke Tepper said after that. I was still recovering from the shock of Lord Sifer's speech when my turn came. Whatever self-aggrandizing speech I had planned left me. I stood and found I had nothing to say. The silence stretched.

"I remember a good emperor," I said. "I can think of no better way to honor him than to say my heart is too full of grief to remember more than that his reign was too short, and that he should be with us now and is not."

The assembled were very still in the wake of my speech. I sank back into my chair, weak with relief.

Queen Aliana waited long minutes before she stood. "As Lord Sifer has done, I shall refer to my emperor as 'Peter,' for so he asked me to call him on the day I first met him."

She drew in a deep breath. "Peter's family and mine had long been at odds, though we were so closely related. Because of this, I did not know him as a child, and spent little time in his presence until he became emperor and I came to the palace as his heir. However, there was a time when we were still young, that he came to Torrea and I was there to meet him with my father."

She looked over the crowd. "I expected him to be cold and distant, as his father was, and mine was to him. It was not so. There before everyone he embraced me and kissed my cheek and said, 'I have so longed to meet you.' I did not know what to say, because I had not prepared myself for such a greeting. He did not seem to think less of me for it. He smiled and the formalities continued. But after dinner that night he came to find me. 'We are cousins,' he said. 'Yes, Your Highness,' I replied. He shook his head and took my hand. 'Call me Peter,' he said, and it was not a command from the imperial heir, it was the request of a friend."

She glared at the rest of the head table.

"In this time of great turmoil, my uncle, the Grand Duke Laudley, stepped up and took charge to ensure an orderly transition to the new ruler you will now suffer. He did this with no concern for his own losses, or the lies he had to tell to maneuver into a weak position those of us who could have opposed him. Nor did he shrink from making enemies of those who consider it a mockery that he would do all of this so blatantly, knowing that many of us are confident he was behind the assassination."

The room was as quiet as a tomb.

"So tonight we mourn the greatest emperor the Empire has ever known, and a great man." She bowed her head briefly before looking up again, facing the crowd defiantly. "Tomorrow he will be succeeded, if it can be called that. He most certainly will not be replaced." She met my eye. "He was the best man I have ever known. He was a better person than me." Her expression hardened. She held Laudley's gaze before turning back to the crowd. "He was better than every one of you."

No one breathed as she faced the assembled, powerful in her position and her anger. She sat. No one moved. "We will eat now," she said, and I heard several people draw breath again. I watched Laudley. His cold, blank expression was exactly as I'd feared, and I wondered if Aliana was ready for the war she'd just started.

Everything that followed the breakfast, the opulence, formality, and ceremony seemed anti-climactic. Part of me was angry that Lord Sifer and Queen Aliana had not only upstaged us, but belittled and shamed us. Anything I said or did now would only look crass and arrogant. I was also grateful to her that she'd taken a stand, and that she gave my silence and reticence an appearance of respect.

I took a place behind Queen Aliana in everything, though I stood ahead of everyone else, even the monarchs of the other imperial worlds. I was given no title beyond 'Duke,' but the hierarchy was clear, and I wore the heir's crown.

At the last, in the great chapel, the ranking member of each of the twelve oldest noble houses in the empire and their immediate family came forward in turn to pay their final respects to the emperor. Only in this did I take precedence over the queen. They came in their groups of five or six, one family of four, and finally Queen Aliana with only her husband, though it was rumored she was pregnant and that perhaps her heir paid respects as well.

In this I was the last, and I approached the bier alone. Every step of the way I felt the weight of the people who were not there. My father and mother, both gone too soon, my wife, long dead. My son, Owen, whom I hadn't seen since he was very small, who was still out of my reach.

Rikhart looked younger than I remembered, as if he had laid down his burdens, placed them on my shoulders instead and now he slept, free of his cares. I had intended to say something impressive. Something that would be picked up on the recordings and played back years later. *This is what Emperor Regent Enryn the First said over the body of his predecessor, the last Killearn emperor.* But all my carefully planned words felt dishonest and disgraceful now. I merely bowed in respect and returned to my seat.

He was paraded out of the chapel and a select group accompanied him to the imperial tomb. There he would be laid beside his father, preserved in stasis for one hundred years. Some future generation, who had never known him, would hold a smaller ceremony. They would turn off the stasis field and lay him on a pyre and there, under the open sky, they would cremate his remains. He would return to the earth, dust and ashes. Like everyone else.

Coronations follow funerals. It is the way of things. It felt disrespectful, though, and presumptuous, as if we discarded an emperor so easily. I spent that day fighting the ice that gripped my chest at the thought that this would someday be my fate.

iv28

The coronation was held the next day. It was to be a smaller affair, a scaled-down version of a typical coronation. Banquets would be laid out from sunrise to sunset, but there were no formal gatherings until the coronation itself, held in the evening, followed by a feast.

I woke very early that morning, too edgy and anxious to sleep. Today I would be crowned ruler of the empire. I wasn't even sure how I felt about that. Such a strange thing to be here again, where I belonged, yet question and doubt everything I'd ever known.

But there was nothing now that would keep me from the throne of the empire itself. And with the power of the entire empire at my disposal, no one was going to keep me from Owen. I would rule, and he would inherit the throne after me. It felt right, in spite of a nagging sense of guilt and uncertainty I wouldn't allow myself to think about.

I was glad I'd insisted on a subdued ceremony. It was good strategy, and there was time enough for all of that when the throne was secure. All the day lacked was Hera, and Owen. The thoughts of Hera were heavy and dragging, all the worse for having been locked away for so long. I'd refused to let Dead End sully my memories of my wife, and it had been years since I'd allowed myself to think of her and acknowledge my grief. At least Owen I could hope to see again.

Sabria had laid out for me a truly regal set of clothes, complete with some of the smaller pieces of the imperial jewelry. It was a bold and decisive gesture I was glad to make, claiming imperial treasures as if it were my right.

She helped me into my things, her face expressionless.

"Are you not happy about the family's good fortune?" I asked her, frustrated that she would feed my mood when I needed confidence I didn't feel.

She regarded me seriously. "Owen should be here."

I narrowed my eyes. "Dawes and the princess as well?"

Her expression hardened. "Is that what you think of me?"

"I don't know what to think of you. You say nothing at all."

"It is how you prefer your servants, Your Grace. Silent and obedient."

I went still, pondering. Why had I forgotten that? Why did I want anything different now?

"I have been a long time alone," I replied, though alone wasn't exactly what I'd been.

She pressed her lips together. "Then would you have me act differently? I shall serve as you please."

The reaction was not deliberate but I felt the fierceness of the expression grip my face. Her eyes widened and I saw the moment she realized the way her words could be taken.

I could have done it. I wanted to. She was a lovely woman, and she could hardly say no.

Sabria went still and waited, passive, expressionless. I turned away. Shame at having even considered it burned my face. I slipped the last two rings onto my fingers and left the room without another word.

I let myself be seen all through the morning and afternoon, though I spoke to very few and never for long. A quietness had stolen over me, insecurity wrapped in solemn purpose, and a restlessness after the encounter with Sabria. I was too long out of practice. The delicate dance of politics taxed and tired me.

By mid-afternoon, I returned to my room, making the excuse that I wanted time to contemplate the responsibilities I was to take on in mere hours. There was truth in that, though I spent the hours until the coronation staring out over the ocean, thinking mostly of forgetting. Before I returned to the celebration, I called up a picture of Hera and Owen as I had last seen them. I reached for them but my fingers passed through the image. I turned it off and left.

For all its importance, a coronation ceremony is rather brief. It made sense in the traditional way of things. It had always been merely a final capping of a child's lifelong training for the role. They would hardly need the seriousness of their responsibilities impressed on them.

I couldn't help feeling it should be different for me. Not from any desire for display, but because I was so unprepared for this. Duke I may have been, and raised to power and influence and a duchy of my own to rule, but that was hardly an empire. And that man was years dead, replaced by some hybrid who had been born on Dead End and returned to the palace for finishing. I felt as though there should be something more, something to wash away the stain of those years, to restore an honor and dignity that felt thin and shaky.

The invited guests filled their places in the great chapel. Sabria attached a long, jewel-studded cape to my shoulders, so that it trailed behind me like a train. I had worn the heir's crown throughout the day but now I removed it, handing it to her before the great doors opened and I made my slow procession down the aisle.

I wanted to look out at the faces, to meet their eyes, to dare them to challenge my right to this, to prove that I needed no one's approval or permission, only obedience. Yet my gaze remained locked ahead, and I saw only the great platform and Queen Aliana standing atop it, waiting for me.

I had been part of the negotiations that had placed her there. The imperial ruler was always crowned by his or her surviving parent, or else another senior member of the family. It was a symbol of the emperor's right to rule by virtue of birth rather than by anyone's grant.

Laudley was perhaps the proper person for the role, but even Laudley knew it wasn't a good idea for him to so obviously place the rulership on my shoulders. I stiffened at the thought and the reminder that it had genuinely been his to give me, since he was the one who had removed—assassinated—the emperor to make way for his own blood. I caught a glimpse of him in the front row and as if reading his thoughts, I could tell that this was not the triumph he had been hoping for. He'd intended Owen to be on the throne. With himself behind him.

My stomach turned to ice. What benefit was it to Laudley to have me take the throne? That I would pass it on to Owen was no doubt his ultimate goal, but he hadn't murdered an emperor merely to step back and cede all power to someone else. He must at least intend to control me as well, no matter what our relative ranks would be after this day.

It was with these thoughts in my head that I ascended the steps of the dais and came to stand beside Queen Aliana. To our right, out of the spotlight but conspicuous enough to draw attention when it was his duty, Lord Naganika stepped forward.

"All in attendance pay heed and serve witness that on this day, Enryn Gambol Avin Ellis Blaine, the first of his name, does take the duties and privileges of Regent of the Empire, invested with all imperial authority until such time as the rightful heir is old enough to reign."

I faced Queen Aliana. "I do take now the crown, and with it, all duties and privileges of emperor of all the citizens and worlds of the Empire."

She held the crown in her hands, her eyes hard on me as she began to lift it. Halfway between us she stopped.

"You will answer me this first," she demanded in a harsh whisper, low enough that no one else could hear. "Did you have a hand in killing him?"

"No."

She didn't move. "Why should I believe that?"

I held her gaze without flinching. "Because Hera was beside me until the end."

Her expression began to relent but then it firmed. "Promise me you will yield this crown to Princess Marquilla or I will not set it on your head, no matter what it costs me."

"Owen is my heir," I said evenly.

"And Molly was his!"

I could hear the faint rustlings and murmurs of the crowd as they watched us gripped in our tableau. I did not look away from her. "I can make you no promises, Aliana."

She sniffed. "Because you are just a pawn. You know this."

"No." I took her wrists in my hands. "I will be no one's pawn. Not yours, and certainly not his."

Her eyes widened a fraction but she kept her control. "I promise you this, husband of my cousin, my niece will be found and she will hold this throne or I will bring the full might of the planet of Torrea down upon you."

"I would expect nothing less."

She stared me down with such a powerful fury and determination that I steeled myself for a blow. But she visibly composed herself and raised the crown, settling it on my head. "Thus I pass the crown to the lawful ruler of the empire." She held my gaze, leaving me in no doubt of what she really meant. I let it settle on my head before I nodded my respect. She turned to face the assembled.

"May the emperor live forever!"

I was thinking of going out to the nebula for our anniversary.

It's a long trip.

It's not worth it?

I didn't say that.

iv29

My husband was buried.

I wouldn't allow my children to watch the live feed. Owen had seen enough images of his father over the years that I was afraid he would recognize him. And I could only imagine all the ways Laudley could make the experience miserable for me if he chose. It was a torture all its own, waiting, as Jonathan edited and compiled the broadcast of my husband's funeral.

When at last it was done, we sat on the bed together, Molly, Owen, Jonathan, and me, and watched the funeral of Emperor Rikhart IV.

Jonathan had offered me the full feed from the palace of all the events of the day leading up to the final ceremony, from the eulogy breakfast to the final interment, but I didn't have the heart for it. It was the laying to rest of an emperor. I mourned a husband.

I tried not to watch but I couldn't help it. I didn't want to see this—this final claiming, putting their seal upon him, locking him away in their mausoleum, their vaults. Closing out his life the way it had begun, with all the pomp and ceremony of an emperor. In the great chapel, the most powerful and important people in the empire sat and watched. It was the same place where he'd been presented to the empire as an infant heir, and where he had been crowned after his father's death; where we had been married, where he had presented his first child and heir to his subjects, and now where he was to be put neatly away, a relic of the empire. He lay there, so pale and still.

I watched Aliana stand before him, her face quiet, but I knew her too well not to see the pain in her eyes. What must it cost her, to stand there and be a part of this farce, knowing how he had died? So powerful and yet so powerless.

Molly lay with her head in my lap, her feet pushed up against Jonathan who, though he sat with us as I'd forced him to, kept an obvious distance between himself and the family. Owen sat on my other side. Though I kept an arm around him the entire time, he was stiff and silent, as if at attention. Molly sniffled into my leg every now and then, but it sounded more like exhaustion than grief. It was all so far away from us now. I thought I'd cry over my husband's funeral, but I was dry, wrung out and tearless.

Pete was carried out of the chapel. The screen went to black, the imperial crest in the center, so that all in the empire could observe a final moment of silence for Rikhart IV.

I turned it off.

I sat on Molly's bed a long time after she fell asleep, petting her hair. She had my hair, thick and dark brown, and it was beautiful on her. Just then I wished she had Pete's quirkier, honey colored hair that would start to curl around his neck and ears when he put off getting a haircut. Maybe it would have been like touching him again, just a little.

"Jake."

Jonathan was framed in the doorway, and I nodded acknowledgment, giving Molly a final pat and a kiss before I joined him in the hall.

"What is it?"

"There's a part of the eulogy breakfast I think you might want to see."

I sighed. "Really, Jonathan, I don't."

He wore a funny half-smile. "Don't be so sure."

With that cryptic hint he got me curious enough to follow him to the sitting room where the vid was already queued up. I watched Lord Sifer rise, frailer than I remembered. Was it because of Pete's death, or had I not noticed before?

Then he began to talk.

I stared at the screen, stunned, as he told a story I knew and didn't know at all. It was one thing to talk to Pete, remembering those first days, all the ways and reasons we fell in love with each other. It was so different to hear Pete's actual words reported by someone who had watched the delight on the young man's face, understanding so much more than what he said.

Jonathan paused the playback when Lord Sifer dropped heavily into his seat. I couldn't move.

"That was brave," Jonathan remarked quietly. I nodded.

"Stupid."

"Brave," he insisted. "And unexpected." I looked at him. "I knew he didn't mind you, but he was so hard to read sometimes. I didn't realize how much he actually liked you."

I huffed a laugh. "I never realized he liked me at all."

Jonathan just shook his head at me then pointed to the stilled vid. "There's more."

It blinked to a view of Aliana as she stood, beautiful and fierce as she always was. A pang of loss gripped me. This too I didn't have anymore. She was one of my first friends at the palace. I hadn't seen her in months, maybe a year. We'd been busy and hadn't taken the time.

I sighed. Then smiled to myself as she spoke of Pete, of the boy I hadn't known, but who I knew just as she described him. As she finished, her voice laced with anger and accusation, I fell back against my chair.

"I can't believe she said that."

"You can't?"

I laughed. "No, you're right. Of course she did." I shook my head. "I hope she can handle what she just started."

Jonathan frowned at me. "The queen can take care of herself."

I nodded, looking back at the still image of her, flushed with righteous anger and love for the man we'd both lost.

"I still miss her, though."

Jonathan said nothing in reply.

I don't want to go, Pete.

I know, but you should anyway.

Hera would understand.

But you should go anyway. You'll regret it later if you don't.

I don't want her to be dead.

I know.

iv30

Late into the night, Jonathan and I sat out on the veranda, lit only by a brilliant moon, drinking concoctions he'd made from juices squeezed from the fruits of local trees and a more than generous helping of something I'm sure he was hoping would put me to sleep.

It did make me tired, very tired, but I fought it. Somewhere in my mind I was sure that I couldn't let this day end, that if the sun rose again, it would be firmly and completely established that Pete was dead and gone, buried, interred, and we would have to go on with our lives without him.

So I fought sleep with all the reason and good sense I'd brought to most of the fights in my life. After a while I simply stood at the railing, watching the roll of wind through the trees, so like the ocean that was somehow different here than at the palace and still the same ocean. Funny how that worked. I scrubbed my face in my hands and drained my drink again.

Jonathan put a full glass on the rail between us, taking up his own vigil beside me.

"He wanted me with him all the time," Jonathan said, and it took a moment for my soggy brain to catch the words. "After you were exiled. He wouldn't say it like that, though he did officially transfer me to his own staff. But he wanted me nearby. He was visibly less in control when I wasn't. So I stayed, all the hours of the day, wherever he was, and I didn't leave his rooms until he was asleep each night. And for half of that time he ignored me, almost as if he was embarrassed to want me around so much but couldn't bring himself to put a stop to it. I didn't mind. I never minded."

He turned his head and I looked over to meet his gaze, so full of his own pain and loss. "I think I needed it as much as he did," he said. "We'd both lost something, with more or less guilt attached to our part in it, but neither of us had anyone we could really admit the depth of that loss to. Not to ourselves, certainly not to each other. So we spent weeks in the same spaces, never talking about it. Pretending it wasn't going on."

I shivered. "He got a bad bargain with me, didn't he?"

"I don't think he'd agree at all."

I huffed. "Pete never did know what was good for him."

"He knew a lot more than you think."

"I should never have let us become friends. I should have kept him at a distance from the first. I knew better. I knew what a disaster it would be for him to befriend an unclass, let alone..." I sighed out what felt like my last breath. "It's my fault. It's my fault he died. If he'd never been with me—"

My ears rang with the sound before the pain registered. Jonathan had slapped me. I stared at him in stunned disbelief. His palm smacked my cheek again. My hand went slowly to my face; my skin burned like fire under it.

"What—"

"When you were in exile, the emperor once said to me that it had all been his fault. If he hadn't taken you out of the IIC, if he hadn't kissed you, if he had listened to you when you said you shouldn't take your relationship public, if he'd done a better job protecting you, if he'd prevented the scenes in the throne room." Jonathan quivered with rage. "I wanted to slap him too. But I couldn't. So that's one for each of you." His eyes bored into me like lasers. "Don't you dare cheapen all you gave to each other. Don't disrespect him and what you had together, those beautiful children, with that kind of complete and utter *shit*. Don't you dare."

He glared at me, his breath harsh and fast. I coughed out a startled laugh. "OK."

I was installed as Regent to the twenty-third ruler of the Empire. Whoever that would be.

iv31

I didn't stay late at the coronation feast. My mind whirled with all that had happened in so short a time. Queen Aliana's words rang in my ears. I retreated to the emperor's office and sank into the chair at the large desk, but turned my back to it, staring out at the ocean through the expanse of windows. The night sky was bright and brilliant and less frightening here than it had been for me in many years.

It was an excellent room for painting. I always had admired the light.

I was stalling, I knew it. The triumph and headiness of power that had made me almost giddy only hours before had waned, and doubts were creeping back in. I didn't want to admit even to myself how much her words had shaken me. I forced myself to turn the chair until I faced the desk squarely, though I didn't take my hands off the armrests.

The throne might be more impressive, the symbol, but this was where the real ruling of the empire took place. I had been in this room many times but always on the other side of the desk. If I'd ever entertained notions of switching places, they felt now like a little boy's dreams. The sort of nonsense we live within as children—harmless but impossible fantasies.

I looked down at the desk. Scrolling readouts, open documents and reports were scattered across the digital surface, like a deck of playing cards. If I let my eyes unfocus, it almost looked like a movie playing. The Story of the Empire. The story of the rule of the House of Blaine.

I shivered and then, angry at myself for weakness, I lay my palms flat and began examining reports with a feverish intensity.

In the notification area, a persistent blinking finally caught my attention and I opened the waiting message.

The face of Rikhart IV appeared. "Hello, Your Excellence."

I catapulted out of my chair, my heart racing. I stared, wide-eyed as a mischievous grin spread across his face. "Still sounds strange, doesn't it? You get used to it. Though every now and then it still throws me."

I looked at the timestamp on the recording: more than seven years ago.

"There's a long tradition of each imperial ruler leaving a message for his successor. I hope very much that I'm talking to my own child, but as I've only just gotten married, and haven't broached the subject of children with Jake yet," he smiled almost shyly, "I know it's possible that I'm not. So I won't assume." He grimaced but then smiled.

"In any case, the purpose of this message is twofold. First, when this message closes, it will open up your private access portal, which will let you into everything in the empire, no exceptions." He grinned. "Including the private network the upper nobility thinks we don't know about." My mouth nearly fell open.

"It's more technical than I can explain, but, essentially, every piece of technology built in the last two hundred years has required a simple base code in order to even connect to the electrical grid. Because of this, there is a backdoor into every single electronic device in the empire. If it can be scanned, recorded, searched, or transmitted, you can find it." He pressed his lips together.

"Be careful with it. Almost everything can be accessed by the highest ISS officers, even more than is popularly believed.

Intelligence and surveillance is their job, and what they do best. Quite frankly, you won't have the time to sit around combing through everyone's private things."

He looked down. "But even more than that, just because you can know something doesn't mean you should. There are some things that aren't worth knowing." His expression was wry. "It actually makes it harder, not easier, to know what everyone really thinks of you. And there's a very big difference between what they think and what they are willing to do."

He smiled. "Not that you won't find the access useful. It may well save your life. It already has mine, once, and as I'm still quite a young man, it may yet again." He sobered. "Just be careful. Make sure you *really* want to know something before you go looking for it.

"Though, if you're like everyone else I know," he said, laughing, "you'll probably end up learning that for yourself the hard way, but I wanted to warn you nonetheless."

He straightened with a sigh, as if he'd set down some heavy burden.

"The second thing is a personal request. That used to be the only purpose of these messages, before the access portal was built, and, in my opinion, it's the most important part. So," he said, blowing out a decisive breath, "each emperor leaves one personal request for the one to follow him." His mouth quirked. "Mine may be a little strange, though if you're Jacob Dawes' child, it probably won't surprise you much."

His expression sobered. "I know I'll be laid to rest in the imperial mausoleum. But I'd ask you, please, to get me out of there." His expression was wry. "I know that sounds odd, but there is a reason, I promise." He sat back, his gaze going far away.

"A few weeks ago Jake and I were at the nebula, and I made a comment about how I wished we could have our remains put into it together after we were both gone. He may have liked the idea a little too much. He took it seriously and he's determined to see it happen."

He sat forward, lacing his fingers together and staring at me intently. "I want to give that to him. I want that for us." He sighed. "I can't know now how it's played out, whether or not he's already dead or if he survived me, but, when both of us are gone, please, I'm asking you to take us out to the Dawes-Killearn nebula and put our remains there.

"I haven't told him about this," he continued. "I don't want to make promises I can't keep, and I have no way of knowing who I'm talking to now. Maybe it's Aliana, who I know would do this for us. Hopefully, you're our oldest child. I don't know you yet, but if there's any of your other father in you, you're probably headstrong and hardheaded." His mouth curved in an unconscious smile.

"But I don't know whether that will translate into you doing this for us or deciding you don't like the idea and ignoring it." He sighed. "Maybe something worse has happened and you're not anyone I expect. So I haven't told him because I know I have no control over what is done with either of us now. But I'm asking this of you. If Jake's still alive, I hope you'll tell him, so he knows you're going to carry it out." He shook his head to himself. "I wouldn't put it past him to try to steal my body from the crypt if he thought that was the only way he could get it. So, please, if you are going to do this for us, let him know, if he's still alive."

He looked down at his hands, silent for a moment before he continued.

"Good luck. I wish nothing but the best for you. Whoever you are. It's a heavy burden, but it's your burden now. I hope you bear it well."

The display went black. I don't know how long I sat there, staring at the blank space, transfixed. I stood, and my knees felt watery under me. I approached the great wall of windows, staring out, unseeing, at the ocean until I was sure I had control of myself and then I left the room, walked away from the emperor's office and through the halls, ignoring everyone, until I came at last to the emperor's rooms. My rooms.

I looked around. None of it was mine. Everything I saw was theirs. The emperor, Dawes, Princess Marquilla, and Owen. My

Owen. Who hadn't been my Owen in so long he probably didn't remember me. I didn't even know him.

I stumbled into the smallest room, the library. I took a chair, turning its back to the door so that there was some semblance of separating myself from this place. From so many things that I suddenly knew and understood and didn't want to know at all.

I was still there when darkness fell and I succumbed finally to sleep.

In the space of two days, the emperor's rooms were cleared of all traces of Killearns and redone in the Blaine colors. They looked bare, waiting.

iv32

I woke in the morning with a crick in my neck and a new resolve. It was time to put my secret access to the test. There was no amount of deliberation or doubt about what I wanted to look for first. The location of the safehouse. I meant to find Owen.

I settled in front of the desk in the private office within the emperor's rooms, still wearing my robe and slippers. My first attempt at finding information produced only one result, and it opened itself immediately. The face of a woman appeared. She looked familiar but her name didn't come to me right away. She didn't look terribly impressed.

"So you've decided to try to find the safehouse," she said. "Maybe you're the first. You won't be the last. But I can save you time. You won't find it. I have taken great pains to set up this sanctuary and I don't intend it to be compromised, whether for nefarious purposes or mere curiosity."

Empress Olga. I recognized the face now. She'd come to power—and held it for five decades—after her father, mother, and three older siblings were all assassinated, one by one. Popular history held that she'd avoided no less than five assassination attempts. I guessed it was more than that.

"The location of the safehouse is secret, for very good reason.

Whether you've come to power through inheritance or murder, you too should appreciate and be committed to preserving the safety of that place."

Her smile was sardonic. "You may find yourself needing it someday. In the meantime, don't imagine that you are the one who will discover the secret. You won't. I advise you to stop trying. You'll only prove yourself to be inadequate to the position if you don't respect the necessity for the safehouse, whether for your predecessor, yourself, or your heirs. Leave it alone."

The screen blanked and I was staring at a search that returned no results at all.

I was surprisingly relieved to know that I couldn't find the safehouse. On the one hand, of course I was frustrated, even angry that I should be the most powerful man in the empire now and still be denied my son. Yet the logic of her position was all too true. Every emperor should treasure that safety net.

And there were perhaps things that were more important right now than bringing my son to this place, and into the life of Emperor Regent Enryn. Empress Olga had reminded me rather forcefully of how I had come to power. Not only that it had involved deception and assassination, but that it had not been my own doing. I held my position thanks to the machinations of someone else. And I wasn't fool enough to think that my own safety or even my life was of any importance to him beyond his own benefit.

I was eating breakfast in the little nook off the emperor's solarium when the servant announced the Grand Duke Laudley. I went still. Carefully I answered, "Show him in."

Laudley seemed at ease for such an early morning after a night of celebration. He was never a man for many smiles, only when they were useful to him, but there was a careless triumph about him that made me grit my teeth. Perhaps he realized that because he gestured to the chair across from me.

"May I sit?"

I regarded him for a long moment, long enough that I could see him grow uncomfortable before I gestured wordlessly to the chair and he sat. The servant poured him coffee but he brushed off the offer of breakfast and we were left alone.

"How did you get in here?" I asked.

His expression hardened for only a flicker before he found his casual pose again. "The way one normally gets anywhere. I came, the servant announced me, and now I am here."

"The Imperial wing is for family only. You shouldn't have made it past the entryway."

Now he made no attempt to appear pleasant. "Are we not family? Are you so quickly grown used to the change in your circumstances that you have forgotten how they came about?"

I settled back. "I haven't." I brushed off his objections with a lazy gesture. "I was merely concerned for the security protocols. I hadn't gotten a chance to give any orders regarding you yet."

He watched me, and I kept my face carefully neutral. He would believe me or not. I wasn't fool enough to think I was better at this game than he was. In any case, I was badly out of practice. Finally his expression softened. "I see. Well, that is a natural concern, of course. If it will help, I can draw up instructions for the guard so that it is clear that I am permitted entrance to the Imperial Wing."

"I think not," I said casually. "No offense, and it's certainly not for lack of gratitude, but I think it is best if we keep our association to a minimum just now. We want to divorce ourselves from any connection in the minds of those who are watching. Otherwise they might think too long on, as you said, how I got here, and they might wonder what else we have done together."

Now his expression was openly speculative. "I see." He settled back into his chair with a broad smile on his face. "Perhaps this is best. After all, it is easily remedied once Owen is returned to us. It is only natural for me to move into Family apartments when my grandson comes home. He will need all the support he can get from those who have his best interests at heart."

Something about the way he said it made me wonder if Owen's

best interests really were what concerned Laudley, or if they were only so long as they paralleled his own. At least Owen had the protection of being Laudley's only grandson. His ambitions were meaningless if the throne did not stay in the family line. One man's rule was nothing.

"And what do you intend to do about the princess?"

Laudley raised an eyebrow. "What brings this up now?"

I sat forward. "You may have been the one behind it all, but they put the crown on my head last night. What you do to further the family interests now, I get blamed for. I need to know what to expect."

He examined my face for a long time. "I intend to find her, of course."

"And then?"

Laudley favored me with an incredulous look, gazing about us obviously.

I sneered. "Do you really think we are being spied upon in here?"

"Do you really think we are not?"

"If the emperor's own bedroom isn't secure, then nowhere is. There will be word games enough from now on, I want to speak openly and to the point in here. Otherwise there is no need for you to come at all."

His pleasant expression froze. He moved deliberately to sit forward, crossing his hands in front of him on the table. "Then speak openly, Enryn."

"Your Excellence."

His eyes narrowed.

"So neither of us learns to become too familiar and slips in public."

His eyes relaxed but his expression didn't otherwise change.

"What do you want to ask me, *Your Excellence*?"

"I want to know plainly and frankly what you intend to do with the princess."

He pursed his lips as if considering. There was not a chance in the empire that he didn't have this thoroughly planned out already. He was considering how much to tell me, and he intended

I know it.

"I would not harm a child."

"You speak of Owen as if there is no doubt that he will be the next emperor. She is unquestionably the legal heir. How do you intend to resolve this without harming a child?"

He favored me with a smile that was more than a little condescending. "She will not always be a child, Your Excellence." The mockery in the title was subtle but clear. I chose to ignore it, for the time being.

"So you will not harm her but you will actively plan her demise for the time when you consider her old enough to kill without compunction."

He made a disgusted noise. "You speak of it as if these things have not been done for centuries, millennia. There are still many years before she will be old enough to rule without a regent. If the people have grown comfortable under your rule then they can be encouraged to forget there was ever any other alternative."

"There will always be those who will remember and resent our rise to power."

"So be rid of enough of them to shut the others up. You speak as if you know nothing about these things. Or have you grown soft in the years spent among unclass and criminals?"

I favored him with a look of icy contempt. "'Soft' isn't a word that comes to mind, no. I think I've gained a valuable perspective. And a few tricks of my own, Laudley." I stood, which forced him to as well, and I stifled a smile. He had stood automatically, out of reflex rather than choice.

"I think you could easily grow drunk on power, and careless." I smiled. "It was wise of you to put me on the throne, rather than try to assume it yourself. Clearly you have factored in your own weaknesses and liabilities." I nodded once to him. "A wise move, Your Grace."

His expression was just short of a glare. "Yes. A man would do well to remember where he is weak," he said. "And where he is vulnerable. You might be more of both than you think, *Enryn*." He gave me a sardonic bow. "Good day, Your Excellence."

On the day that my ally and nemesis liberated me from that prison, I took nothing away from Dead End, not even myself. I wasn't the man who had arrived there so many years before.

iv**33**

I left my rooms, not at all sure of the wisdom of baiting Laudley as I had just done. Had power gone to my head already? It was far too soon, and I was still tied too inextricably to him. If he went down, I did too.

I pondered that all the way to my meeting with Lord Naganika. Already it sat in the first position of my schedule each day, as it had for Rikhart. It seemed a good pattern to keep up, if only because Rikhart had clearly found value in it.

Not that I trusted Naganika. I still didn't know where his personal loyalties lay. I was more and more convinced any glimpse he gave into what might be considered his true feelings were as calculated as his non-reactions. But I did trust his professionalism. Not only had old Sifer picked him personally, but Naganika was a younger son of the king of Carolis. He had been weaned on court politics. There was a reason he was in one of the highest positions in the empire before he was thirty years old.

After my unexpected breakfast meeting with Laudley, I found myself looking forward to the meeting with Naganika. I had a feeling that the juxtaposition would be as informative as anything either man said himself.

"Good morning, Your Excellence," Naganika said, bowing properly as he entered my office.

"Good morning," I replied. "Have a seat." His brow cocked as I gestured to one of the chairs in front of my desk. "Would you prefer not to?" I said.

He smiled, settling into the chair with a casualness that was in no way disrespectful. Just the proper amount of deference and the ease his emperor had asked for. I set my chin in my hand. "You seem surprised? Did Rikhart never ask you to sit?"

His expression sobered briefly before he smiled again. "On the contrary, he asked me to sit from the first day I met him, long before I was appointed as his Minister."

"So I'm the one who surprises you. Is it that we've met more than once and I've only just asked, or that I asked at all?"

His smile settled into a comfortable pose. "I expected you to ask me eventually. I'm surprised that you have this soon."

I watched him, letting the silence stretch for a long time. He returned my appraisal with a frank, expectant look, never once fidgeting, his expression not even twitching. I smiled.

"You intrigue me, Lord Naganika. I think you are a more valuable asset than I realized."

He smiled. "I hope so, Your Excellence, and I hope that I will intrigue you many more times over the course of our association."

"Will that be good or bad?"

He laughed. "Both. And neither. And everything. The universe is infinite and complicated, Your Excellence, and humans much more so."

We talked of minutae on his report until I came to the final line. "Laudley has ordered changes in the chain of command among the palace guard?"

His expression firmed. "Yes, Your Excellence."

"He *ordered* them?"

He gave me a careful shrug. "Perhaps it is merely force of habit."

"Is that what you think?"

He weighed his words. "I think he would like for things to continue to be that...easy for him. I think he would like to be able to issue orders and have no doubt they will be approved."

"What do you think of these substitutions? I don't recognize most of these names, but he's trying to replace Samson Illiane, the head of the Imperial Guard? That's quite a change. Has there been some complaint about him, or report I haven't been made aware of?"

"Other than the fact that the last emperor died under his watch?" Naganika replied, with no emotional coloring except perhaps a hint of sarcasm. "No, there has been no concern or complaint."

"This woman he wants to install as guard captain, she is loyal to Laudley?"

Naganika cocked his head. "Not that I'm aware of, and I seriously doubt that would be the case."

I steepled my hands in front of me. "Why is that?"

"Because it's too obvious. I have no doubt he believes she will be malleable, but I cannot believe she would be his creature already. It would be a careless and stupid thing to do, and if he is anything, the Grand Duke is neither careless nor stupid."

"But these others?"

"The other substitutions? Some of them will be his men, of that I am certain."

"Which ones?"

"I do not know, Your Excellence. Not yet."

I sat in silence, considering. "The captain will not be replaced. As for the others, approve half of them."

"Which ones?"

"That I will leave to your discretion, Lord Naganika."

He gave me a smile, and I felt sure it was the most genuine one I'd seen from him. He stood.

"Thank you, Your Excellence. I will do my best to protect the interests of the Empire." He bowed to me, indicating, as was proper, that the empire and I were one and the same. But long after he left I was still pondering his choice of words. Wondering.

Laudley's words from the morning churned uneasily in my gut, sloshing together with Naganika's warnings. Cautiously I opened the secret data link. I searched first for Laudley's location. He was in a garden in the noble wing, and he wasn't alone. Naganika was also there, though they were on opposite sides of the lawn. I scanned for possible surveillance devices that might allow me to eavesdrop.

There were two, and I sat back, stunned and appalled to realize what they were.

Most people carried personal comm devices, but nobles rarely did. That was what servants were for. Of course, when plotting treason, the privacy of a com device was more attractive than go-betweens. I had carried one myself for years. Enough powerful men used them for virtuous reasons that it wasn't immediately suspicious for those of us with nefarious purposes to be seen with one.

The two surveillance ports the computer was reporting were the two men's personal com units. I could access live feed of anything they could hear or see.

Cold sweat drenched me even as a hot flush swept up my neck. Adrenaline set my heart racing and my pulse pounding in my palms. Our personal com devices. We had plotted murders, atrocities, and treasons. The emperor could have accessed us at any time. How had we remained undetected so long? How had Laudley managed to *kill* him?

I shook my head. Perhaps Rikhart's advice on cautious use was less wise than he'd believed. I let out a slow, deliberate breath, and tuned in to Laudley's device.

"Good evening, Your Grace," Naganika's voice came to me clearly. "This is one of my favorite gardens. Do you come here often?"

"We will keep this brief," Laudley said. "What is so important that you asked to meet me here, where anyone can see us together?"

There was a smile in Naganika's voice. "There is no one but us here and if anyone comes within fifty yards of any entrance to the garden, I will be alerted. It is not as dangerous as you think."

"It is always more dangerous than you think. Was there a point to this?"

Naganika cleared his throat. "Yes, Your Grace. I met with the regent this morning and he would not approve all of your guard transfers."

"Which ones?"

"I believe he was reluctant to approve any of them, though he did eventually authorize a select few. Mostly the guards who have little access to either him or you."

Laudley scoffed. "And the guard captain?"

"That one he did not approve."

Laudley was quiet for a moment. "It makes no matter, though his initiative concerns me. What have you done to make him suspicious?"

"Me? On the contrary, Your Grace, I got the impression that he suspects *me* not at all."

He made a noise of disgust. "He is not a complete fool. Never mind, I will handle it. Is that all?"

"Is there anything else you would have me do about Blaine?" There was a long, charged silence. Naganika broke it with a laugh. "There are no recording devices here. You checked before you came and you scanned me before you spoke. I'm not trying to trap you, Your Grace."

Laudley made a rude noise. "It is careless just the same. Continue as you are. At present you need only concern yourself with making sure my *son-in-law*," the words dripped with contempt, "does not learn too much, either about me or about how to be an emperor. The less he accomplishes, the less he will believe he is able to do. Anything else is of no matter until Owen is found. After that, we will speak of Blaine again."

"Yes, Your Grace."

I stared out the window for a long time, a heavy, sinking feeling in my gut. And the worst realization was that I wasn't surprised, or even disappointed.

Laudley had been planning this for years. He was prepared for anything I could throw at him and I had no idea what traps he had already set for me. He didn't need time, or for me to be careless enough to give him an opportunity. He only needed Owen. After that, I was worse than expendable. I was already dead.

Don't forget, dinner tonight with the Blaines.

Ugh.

Hera will be there. And she asked me if she could bring Owen.

What does a baby do at an official dinner?

Sleep, I imagine.

iv**34**

I spent the next two days in the lab. Jonathan helped me set up an area for the children, so that we could establish some sort of routine for them, some semblance of normality. So while I worked at my table, and Jonathan at his console, the children did their schoolwork for a couple of hours each day. It seemed to soothe them from the first, this pretense at a normal life. I didn't like to think of how easily they adapted to the change, or how much it hurt me, against all logic.

I scowled to myself. What did I want? For them to be uncertain and miserable?

I watched their faces, intent on their work. They were my life, and this was our life now. Pete was dead. Pete was dead and there was nothing I could do about that. Wherever we went next, whatever we did next, we had to do without him.

The children understood it better than I did.

I watched Jonathan working nearby, quiet and intent. It occurred to me that I'd never seen him work like this before.

Always these things had gone on behind the scenes. The invisible backdrop that allowed him to work his magic and remain almost unseen. I'd always hated that. The sight of Jonathan like this, with us, warmed me and I went back to work with a smile on my face.

About mid-morning, I released the children to play for a while and I made my way to the kitchen, grinning at the thought of what Jonathan would say when he realized I'd come in here and fixed my own snack while he was working on something else.

As I was rummaging through the cabinets I heard what sounded like knocking. I turned, trying to locate the source and found myself standing in front of the door to the garage. Had one of the children gone in and gotten stuck? I opened the door.

Blaine was standing there.

"How funny," he said, "it won't open the door for me because you were here first."

I catalogued the fact that I was still standing there, in the safehouse, that Blaine was in front of me making meaningless conversation. I expected to blink and the illusion would be gone, the mirage created by too little sleep and not enough sanity.

The reality of what his presence here meant slapped me across the face and my heart stopped. A rush of pure fear nearly drove me to my knees, but it was washed away in a strange calm and certainty that settled over me. I stepped into the garage, closing the door behind me.

"I'll come with you right now, no fuss, if you leave the children alone. I'll do whatever you want—" I swallowed hard, "if the children are left out of this."

Blaine's eyes widened only fractionally before a smile teased the corner of his mouth.

"Anything I want?"

"Yes."

"You'd confess to killing the emperor?"

My gut bottomed out, my heart clogging my throat.

"Yes," it was hoarse but audible. "If I have to. But only if I have a guarantee that the children are safe, and I don't mean with you."

Blaine's eyes narrowed. "One of those children is mine."

The strange thing was, that hadn't even occurred to me. It took me a moment to recover. Maybe that's why I didn't hear the door opening.

"Daddy?"

I reached back for Owen as a reflex but I was watching Blaine. He went very pale, his eyes devouring Owen like a starving man.

Pete wore the emperor's mask better than that. At least, he had.

Blaine's expression tightened and blood flooded his face. It was only then that I looked back at Owen. My hand was on his chest and he had his hand over mine, giving Blaine a puzzled frown. Owen looked at me.

"Who's here, Daddy?"

My brain had gone into hibernation. It took me another several painful moments to realize that Blaine had heard Owen say "Daddy" and mean me. I turned my back to Blaine, moving to put my body between him and Owen.

"I'll explain later, buddy. Can you go check on Molly for me?"

Owen cast a suspicious look up at Blaine. He went pale and gasped, turning wide, wet eyes on me, his face crumpled, all his preternatural calm lost to panic. The words began to tumble out of him. "I don't want to go with him. Don't let him take me, Daddy. Please." He was clinging so hard to my hand that it hurt.

I knelt in front of him and took him by the shoulders, giving him a little shake before I pulled him close. He burrowed into my embrace like a much younger child.

"No one is taking you anywhere, Owen. I won't let anything happen to you, remember?" He was trembling so hard that I wasn't sure if he'd nodded. He clung to me as if proximity could make the words more true. "Besides, do you think Molly would stand for it?"

He shuddered out a laugh that sounded more like tears than anything else, but I felt his smile against my neck, weak but there. More quickly than I expected, his trembling eased and he slowly extricated himself from my grip. He turned to face Blaine, though his body was angled subtly behind mine. His expression turned to stone, his eyes glittering hatred as only children can do it, so pure and so innocent.

"Did you kill my Papa?"

I glanced at Blaine. He looked like he'd been kicked in the stomach. I turned back to Owen and took his hand. "Will you do something for me?" He tore his glare from Blaine reluctantly and nodded. He was still shivering. "Go tell Jonathan who's here and that we're going to be out in the garden. OK?"

"OK," he said quietly, cutting a quick look at Blaine before he turned and ran back into the house. I shut the door.

I was strangely reluctant to meet Blaine's eyes. He was pale. For a moment he looked so much like Owen that my heart ached. I had a bright flash of memory, so clear it overlaid everything else. Hera sitting in bed holding her newborn son and Blaine looking down at both of them. At the time, I'd labeled the expression on his face as "fond," which I thought was charitable of me, even as it sickened me.

Now I knew I'd been far too stingy. That look was pure love. I hadn't wanted to believe Blaine was capable of any such emotion. It was impossible to deny now. He was staring at the door where Owen had been only a moment before, raw, stark longing on his face.

I gestured awkwardly. "Maybe we should go outside."

He gave no indication he'd heard me, but he followed me through the house when I led the way.

I sat down on a carved bench and Blaine took a chair across from me. He had none of the polish and arrogance I'd always credited him with. He looked tired, strained.

I'd hated Blaine for as long as I'd known him. Maybe my attitude had softened over the years he'd been in Dead End, though I think it was more the lack of new things to hate him for than any active efforts on my part. Maybe just knowing he was on Dead End had made it hard to hate him as much as I wanted to.

Maybe all that time with Owen, the stamp of Blaine on his face even when I hadn't consciously seen it, had done something. But in this moment, all I could see was the father, not the man. And that set empathy tangling in my gut with guilt.

It also quenched the fear. When I'd opened the door to find him, I could almost see the ISS ships landing, the soldiers coming for us. Now I knew they weren't there.

"He doesn't even know about me, does he?"

He wasn't looking at me, but for once I was sure it wasn't because of me. He was starting off into the distance, a closed look on his face. Seeing the past, perhaps, or might-have-beens.

Or maybe he didn't want me to see too much. The thought tipped me off balance. I wasn't used to thinking of Blaine with emotions, not human ones, anyway. It was easier when we were both angry. This was all wrong and I didn't know how to think or feel anymore.

"He knows what he has to know," I said. "He knows he's not ours—" The word sent a stab of pain through me, keen as a knife. No, there was no "ours" anymore. And yet I couldn't voice the alternative.

"He knows who his parents were, and he's heard of what you did, more from others than from us. He knows a lot about his mother. As much as I can remember, and whatever anyone else can remember too. He thought you were dead. I didn't intend for him to know you weren't, but with all that's happened..." I spread my hands in a helpless gesture. "I can't keep him entirely ignorant of what's going on around him. It's too dangerous now. But I did censor what he's seen so he wouldn't find out you were alive and in the thick of all this during the funeral of the man he called Papa." Blaine stiffened, but I didn't relent. "He's always had nightmares about you coming back and taking him away from us. So maybe he knew on some level long ago."

"He's afraid of me."

"I think he always has been. Though we've tried to discourage that. Neither Pete nor I wanted him to hate you. It wouldn't do any good and would only hurt him. But he's taken what he knows and formed his own opinion about you. If there's much in it that's charitable, he hadn't told me."

Blaine absorbed it all in impassive silence. Finally he turned to me, the emperor's mask falling flawlessly back in place.

"I think this discussion will be much more productive if you understand that I didn't have anything to do with your husband's death."

It felt like he'd tossed a bucket of cold water on me. "And now you're going to tell me you didn't kill the emperor's unborn children either?" My throat was closing around the words.

Blaine went oddly still. "I was not behind the miscarriages."

I made a rude noise, though it didn't come as easily as it should have. I wasn't even sure why I was baiting him. "You weren't behind the assassination, you weren't behind the miscarriages. What *were* you behind, Blaine, or am I supposed to believe you did nothing and that it was all a misunderstanding when we believed you were The Patriot?"

His face and voice were emotionless. "I was never The Patriot, I think you know that now. That was the name Laudley created for his anonymous messages. I personally was behind all that happened with Kafe and Revan. And the fire in Abenez."

I caught my breath.

I hadn't expected him to claim responsibility for anything, much less acknowledge openly that he had taunted me with my rapist and kidnapped the child I hadn't even known about and murdered millions of people just to destroy something of mine.

The anger went out of me all in a rush. Molly. Owen. My reply, when it came, sounded too much like capitulation. "Just that."

"I understand those are not inconsiderable obstacles to any sort of arrangement between us," he said softly, "but I can offer you a pledge of good faith."

"Oh? What would that be?"

"His remains."

The whole world screeched to a halt with an ear-piercing clarity that stole my breath and clouded my vision.

"What?"

Blaine folded his hands, calm and regal, though he didn't look me in the eye. "Every emperor leaves a personal message for his successor. In his, he asked for his body to be given to you, if you survived him. He wanted to be put into the Dawes-Killearn Nebula with you." He paused, as if he thought I was capable of making some response. "I will carry out his wishes, and give his remains to you as soon as I can."

The overwhelming need to cry clenched so hard in my gut that I doubled over, gasping for breath. I stared at my feet, wondering what dream, or what nightmare, this was.

"I give you my word," he said, quietly.

He waited as I straightened, but this time I leaned against the back of my chair for support.

"Thank you," I said, breathless. "Though I suppose you realize I can't go anywhere near the nebula right now. I can't go anywhere at all."

He nodded. "But that won't always be the case."

I raised an eyebrow. "Really? Because I would have sworn..." I gestured around me, floundering. "Well, you sitting here doesn't bode well for our chances of remaining hidden long. We're not hidden at all, now." I leaned toward him. "The Empire has found us."

"No," he said. "I am not here as the Empire, though there is a much more precise explanation. I don't know where we are right now, either, and I've sent no signals to anyone of my position. I came here as you did, on the transport."

"There's another one?"

"As I understand it, the departure of one transport triggers the construction of another. The one I came in was seaworthy, but incomplete. For example, I understand that it is supposed to alert the caretaker of its departure. That component had not been installed yet."

"I see. So no one knows you're here but us, or knows how to come for you?"

"No."

I just stared at him. "So if I decided to strangle you right now, no one would even know what happened?"

He huffed. "Yes, if that's what you want to take away from this conversation."

I threw up my hands. "You expect me to believe you just handed me that enormous advantage?"

"You mean the way you handed me an unconditional surrender before you even knew what I was here for?"

I scowled. "No one ever said I was any good at this stuff. You, however, *are.*"

He nodded a sardonic bow, his lips twitching. "I used to think so." His expression sobered quickly. "Though I'm surprised you haven't doubted that, yourself. I still ended up on Dead End." We sat there, locked in silent acknowledgment of our tangled past, and all the pain we had inflicted on each other. "This isn't a game, and it's not about you and me anymore. You laid down your cards before you even looked at them, for the same reason that I just exposed my vulnerability to you."

I looked down with a sigh. "The children."

"Yes. I'm not here as the emperor or as your enemy, or for any reason having to do with you or your daughter. I came for my son, and for no other reason."

My whole body went rigid. He held up a hand. "No, don't take it like that. I mean I'm here because of him. In truth, I have no intention of taking him with me when I leave."

"Assuming you can leave."

He inclined his head in acknowledgment. "I have made arrangements."

"They won't work." Jonathan approached, taking his place behind me. "Unless you intend to bring an army."

Blaine's face was a picture.

"*Jonathan?*" He stared at me. "*This* Jonathan?" He shook his head, stunned, and looked up at Jonathan. "I thought you were dead."

"Your spy network clearly isn't what it used to be."

Jonathan's reply drew a snort of amusement out of me even before I'd processed the absurdity of the situation, or what was really niggling at my thoughts. Something Blaine had said.

"You didn't come to take Owen? You didn't come here to do anything to any of us?"

His mouth twisted. "It's interesting to me that you would go immediately back to how this affects your family as a whole, rather than merely yourself or your own daughter. That's not something you would have done all those years ago."

"Well I'm also not fifteen anymore. But you're wrong anyway. I always loved Pete, even when I was stupid. You know that because you used it against me."

"Too true," he said.

Jonathan's presence at my back was like a nagging itch. "Oh for fuck's sake, Jonathan, sit down. There's no protocol for a meeting of Traitors Anonymous. The only rule here is sit your ass down and be part of this conversation. We all know you know more about any of this than I do."

Jonathan gave me a half bow. "Yes, Your Highness."

"Jake."

He huffed amusement. "Jake."

Blaine was watching us in silence, his expression pensive. "I have to say, this development has taken me completely by surprise. Jonathan being here was something I never even considered. And you seem to have reconciled."

"It's none of your business," I snapped.

He inclined his head in acknowledgment. "So long as we understand each other, if we are to work together."

"I didn't say I was going to work with anyone, yet. I still don't get why you're here."

"Then I shall explain." He waited for an objection, but it didn't come. "Everything that has happened, starting with your husband's murder, has been orchestrated by my father-in-law."

"Laudley," I spat. "Yes, we figured that out already."

He didn't react. "Then you have no doubt also guessed that his motives are entirely self-serving."

"Which would include your interests as well."

"Why should it?"

I frowned. "What do you mean? Clearly he intended to incorporate you in his schemes. He took you from Dead End. *You're* the Regent now, not him."

"He's only using me now to stand in for the one he intended to have already. Owen."

Jonathan nodded. "Your usefulness to him ends when Owen is recovered."

"Yes. And this is not only supposition and logic. I have evidence that makes his intentions clear enough. With Owen on the throne, he could serve as Regent as well as I could, and he intends to. At that point, I am in his way. We have all seen how he deals with people who are in his way."

Slow anger burned like fire in my gut. "So what is it you want from me?"

"I want you to do nothing."

"I beg your pardon?"

"I need to know my son is safe with you, and out of Laudley's reach. I can't act effectively if you are an unknown variable. If I succeed, you will win as well. But I need to know that we're not, even unwittingly, working against each other. Especially in any way that would put Owen at risk."

"You want me to sit here while you decide the fate of me and mine?"

"Yes."

I laughed. "If there's one thing to be said for you, Blaine, your honesty is refreshing. Or at least, your straightforwardness. I suppose it would be stupid of me to assume those aren't lies."

"Yes, it would," Jonathan interjected. It made me laugh again.

"We'll have to discuss this," he said to Blaine, "before we make any decisions."

"How does this end?" I pressed. "What happens when you've

got Laudley out of the way?"

"I'll come back for all of you. You will be cleared of all charges and be free to do as you please."

"And who rules the empire?"

He cocked an eyebrow. "You have ambitions, Prince Jacob?"

I glared. "In the two decades you've known me, what did I ever do that gave you the impression I wanted to rule the fucking empire?"

"Then why do you care?"

I bit back the reflexive response, the one that said I didn't care, that he could take his imperial throne and shove it up his ass so long as he left my family alone. I looked away.

"Because I won't sit back and watch all of Pete's work undone." His mouth quirked but he didn't interrupt. "Because Pete's daughter is the rightful heir." I sighed, feeling defeated. "Because he would care."

He nodded, as if satisfied. "I see. Believe it or not, I'm impressed. I wasn't sure you would be so forward-looking. You've always struck me as a man who lived in the moment, and didn't consider the consequences past the end of his temper."

"And I've always believed you were a narrow-minded, arrogant asshole ready to run over anyone who offends you."

"Or you're clueless with a temper and an overblown idea about your own intelligence."

I barked a laugh, though I wasn't sure if I thought that was funny or if it had just startled me. "That too. So why did you change the subject?"

He sat back, his eyebrows raised. "You really are better at the game now, aren't you?"

"I don't know. I survived the last five years without much of a fuss from anyone, so that could be true. But I think there's something to be said for this non-confrontational curve ball you're throwing me." He gave me a long, considering look and sat back. "What happens after we win is negotiable, to some extent. My only stipulation at this point is that Owen is safe and that he acknowledges me as his father. I won't go away. And I won't give up all the progress we've made so far."

"Progress?"

"Power." He was very still. "I won't put myself in someone else's power. Not again."

"You expect me to agree to that?"

"I don't expect you to agree to anything at all. I only ask that we work together to protect all of us, and eliminate Laudley."

"Ridiculous," Jonathan said. "Even Jake's not stupid enough to make an agreement like that, open ended and with no assurances or protections."

I scowled, wanting to protest some part of that.

Blaine spread his hands, ignoring my reaction. "I am in no position to make promises at this point."

"And Molly? I notice that her interests have been almost completely absent from this conversation."

"Molly?"

"Princess Marquilla," Jonathan clarified.

Blaine pursed his lips, but replied too quickly. "We have been put in a difficult position, all of us. I must get back as soon as possible. In the meantime, I'll—"

Molly screamed.

What about Ella?

As a first name? No, there's no imperial tradition for that one. We could use it as a middle name, though.

There's no imperial tradition for Marquilla, either.

But it was your mother's name, so there's precedent.

I don't like it, Pete.

Why?

It's hard to explain.

Let's talk about it tonight.

iv35

We ran toward the house. Through the window I saw Molly, struggling and kicking in the hands of three armed and armored men. Something hit me hard in the back and I fell to the ground, a heavy weight on top of me. I struggled but someone hissed in my ear.

"Be still. They're ISS."

Power surged through me on a wave of pure rage and I rolled us both over, crashing my fist into Blaine's face. Someone else grabbed my arm.

"Stop!" Jonathan whispered. "Wait."

"He—"

"They're not mine," Blaine grated out, swiping the blood from his mouth with a fist. "They're not with me. I didn't bring them."

I glanced up helplessly at the house. "Then who—"

"Laudley," Jonathan said.

"Check outside!" The shout jerked all our heads up.

"Quick!" Jonathan grabbed my arm and together we scrambled up, dashing into the pitiful cover of the trees, Blaine crashing behind me.

"Where are we going?" I demanded. "The children are in the house!"

"And they've already got them," Blaine spat.

I whirled around but Jonathan had my arm and wouldn't let go.

"Stop that! Stop bickering and run. We're almost there."

The noise from the direction of the house was all the encouragement I needed. I ran after Jonathan but in moments he disappeared. I jerked to a stop but Blaine pushed me ahead of him.

"There," he said, pointing. I followed his finger to where Jonathan had disappeared and I could just make out a faint shimmer around what looked like a bush. I dashed toward it, closing my eyes when I hit it. Nothing stopped me and I passed through the camouflage field, Blaine on my heels. Jonathan smacked his palm against the wall and the shimmer hardened and went opaque.

"All right," he said, panting. "We're safe for now."

I stared at the poly walls, the drawers and cabinets and the occasional dark screen of a simple bunker for a moment, getting my bearings, before I rounded on Blaine. "They followed you."

Jonathan grabbed Blaine before I could, and for a moment I thought he was holding him still so I could hit him. But then I realized he was trying to get Blaine's jacket off.

"What the—?"

"What are you—?"

"Get it off." Jonathan cut us both off, jerking hard at Blaine's collar. It shocked me how quickly Blaine stopped arguing and slipped out of the sleeves, a look of realization dawning. His hands went to the buttons of his shirt. I stared with a sort of horrified fascination at a long, thin scar that traced from his collarbone all the way down his chest to disappear below his waistline. Within moments Jonathan had him stripped down to his underpants.

"Oh, please don't," I said when Blaine reached for them.

"Turn around if you don't want to see," Jonathan snapped. I did as I was told. Moments later, Jonathan moved past me with a bundle of clothes in his arms which he dumped straight into an incinerator chute, slamming the door and hitting the igniter. He went to a drawer nearby, jerking it open and grabbing pants and things and throwing them in Blaine's direction. He disappeared again, moving behind me until finally he said, "It's safe now, Jacob," with only a hint of wryness in his tone.

I turned to find Blaine fully dressed again, though the sleeves and pants legs were too short.

"Trackers," Jonathan said. "They were probably in his clothes."

I took a minute to make sense of that.

"He didn't bring them so they had to have followed him," Jonathan explained. "The only way they could do that is if they had a locater on him. There's no way they could have followed the transport."

"How do you know he didn't bring them?"

"Because he was as afraid as you were when he saw them with the children." I glanced at Blaine but he was watching Jonathan.

"We have to go back," I insisted. "We have to get them."

"How do you propose we do that?" Blaine's dry tone made my hands clench into fists. "Do you have an arsenal and an army stashed on this island, too?"

I advanced on him but Jonathan stepped between us. "Stop acting like children! Can you two do that?"

Jonathan glared at me and I snapped my mouth closed. Blaine straightened. "Yes, of course."

Jonathan didn't wait for my answer, he gave a curt nod. "Good. Now," he turned to Blaine, "how were you planning to get off the island?"

"I have someone at the palace waiting for my signal to activate the return transport."

"Well there's a fantastic plan. Only one way out, which you leave right in the hands of your enemies and expose the location of the safehouse at the same time."

Blaine glared at me. "There's almost no information about this place to plan from, in case you hadn't noticed. I had no other options."

"Then why did you even come?"

"Because that's my son!"

All argument died on my lips as my heart sped up again. I rounded on Jonathan. "We have to go get them."

His eyebrows shot up. "How?"

I stared at him. "What do you mean, how? I don't know. That's your job." I waved my hand around at the vid screens in the bunker. "You and all this stuff."

Jonathan made a noise that sounded like a growl. "In spite of what you seem to believe, I can't actually perform magic."

"They have my children!"

His voice softened. "I know that."

"Then what are we going to do?"

He turned away, switching on a vid.

"We're going to get out of here. Jake, I hope that transport of yours is as far along as you said. We can take a tunnel from here."

I grabbed his arm, whirling him back around to face me. "We're going to rescue the kids first. They're coming with us."

"We can't possibly help them now. We'd only be captured ourselves."

I shook him, hard. "My children!"

He jerked away from me.

"I know. But you can't help them by crashing back in there. The only way you can do anything for them now is by escaping so you can fight another day. Not today. Today is already lost."

"But—"

I sought Blaine but he was glaring at the floor, his jaw tight. When he raised his head and his face was carefully blank. "He's right."

"Can't you do anything?" I demanded.

He gave me an incredulous look. "Don't you think I've done

enough already?" His tone was sour and full of contempt. But for once, it wasn't for me.

"The transport, Jake?" Jonathan prompted. I nodded tightly. He gave me a long look full of sympathy. "We have to go."

"Wait," Blaine said to Jonathan, "you have a port comm?" Jonathan held it up wordlessly. "You'll have to leave it." Jonathan's expression hardened but he hesitated only a moment before chucking it in the incinerator.

Blaine turned to me. "You?"

I shook my head. "He can track us with those?" I asked.

"Or worse," Blaine said grimly, but looked at Jonathan rather than me. "There's a transport, you said?"

You'll be at the game today, right?

Pete...

Please?

They're all going to hate me.

Since when have you cared about that?

I cared whether or not you hated me.

Well, yes, but that was because you were afraid of me.

I'm still afraid of you.

You are not.

That's true.

iv36

The garage was further below the waterline than I'd realized and we dove quickly to a depth that would make us invisible from above to the naked eye. Thankfully, the things that had not been affected by the transport's deactivation on arrival were the majority of the camouflage and defense mechanisms.

I set the autopilot for somewhere in the middle of the ocean and stepped back into what was more a cargo area than anything else. "Jonathan—"

"What are you doing back here?" Blaine snapped.

I cocked an eyebrow sarcastically. "Whatever I choose to do. What business is it of yours?"

"If this thing goes down or runs into something, I drown too. I think that's very much my business."

"Do you want to drive it?"

"No, I'd like you to drive it."

"You know what, Blaine? My husband just died and now I've lost my children. You think you could leave me alone just once?"

He went very still, his voice cold and hard as ice. "You think I don't know what that feels like?"

I froze, startled. A familiar grief descended over me. "Did you really think I had anything to do with it? When Hera died?"

"No. And yes."

My eyebrows climbed but I waited.

"I didn't think you actively had anything to do with it. But you were like a disease. You infected everything around you. You killed things that were good and proper just by existing."

Anger smoldered in my chest. "And now?"

He laughed. "Now? Of course I think that. More than ever. The emperor is dead. That was entirely because of you."

In a flash I was standing so close to him I could feel his rapid breaths. He sneered. "Aren't you going to punch me?"

I could imagine my fist crashing into his face. Breaking his nose. I'd done it once before, and I wanted more than anything to do it again. But my gaze flickered unwillingly to the scar that cut through his eyebrow and my stomach went cold. With a force of will I slowed my breathing, and finally stepped back, blowing out a long breath. "How did that arrogance survive Dead End?"

He froze but then started to smile, a weak, sickly thing.

"The same way yours did, I imagine."

We drove in an awkward, angry silence for a while before I turned to Jonathan with a sigh.

"What now?"

"There is another safehouse I know," he said slowly.

"Another?" Blaine said. "Why don't I know about it?"

Jonathan's expression was bland and dry. "Because it's not an Imperial safehouse. Quite the opposite, in fact." His mouth twitched. "And I think it is the last place anyone would look for you." The emphasis on the last word was clearly meant for Blaine, though I got the feeling Jonathan meant that just as surely for me.

"Where is it?" I asked.

He shook his head. "I'm not going to say. Not yet, anyway."

I scowled. "Why?"

"Because it's not my sanctuary to offer you. I can take you there, but they are the ones who will decide if you may refuge with them or not."

There was a long moment of silence. Blaine's voice was icy. "I refuse to blindly follow you wherever you've decided is best for us to go. Tell me where you're taking us."

Jonathan cocked an eyebrow. "You refuse? On what position of power do you base this demand? Your authority as emperor?" His tone left no question as to what he thought of Blaine. "You require protection. If you want it from these people, you will do what I say, or you won't have it."

"What people? I said.

Jonathan ignored the question. "We will have to drop him off somewhere first."

"Stop!" Blaine bellowed. "I will not be dismissed so easily, certainly not by you."

Jonathan's expression was an odd mix of amusement and annoyance. "Me? What difference is there between you and me at present, *Your Excellence*," he made the title a mockery, "except that I have connections and information that will protect me, and you don't?"

Blaine whirled around, storming the whole five feet across the transport. A long, heavy silence passed before he grated, "I don't owe you anything."

"You owe me a great many things, my life not the least of them." Jonathan's tone softened. "Yet I'm willing to help you. Because I'm not like you."

"No, you're not," Blaine said. There was something in his tone I couldn't make out at all. Finally he turned. "I accept your offer," he bowed his head regally. "Thank you."

Jonathan pulled out meal packets for us before he disappeared into the forward compartment to enter the new coordinates. I laughed at the simple practicality of it. Of course Jonathan would make sure we were fed.

If Blaine thought anything of it, he gave no indication. He sat down across the cabin from me and began to eat with a straightforward purpose, though it almost seemed like he didn't realize he was doing it.

"Kafe's dead."

My head jerked up and I stared at Blaine. He was holding a cracker between two fingers, painting swirls in the hummus, not even looking at me. And yet I felt like he'd punched me in the face. I went hot and cold all over. I wanted just to nod and move on, as if I didn't care. I didn't want to care.

"When?"

He sat there, still and unresponsive. Without looking up he finally answered. "When Laudley came for me, he took Kafe as well. Once we were on his ship he spaced her."

I grunted, as if this time he'd punched me in the gut. I'd imagined it before, Kafe's death, many times in many ways. I'd imagined that one, her being spaced while still alive. The moment of panic before the cold vacuum of space ended all the rest of her moments. Somehow there was no satisfaction in hearing that it was done. Or even relief. Mostly I felt sick.

"She protected you, you know."

Blaine's words seemed to echo in my ears; ridiculous, unbelievable words. I laughed, an unhinged, desperate sound.

"Protected? Is that what you call it?" He knew what had happened to me on Dead End. He'd arranged it and watched it, collected the security footage and used it against me more than once.

He snorted. "You have no idea how protected you were. When I contacted her to make sure your stay on Dead End was..." he looked up at me with a malicious smile that still managed to be wan and halfhearted, "memorable, she said she knew how and would take care of it. And I was happy with the results."

My hands clenched and unclenched in my lap. I struggled not to reach across the cabin and strangle him.

"It wasn't until I went there myself that I realized how much she sheltered you."

"Sheltered?" My voice shook.

"She warned everyone else off of you. She thought it would have more of an impact and make you feel more isolated if you thought your suffering wasn't simply the normal way of things. If you thought that no one else went through what you did."

"Did you ever even spend one day on solitary?" My voice trembled with fury.

"Of course. Two days."

I snorted. "Twenty days, Blaine. I spent twenty days out there. Do you think that was fun? Do you think I felt protected? Would you even be alive right now if the same thing happened to you? Over, and over, and over."

He slammed his hands down on the bench, rising on a rush of fury. "How many times were you gang raped?" I sucked in a startled breath. "How many nights did you lay awake, in too much pain to sleep, wondering if it was going to happen again tomorrow, when it would stop—if it ever would?" He sneered at me. "Highness."

I fell back against the seat. Long before I was married to the emperor, Kafe had called me that. She'd denied me even the threadbare dignity of the names the people on Dead End made for themselves, cobbled together from the identities they'd lost. She was the first one to call me "Highness," and I'd heard it every day for six months in that hellhole, a mockery of what I'd had, and what I'd lost. Blaine hadn't punched me, he'd reached down my throat and pulled out my insides, holding them up for me to see. Rage pooled in my chest, a hot, hard thing. I jerked to standing, clenching my fists in fury.

"How many nights did you lay awake, E—whatever, trying to cling to sanity after days and days of solitary, knowing you'd just be going out there again tomorrow? How many nights did you spend wondering if you'd get a day or two before they did it to you again?"

"There are worse things than solitary," he sneered.

I sucked in an angry breath. "There are worse things than—" but the words got stuck and I couldn't say them. As much as I wanted to stab him with the memories, hurt him as much as he'd hurt me, that was a two edged sword, and I didn't think I could survive the blow. I sighed.

He was very still. "You don't know what they called me?"

His quiet shock drenched me and I sat back down. "No. I told you I'd leave you alone out there and I did." He watched me in silence. I looked away. "And I didn't want to know what was happening to Owen's father." I glanced up at him, and the look of blank shock on his face. I sighed. "We've spent a lot of years trying to hurt each other. Look where it's gotten us." He said nothing. "Maybe we should stop trying."

It felt like hours, days in which neither of us even breathed.

"Eight." I raised my head but he wasn't looking at me. "That was what they called me." He straightened, brushing away wrinkles in his shirt. "Eight."

And then he walked into the forward compartment, leaving that peace offering like an unexploded bomb at my feet.

So quickly I was powerless again.

iv37

We traveled for some hours. Anger and humiliating helplessness washed over me. It was almost unbearable.

Only days ago I had been crowned emperor, and now I was nothing again. Discarded as easily as any unclass. I kept my hands in my pockets so no one would see them shaking.

Dawes paced in the back cabin, with Jonathan always nearby, accessible, as was proper for a servant. And yet there was something different between them now that was hard to define. It wasn't the cold distance of betrayal. It was more like the comfortable familiarity of friends. It was wrong, and strange. Yet somehow I also felt a pang of jealousy. In the face of his losses Dawes still had *someone.* I looked away, staring at navigation controls that meant nothing to me, trying not to think about loneliness.

We docked, finally, at a small, grubby, dilapidated marina that the nav said was in Mexico. Not the closest approach to Mexico City, but not far from it, either. I scowled in disgust.

"You're going to hide us exactly where everyone expects him to be?"

Jonathan's expression was cool, and that of a man to an equal, not a middle class former servant to a noble. "Yes. Exactly where they've already looked." He held my gaze for a long time, and when I didn't reply he continued. "In any case, we're not going to Prince Jacob's estate, or where anyone would think he would choose to be."

I glared at him but decided not to say any more. I had agreed to this ridiculous scheme, and I would not let them see a coward.

"Here," Jonathan said, handing us each a small device. "Stick it in your pocket and activate it. It's a holo-disguise." Dawes and I both took them. I nearly choked when Dawes suddenly changed from a relatively young man to a homely old woman. He wore a smirk that made me think my disguise must be similarly ridiculous, and I scowled. "This way," Jonathan said, gesturing for us to disembark.

Dawes gave a sharp nod of his head. "Lead the way."

We were scant moments on the docks before we entered an empty warehouse. There we passed through a hidden door and into a tunnel. It was plain and nondescript, with no markings to indicate its purpose or any destination. It might have been anywhere in the empire. We walked several hundred meters before another door came into sight. This one was locked. At Jonathan's direction we deactivated the disguises.

He keyed in a code on the pad by the door and we waited in silence. There was nothing identifiable about the woman who joined us in the tunnel, emerging from a door behind us that I hadn't seen. She had no distinguishing features, no discernible racial influence, and she wore gray from head to toe. Even her hair was gray. She didn't speak to us at all, merely handed Jonathan a tablet. He turned to Dawes and me.

"Before you can go any further, you must swear and document your promise not to reveal this location, or anything about those who maintain it, their activities, and their organization."

"What do you need?" Dawes said. I gritted my jaw.

Jonathan extended the tablet to Dawes. "Swear that in exchange for their help, you will reveal to no one anything you know about this location, the people who have helped you, their confederates, their methods, resources, and plans. You will protect their secrets as your own under pain of death."

Dawes nodded without further complaint, placing his hand on the tablet to record his agreement. A flicker of a wince passed over his face before he pulled his hand away.

"That also implanted a passive tracker. It is usable to no one or nothing that does not have the highest clearance among this group. But should you break your vow, it gives them the ability to find you and mete out the consequences you just agreed to."

My breath caught. Dawes stared at Jonathan for a long moment. Jonathan merely stared back. "You wouldn't betray the people risking their lives to avenge your husband and protect you, would you?"

"No," Dawes replied in a hoarse whisper.

"Then you have nothing to be concerned about." He gave Dawes a wry look. "It has a limited lifespan. It will need to be refreshed over time if you continue to work with them."

"How long?"

He arched an eyebrow. "If you knew, it wouldn't be very secure, would it?"

They exchanged private smiles. "It also enables me to find you, should we become separated."

Dawes huffed. "You could do that anyway."

Jonathan turned to me and I backed away before I could stop myself. "No." My voice was too strained. "Absolutely not. I will not allow you to implant a tracker in me. A *termination device.*" It came out in a rasp and I forced myself to breathe deeply, find some measure of calm. "No. I am not a fool."

He and Dawes exchanged looks between them. Adrenaline and anger rushed through me like a summer thunderstorm, raging and powerful. "No," I said, firm and sure. "I will not put myself so entirely under the control of anyone, much less a group of traitors." I looked at their faces again, so still and uncompromising. My resolve weakened even as my heart rushed faster. "You ask too much."

Jonathan's face softened, and my anger flared. I didn't want his pity.

"Look," he said, his voice gentle but insistent. I couldn't help but glance at the tablet he held out in front of me. "It is a temporary but necessary safety measure for people who take a great risk helping you."

I couldn't take my eyes away from the display. Temporary, he'd said. I wouldn't be so vulnerable forever. Unless it was a trick. A trap. I examined Jonathan's face, but what did I expect to find? I knew better than to believe what I might see in his expression.

I took a deep breath. I didn't have a choice. I could do this and enter the safe haven on the other side of that door, or I could refuse and be left out here alone, to fend for myself for as long as I managed to hide from those searching for me with the full resources of the empire.

I slammed my palm against the tablet, almost knocking it out of Jonathan's grasp as it recorded my scan and inserted the tracker. I closed my eyes briefly and then forced myself to open them.

"Very well, it is done. Proceed."

The woman in gray wore a pinched expression but didn't look at me. She turned back to the door and entered a code in the pad, scanning in the data from her tablet. With a clank the doors opened and we proceeded.

On the other side things were subtly different. There was still no declaration of what this place was, or where it was taking us, but it began to look like it belonged to something. A door here, a computer panel there. Nothing declarative and everything locked down, but it was clearly a place with a purpose.

In a small garage a few hundred meters past the door, we found a transport. The woman gestured for us to enter.

We sped along for an hour before she parked and we all got out. There were no more identifying marks in this part of the tunnel than there had been before, and I wondered how much longer we'd travel this way. I didn't ask, because I had a feeling I was the only one who had no idea where we were going.

Fifteen minutes of walking brought us to another door. We were required to submit to a biometric scan, one that no doubt looked for the implant as well, before we were allowed to pass through.

On the other side was a war room. Everywhere were vid screens and terminals and panels, all active and in use. Five or six people bustled about, intent and purposeful. All of them stopped to look at us when we entered, but unlike the gaping, common response I expected, most simply went back to their work once their curiosity was satisfied. One woman, however, wearing the plain blue colors that seemed to be their uniform, approached us.

It was Lady Chou.

I realized then that there were many ways to betray one's country, one's friends, and oneself. I wasn't sure which one I was doing anymore.

iv**38**

I stared at her. "How in the empire did you get here?" I demanded.

She smirked at me. "You mean, after you confined me to your estate so your associates could easily find and kill me at your convenience?"

I didn't bother to reply to that. There was an edge to her voice that made me sure she knew exactly how much control I'd really had over anything since my release.

Her grin grew wider. "So interesting to find you here. Among the rabble."

I refused to take the bait.

"You are TG?" Dawes asked. It meant nothing to me.

She gave him a considering look. "I am not. Not for lack of willingness. I simply haven't the resources to set up and maintain an operation like this."

"Who does?" he asked.

"I do." I recognized the voice even before Lord Naganika came into view, a smile lighting up his face.

"Lord Naganika?" Dawes said, his tone somewhat relieved. It occurred to me then that Dawes would have last seen Naganika before, or perhaps just after, the emperor's murder. I wondered what he would think if he knew everything of the man that I did. "You're TG?"

He essayed an ironic bow. "I am."

"What does it mean?" Dawes asked. Naganika raised a brow in question. "Your alias," he clarified.

He smiled. "It's a long story."

"Did Pete know about this?" Dawes pressed. I wished fervently that he would stop with the inane questions and get to the root of the issue: that we were fully in this group's power and we needed to know who exactly they were, what they were doing, and what that meant for us.

Naganika pursed his lips. "I would never wager on Rikhart IV being ignorant of anything. But if he knew, he didn't tell me."

In the silence that followed, Lord Naganika nodded to me. "I'm am glad to see you are alive and unharmed, Your Excellency."

Dawes made a rude noise, thought it was clearly for the title and not the sentiment.

"What do you know of all this?" I demanded. Naganika's fluctuating loyalties frustrated me, and it made me angry that I'd begun to trust him, before. "What is Laudley doing now?" I doubted he was unaware, but I added, "He has the children."

Naganika's expression was somber. "Yes. I know. And I apologize," he looked around, "to all of you. I was not aware Laudley was tracking the emperor."

"Blaine," Dawes said, and we all looked at him. "You mean he was tracking Duke Blaine."

Naganika's eyebrows rose, but he stepped back as I closed on Dawes. "I've had enough. If you want to snip and snipe at someone for holding a position of power then perhaps you shouldn't have married an emperor."

There was a long silence. I expected fury, that he would even try to hit me again, but his shoulders sagged.

"Pete was always an emperor. Even when I didn't want him to be. He was born to it and he was wonderful at it. No, I don't respect anyone who would aspire to be an emperor at the expense of others. But that's not what he was, or what he did."

Every eye in the room was on him, and there was respect, uncompromising and unanimous. I looked away, unaccountably jealous. Of Dawes, no less.

I sought Naganika. "What will Laudley do now that he has the children?"

In the heavy pause that followed, Naganika sighed. "I can only tell you what little I know, and what I suspect."

"Then do it."

He met Dawes' gaze rather than mine. The acknowledgment of his right to the children rankled me. "They have returned to the palace. He intended for it to be quiet, but there were too many people involved. It is known among the guard, and I expect it will soon be known by many more, that both Princess Marquilla and Prince Owen are in residence again. I believe both children are safe for now."

Naganika turned to me. "Prince Owen is safe because the Grand Duke needs him, and Princess Marquilla because the Grand Duke knows he will lose Prince Owen if he acts against the princess."

That all of these people knew more about my son than I did, that they knew I needed them to explain how my son would react, doused the rest of the anger I was sustaining myself with. "So, what now?" Dawes asked, his tone bordering on sarcastic, as if Naganika were avoiding what was truly important. Naganika seemed to accept that without questioning it.

"My guess is that he will acknowledge the return of both the princess and Prince Owen, and that he will not deviate from the expectation that the throne is Princess Marquilla's by right." He paused. "For Laudley, that is a small enough detour from his original intention. She will need a regent as Prince Owen would. Laudley intends to be that regent. He has many years to bend her to his will, or, if he fails at that, to find a quiet and convenient way to be rid of her."

Dawes sucked in a breath. Naganika met his frantic gaze. "He would only harm himself to act against her now. He has too much to lose and almost nothing to gain."

"Nothing?" Dawes demanded, incredulous.

"Nothing," Naganika insisted. "There is no one to challenge him for the regency now. Especially in light of the fact that the princess has no close relative available."

"And he will kill us as soon as he finds us," Dawes said flatly.

Naganika nodded to him. "That goes without saying." He looked at me, "Though Emperor Regent Enryn's death would have to be quiet and easily explained away." He focused on Dawes. "You, he wants to dispose of publicly. He intends to have you executed for the crimes you have been accused of on record." Into the silence he continued. "It is a convenient setup for Emperor Regent Enryn to disappear now. He can easily claim that you took your revenge before the emperor could be rescued, and lay Emperor Regent Enryn's death at your feet."

"He's not dead," Dawes protested stupidly.

Naganika's reply was quiet. "He could be."

A long moment followed, in which everyone digested that information.

Jonathan was the one who spoke. "We have things to decide now."

I gestured to Naganika that I intended to speak to him. His eyebrows quirked upward for a moment but quickly he nodded and followed me to a corner of the room. I wondered which face of Naganika that I'd seen so far was closest to the real one, and where his loyalties truly lay. I imagined they were with himself.

He turned to me. "Your Excellence?"

I frowned. "I think we both know that I am merely Your Grace, at best. Considering the circumstances."

He gave me a nod of acknowledgment, with no opinion or judgment apparent. I forced myself not to rub at the spot on my palm where they had inserted a tracker that would allow this group of people—this man—to kill me as easily as Laudley might wish.

"You seem to be a man of many allegiances," I said. "I'm not sure what I can expect from you."

He smiled faintly. "I am a man who would see the empire strongest and at its best. Is that not explanation enough?"

"It's no explanation at all. The throne of the empire is constantly in transition these days. You support whoever manages to claim it for an hour or two? It's the same as supporting no one. I would know where you stand before I can work with you." He glanced at my hand, and I resisted the temptation to rub it.

He regarded me frankly. "What choice do you have, Duke Blaine?" I froze. "What choice do *I* have? If I am to be useful to anyone I must appear to be useful to everyone. There are many who would take sides in this. And there must be. Some cannot survive if others don't fail. If I am smart, I can remain a vital piece in everyone's game. That isn't just self-preservation, Your Grace. I can only work toward my goal if I am alive."

"As can I!" This time we both glanced at my hand. I burned with indignation. "You will have to pick a side some day."

"Why do you assume I haven't?" he replied almost sadly. "If I am lucky, I won't live to regret it." He gave me a funny smile. "Your life is safe in my hands, Duke Blaine. I'm sorry you doubt that." He stood, bowing to me with the proper affectation of respect. "May I go, Your Grace? There is much work to be done now."

I waved him away, disgusted and shaking, wondering which one of us was wrong.

The clock said night had fallen long ago, but there was neither day nor night in these tunnels.

Lady Chou turned to me, a look of amusement on her face. "How are you enjoying the hospitality of Abenez, Your Grace? You have only to climb the stairs to find a large population of those displaced by the great fire many years ago." Her gaze was piercing, as if she blamed me for the fire. She was not wrong. I didn't deign to answer.

"You have found sustenance and shelter among the unclass." Her eyes glittered with malice, and I refused to give her the satisfaction of a reaction. She frowned and pressed on. "You should be grateful that the fire did not kill everyone, and that they allow you here among them."

I stepped closer, needing to reclaim some measure of power, even if it was only illusory. "Does that bother you, Lady Chou?"

She seemed unsure of what to do with my response. "It doesn't surprise me that they would shelter you," she snapped. "Only that you do not disdain their generosity."

I looked at her for a long moment. "I think there is work to do now, my lady." She gasped in surprise and I turned away, savoring my small triumph.

Abenez felt like an avalanche above my head, poised to fall on me at the slightest mistake.

iv39

We stood around the center console, strategizing.

"Our options are severely limited now," Jonathan said.

I turned to him, curious. "What options did you have before that you don't have now?"

"I had hoped to use you, in your position as regent, to play on your sympathies for your son."

I glared at him. "You intended to use Owen as a hostage."

Dawes stiffened. "Owen is my son and I—"

"Not a hostage," Jonathan interrupted, blunting the moment in which I would have lashed out at Dawes for claiming my child, again, "but I intended to appeal to your feelings as a father." He examined me for some time. "I think it would have worked, had you still been in power."

I looked away, frustrated and ashamed that I was not still in power, that he couldn't simply offer me my son in exchange for protection. How much easier that would have been. I glanced around the table at this strange combination of people who somehow had the same goal.

"What do you think, Prince Jacob?" Naganika said. Dawes looked pensive.

"A simple power grab would never work. It would be nothing more than infighting among the nobles. We're on the losing side there. No matter what the nobility thinks of any of us, they're set in their ways, and will follow the one with power rather than think for themselves."

It was on the tip of my tongue to protest but it struck me as amusing that Dawes would use the same phrasing to criticize the nobles that Laudley had used to disdain the common people.

"Then what do you suggest?" I asked.

"Everyone else."

I stood there, waiting for clarification. Jonathan wore a faint smile.

"Everyone else," Dawes repeated. "This isn't about the nobility, or even the throne anymore. This is a coup by a man who has taken powerful and precious hostages to secure the throne for himself. The solution isn't within that power structure anymore. We can't fight the status quo with the status quo. It's time to turn to the most powerful force in the empire."

I stared at him. Did he think he would take control of the ISS somehow?

"Everyone else," Jonathan answered.

That made no sense, yet others around me seemed to understand him. "Not the nobles," Dawes explained. "All the rest of us. The high class, the middle, low, and unclass. The real power in the empire lies with the people. They just don't know that yet."

I glared at him, angry and betrayed. "You mean to destabilize the very empire you claim to fight for?"

"No," Dawes said, striding toward me, his voice steady and hard. "I mean to take back the empire that serves and protects all these people. And I mean to use the people to do it."

I refuse to speak to that Lord Whatever His Name Is again

You're the emperor's consort now. Confront him directly and he will have to stop being such an ass or expect retribution from me.

Couldn't you just skip straight to the retribution and leave me out of it?

I won't always be here to take care of you.

iv 40

Do you mind explaining what you mean, Jake?" Jonathan said, glancing subtly at Blaine. I grinned at him, but the smile faded.

"I never wanted to lead anyone. I wanted to marry the man I loved and go on with our lives. But I fell in love with the emperor and that changed everything."

I stepped closer to him, as if pretending this were a conversation just between us would make it easier to explain. "He tried to make me understand what a powerful symbol I was, how much I could accomplish merely by taking a stand and giving others a rallying point, and hope." I chuckled sickly. "Pete was right, and I knew that, even though I never wanted to admit it. But now I intend to use it." I looked up at Naganika. "Can we broadcast from here?"

His eyebrows climbed. "You mean, to the empire?"

"Yes, the way The Patriot did." It went very still around us and several people cut glances at Blaine before looking quickly away.

Naganika nodded slowly. "It could be arranged. I'd need a few hours. Maybe a day."

I nodded. "That's fine, because I don't know what I'm going to say yet." My face was heating, but the others' expressions were more encouraging than mocking. "In the meantime, I have something Laudley won't expect." They all turned to me and waited. Blaine had a funny look on his face. "The blinders," I continued. Jonathan's mouth thinned. He knew what I was talking about. He glanced around the console at the people gathered there. Not just Blaine and Naganika, but Lady Chou and a man with her I didn't know. Yes, I was taking a big risk and I knew it. But it was the time for risks.

"I beg your pardon?" Naganika said.

"They're called blinders, but they're really just disguises. Advanced camouflage devices."

Blaine scoffed. "An ISS team will have scanners sophisticated enough that they won't be fooled by your camouflage devices."

"No," I said, "that's what you don't understand." I glanced at Jonathan. "These technically don't exist. That's why Jonathan doesn't want me to talk about them. They're an official Imperial secret, available only to the Family. These don't just project a hologram, they fool the sensors into seeing the bone structure, flesh, and fat to fit your false image. They won't see past it. They'll see what you want seen."

There was a long silence.

"Yes," Naganika said quietly, "I can see why that is kept secret."

Even Blaine looked like he thought I shouldn't have said anything. "We have some with us," I went on, ignoring the glares. "Jonathan brought them from the safehouse. We can use them as templates to create more."

"Jacob," Jonathan said, a quiet warning in his tone.

"No, listen," I said, "I know this is a big gamble. But the fact is that we're at a huge disadvantage, and I'm not talking about some nebulous 'our side.' I'm talking about the imperial heir herself. My daughter." I turned to Blaine. "Owen. *This* is how we protect the Family, by beating those who have the children." I looked around at all of them. "Isn't that the point of the devices?"

No one answered. "That's not the only purpose I have for them, though. I examined much of the tech found on the safehouse transport and I think I can combine a small shield into the projection. Not enough to stop an army, but one that should hinder a bullet or beam while you get the hell out of the way. These shields won't make you bulletproof, but they'll give you breathing room and an extra level of protection while you get away."

"All right," Jonathan said, "now that you've told all of us about these Top Secret devices, do you mind explaining why?"

"I don't intend to just send a broadcast and then leave the people to fight alone. I intend to go out there, be with them. I can be that symbol and rallying point not just from afar, but right there among them."

Blaine raised a brow. "And make it very easy for the ISS to simply swoop in and collect you."

I gave him a mischievous look. "That's the point of the blinders. I can be in several places at once." A dawning look of understanding lit Naganika's face. I could tell Jonathan had guessed my purpose already. "I would need volunteers. I can modify the blinders to provide some protection, but there are still plenty of ways the wearer can get hurt, and it won't do anything to prevent capture. Though turning it off would be a simple solution for anyone but me."

"Then you want volunteers to..." Jonathan prompted.

"I want to broadcast a call to action, to challenge everyone who loves the empire to come together in force in all the major cities all over the empire. I'd like for some people to volunteer to go to some of the bigger cities wearing the blinders. I'll go too, I just won't need a disguise. I don't intend to lie about the fact that they aren't all me, once that becomes apparent, but if I'm going to make myself a symbol, even my doppelganger will be a powerful rallying force for the people who take the risk of standing up to take back the empire."

"Take back the empire?" Blaine's voice held an edge of danger. "What exactly are you proposing? A revolution?"

"No. I mean to take it back from the man who stole it from the rightful emperor and his heir." There was a long silence in which Blaine and I locked eyes, both of us aware that I could be referring to him, though we both knew I wasn't.

"I mean to publicly denounce Laudley and expose his crimes, and call the people to band together and act." I looked around at all the faces. "He has Molly. She's the heir and everyone knows it. I'm not asking anyone to do anything but support the legitimate ruler of the empire, and pull down the traitor who assassinated Pete."

"You probably shouldn't call him that in the broadcasts or no one will know who you're talking about," Naganika said, the faintest sarcasm in his voice but a grin of pure delight on his face. "This is the sort of catalyst we've been looking for. We always planned to leverage the power of the common classes to oppose Laudley. We were missing a way to light the fire, and make people angry and brave enough to act."

I spread my arms. "Here I am. I've always been good at making people angry."

He grinned. "Here you are, indeed."

I forgot to tell you, Chuck would like to come for a visit, if that's all right?

It's always all right.

Perks of being friends with the emperor's husband, right?

Perks of being the friend of Prince Jacob.

Same thing.

It may not always be.

What does that mean?

iv 41

Naganika introduced me to a young man named Jesus. "He's our techie. If anyone can help you adapt and build your devices, it's him."

"I've never met anyone named Jesus," I said to the man. "I thought that name went out of favor after the Religious Wars."

He grinned at me. "My mother was always a bit of a rebel."

Naganika patted him on the shoulder. "I have to get back to the palace," he said to me. "I'm on important official business right now," his mouth quirked with irony, "but I'll be expected back soon."

I nodded and turned away, but his voice stopped me. "Prince Jacob," he began, oddly hesitant.

"Jacob will do."

He quirked an odd smile. "I don't think it will, actually."
I stifled a laugh and decided not to point out the paradox of
ignoring my request even as he acknowledged me as his superior.
"May I speak to you before I go?"

I nodded an apology to Jesus and followed Naganika from the
room. There were very few people in the hallway and he led me
to a nearby offshoot that showed no sign of use. "My alias means
'That George.'"

"I beg your pardon?"

He huffed a laugh at himself. "I wanted to explain myself to you."

I frowned. "Why?"

His smile was halfhearted. "Because the emperor is dead." I
waited, but he seemed to believe that explained it. He smiled weakly.
"You know that I'm just one of many sons of the king of Carolis."

I nodded.

"Perhaps you don't know, but I was also a twin. I had an
identical twin brother who died when we were seventeen."

"I'm sorry."

Naganika nodded acknowledgment. "Thank you. But the
real tragedy of it is, he and I were never close. We were both
too competitive. Fought constantly." He shrugged. "For some
reason, known only to them, my parents named us both George."
He grinned, a twinkle in his eye, though I got the distinct
impression that the emotion was an impressive lie rather than
true amusement.

"We went by our middle names, naturally, but when we were
still young, a cousin of ours thought to be clever and began calling
us This George and That George."

"Which were you?"

"This," Naganika replied. He smiled at me. "Per normal for us,
my brother took that as a slight. You see, 'this' implies the preferred
or selected option and 'that' becomes the alternative, or even the
discard. I used to call him That when I wanted to make him angry."
His smile turned sheepish. "In any case, he died and I took it very
hard. You never know what you have until it's gone, as they say."

"*They*," I said, "are often morons."

His grin spread. "Indeed. But I was seventeen and he was my brother, after all. So I asked them to put 'This George' on his memorial stone. And I took 'That George' as my alias when my life took a turn that required me to have one." He shrugged. "Because I'm the 'that' after all, the one left over." He pursed his lips, a faint blush rising. "I've never told anyone that before."

"Why did you?"

His grin was faltering. "I'm still not completely sure. I think I wanted you to know about him, because of his stance on you."

I raised an eyebrow. "Which was what?"

"Not much, honestly, until the rebellion in Wildflower Hill."

The name sent a cold shiver down my back, but I steeled myself and nodded. "You would have been, what, fifteen or sixteen when it was razed?"

"Seventeen," he replied. "I expressed...a negative opinion of you, so naturally my brother took your side. I thought you deserved your exile—honestly, I thought you deserved the execution—and I said so, and argued that with him more than once."

"He didn't agree?" My tone of skepticism wasn't lost on him. He snorted.

"No. Though, as he'd expressed no populist sentiments before that, I can't say how much was genuine opinion versus one he came to hold because he kept arguing it with me."

"Maybe he never really held that opinion at all. You don't have to believe something to argue in favor of it." I made myself smile. "I'd be surprised if anyone on Carolis had a positive opinion of me back then."

He laughed. "True. But I think he did believe you were in the right, eventually, at least." He shrugged but there was a heaviness to it that belied the gesture. "It was one of the last things we said to each other, before his accident. Just another stupid argument about the unclass and the emperor and you."

He met my eye even though he looked embarrassed. "It stuck with me. I had a lot of guilt over his death and the relationship we had. Or didn't have, I suppose. I found myself picking up some of his causes," he chuckled, "even when they were directly contradictory to the ones I chose to take up for myself." He paused, taking a deep breath. "I started UpClass for him."

I wasn't sure what to say to that. He laughed at himself.

"Sounds a bit like a split personality, doesn't it? That should be comforting, knowing your safety is largely in the hands of a lunatic."

I shrugged, turning away. "I think we're all a little bit crazy, Lord Naganika. Anyone who would choose to get involved in imperial politics probably is. You'd have to be to survive it." A heavy stillness crept over me. "Which is probably why Pete is dead and we're still alive."

Before he could reply, I looked away. "Have a safe trip, Lord Naganika."

"George," he said quietly.

I looked back, confused. "I thought you didn't go by that name?"

His smile flickered and died quickly. "I do now."

I rejoined Jesus and together we worked out how to alter the blinders to add a level of shielding as well.

"If you don't want the tech getting out," he suggested, "we could rig them so that once they're turned off they self-destruct. It might limit their effectiveness, but no one would be able to copy the design if they got their hands on one."

"That's a very good idea. Would it take long to add to the design?"

"Nah," he said and froze, blushing a hot red. "I mean, no, Your Highness."

I laughed. "Don't worry. I don't care." I took a deep breath, fighting the pain of memories. Of Pete when we'd first met. All the times I kept forgetting to speak to him as an emperor. All the times he laughed and told me he loved it when I did that. I shook my head. There was no time for my grief.

"Where are you from?" I asked Jesus.

"Here." At my look of shock he said, "Well, one of the low class neighborhoods of the city. La Puerta." He gave me a funny look. "I may not be unclass, but I believe in the cause."

I stared at him and laughed in shock. "I don't think I have ever heard anyone apologize for not being unclass."

He made a soft sound of amusement. "A lot of things are different now than they were just a few years ago. You changed things."

"I think the emperor changed things, really."

He shrugged. "Sure. He married you, didn't he?"

"It wasn't just that—"

"No, I know." He blushed again at having interrupted me. "I just mean that it's a good example of how he thought differently than emperors before. But mostly I think... Well, I don't know. It just sounded wrong when you brushed off your own contributions. You did good things. Both of you." We worked a bit longer in a somewhat uncomfortable silence. "The number of new recruits in the Resistance tripled in the two days following his death." He looked at me sheepishly. "I don't know if you think that's disloyal to the empire, or anything."

I laughed. "Considering where I am and what I'm doing? No, I don't think it's disloyal at all." We both went quiet. "Pete wouldn't think so either."

"Pete?"

"The emperor."

"Oh." He blushed again, fighting a smile. "That's good to know."

When are you leaving?

In an hour. If Molly's ready by then.

I wouldn't hold my breath. She worked up quite a temper this morning.

I've seen worse.

I think you've done worse yourself.

iv **42**

W e worked together for some hours until the tiny pieces began to blur together. "How long since you slept, Your Highness?" Jesus asked.

I stood up, stretching my shoulders and rubbing the back of my neck. "What day is it?"

"Wednesday. Afternoon."

"Then it was the day before yesterday, I think."

He shook his head. "You should get some sleep. I've got a couple of friends here who could help me with the assembly. Now that we've figured out how to work them, it's just a matter of putting the pieces together. They can do that."

I nodded, too tired to argue. "You should get some sleep, too."

He smiled. "I will. I'll get them started and find my bunk. We've got a lot to do in the next few days. Might as well sleep while we can."

Lady Chou led me to a standard-issue barracks room, complete with bunk beds lining the walls. For some reason that made me smile.

"I'm sorry we don't have anything better to offer you," she said, but I waved away her objection.

"This is plenty. Thank you."

She bowed to me before she left and my brain was so sluggish that I didn't think to ask her not to until she was already gone. The room was mostly in darkness, dim safety lighting at the doors provided the only illumination. I found an empty bunk and fell into it, so tired I felt drunk.

Yet I lay there, staring up in at the bunk above me, unable to sleep. How long had it been since my children had been taken? I fought a wave of anger and panic. It would do no good now. A whole team was working to get them back. And I needed sleep.

The door across from me opened and a figure was outlined briefly in the doorway before it closed and the room went dark again. But I needed no more than that to recognize Jonathan.

"Over here," I whispered. He followed the sound of my voice, stopping in front of me.

"I'm glad you found your way to a bed, finally. I was hoping I wouldn't have to drag you."

I chuckled. "You should sleep, too."

"That's why I'm here." He put a hand on the bunk above mine but paused. "Is there anything you need before I do?"

That hurt, the way he was distancing himself again.

"Why do you have to do that?" I snapped.

He paused, but didn't ask for an explanation. "Because I'm the servant."

I scoffed. "And I'm the nothing whatsoever." My throat tightened. It was true. What was I? A married man with no husband. A father whose children were lost. The consort to an emperor who had been killed.

Jonathan climbed into the bunk above me silently. But when he was up there he leaned over and looked down at me. It was such a boyish thing to do that I almost laughed.

"You're my friend," he said. "That's something."

I blinked back stupid tears. "Yeah. That's something."

I woke several hours later to find that Jesus' friends had fifteen finished devices. My eyebrows shot up. "That's amazing." They both blushed, the boy staring at his feet, fighting a grin.

"It's nothing," the girl said. She looked incredibly young to be part of something like this. If she was eighteen years old then I was a grandfather. "We could have made more but we've cannibalized all the non-essential equipment they let us have. Lady Chou is trying to find more components for us." She had gone completely red. "They're not that hard to put together. Once you know how."

"You've done better than I expected," I said. "Thank you."

An older woman nearby rescued me from their embarrassment, asking if she could borrow them and then redirecting their efforts elsewhere. Jonathan came to find me, handing me a ration pack. "Breakfast," he said. I cocked a brow, smiling.

"Do you know if we have any volunteers yet?" I asked. He raised his eyebrows.

"No one told you?"

"Told me what?"

"We have more than 'any' volunteers," he said. "Everyone has volunteered. Lady Chou is drawing up a plan to keep all the essential functions here manned while allowing as many to go as possible."

"Oh." I shook my head. "They do understand it's dangerous, right?"

He gave me a steady look. "Life's dangerous, Jake."

I snorted amusement. "All right. If that's what they want I'm not going to argue."

Lady Chou came to collect some of the devices, apportioning them out to people who would be traveling to the imperial worlds within the perimeter we felt we could reach. "We'll have to send them more specific instructions once we work out all the details," she said. "But we can't lose travel time."

"Jake." I turned to find Jonathan pointing at a vid. "You need to watch this."

Citizens of the Empire. Naganika's familiar face and voice in front of the imperial seal was startling now. Only hours ago I'd talked treason with him at a headquarters for the Resistance.

In this time of turmoil, good news is always welcome, and today we have for you the best news of all. Princess Marquilla Killearn, heir to the throne, and Prince Owen Blaine have returned safely to the palace. Naganika beamed as if personally responsible for the rescue. I wondered whose idea it was to chop 'Dawes' out of Molly's name. *Both children are well and have not suffered from their unfortunate abduction.*

Abduction? Was that what they called a father rescuing his children from murderers? In Laudley's empire, no doubt it was. *They are home and resting. As soon as possible they will make an official appearance, but for now they are recovering from their ordeal and the palace will not allow them to be disturbed.*

His face and voice sobered. *We will need the joy of that news to carry us through another unfortunate loss for the empire. Our newly crowned Emperor Regent Enryn was murdered by the former imperial consort. How Prince Jacob managed to abduct him from the palace is still under investigation, but only yesterday as the children were being rescued, the former prince tried to use the emperor regent as a hostage in exchange for his life. As a father and as an emperor, Enryn would not stand for it and he forced Prince Jacob's hand so that the children could get away safely.* Naganika bowed his head. *We will now observe ten minutes of silence for our late emperor regent.*

All around us people were frozen in shock, some staring openly at us, some trying not to be seen doing it, some simply staring at the screen, lines of confusion in their faces. I'd always been terrible at this game of politics but when I realized that I understood what was going on and others didn't, I laughed.

Those who hadn't already been staring at me did so now. I turned to Blaine, grinning.

"Well, Blaine, I heard my execution order. Did you hear yours?"

His tone was dry. "Yours is old news." But then he gave me a conspiratorial smile. "Mine was masterfully done, though. Don't you think?"

"Well, sure, if you want to admire the way we just handed him everything he wanted on a silver platter." I waved in the direction of the vid, where the imperial seal still filled the display as the backdrop to the moment of silence we weren't observing for the man we were having a conversation with instead. "Because of that, he's rid of you exactly the way he wanted to be and with no effort on his part. All he has to do now is quietly kill you and he wins. He's already won."

"Which is exactly why he's going to get quite a shock when we make it all blow up in his face, firmly and publicly." Before I could answer, Blaine turned to Lady Chou. "Do we have everything ready for our own broadcast?"

Understanding began to dawn slowly, and with it, a grin spread across my face. "Oh, I think this is going to be the most fun I've had in a long time."

My rule, such as it was, was no more than an ink stain in the book of history.

iv 43

Naganika sent a series of coded messages to Lady Chou that helped us set up for a broadcast of our own. Dawes and I worked separately and together, crafting a message that would expose Laudley and bring him down.

Less than twenty-four hours after the palace's broadcast, everything was in place for us to break into the official broadcast channels, as Laudley had done in the years he hid behind his assumed title, The Patriot.

"Naganika has hidden the hacks well," Lady Chou said, "and you might have as much as an hour before the palace teams shut you down. But you can count on fifteen minutes, and be reasonably confident of a few more past that. Shorter is best, but say what needs to be said. You should have time."

I nodded my thanks, folding my hands together to disguise my unease. Now that it had come to it, what I was about to do struck me as absurd and impossible.

We took our places and a pimple-faced kid signaled for us to begin. The official news outlet suddenly blanked. The imperial seal and the alert that important and mandatory information was coming from the palace replaced it. It faded and my own image appeared.

"Citizens of the empire," I said, my voice calm and controlled as I had feared it would not be. "As you can see, the recent reports of my death were a lie. Not only am I alive, I am in no danger from any except the palace itself. A powerful duke there, the Grand Duke Laudley, has been behind the workings of a network of traitors for some time. You once knew him as The Patriot, and now he has finally seized power. Power he means to keep at any cost."

I paused to let that sink in, and met the camera squarely. "He arranged and carried out the assassination of our rightful emperor, Rikhart IV. His goal is to see that his grandson, his blood, holds the throne after him. In the meantime, he means to hold that power himself, ruling through innocent children he can manipulate and warp to his own ends."

I paused for the effect. "Take note, his goal is to see Prince Owen on the throne. To do that, he would have to eliminate the one who still stands between Owen and the throne: Crown Princess Marquilla. A child, and the last surviving member of the true imperial line."

I almost didn't recognize my voice, gone low and dangerous. "Shall we stand for this? Will we stand by and pretend we are powerless to stop him, turning a blind eye as he murders again, this time a child? I for one, will not. And it is to that end I have joined my efforts to another who fights for our rightful ruler with at least as much passion as I do."

I gestured for Dawes to join me. "Prince Jacob did not murder me, as you were so recently told. Nor did he ever intend to. It is to his protection that I owe my life, for he helped me escape when Laudley would have killed me as well." I turned to him. "Prince Jacob?"

He bowed to me, the formal acknowledgment between equals. We hadn't agreed on that and it surprised me. Yet, with everything so out of control, so confused as it all was, it was the perfect gesture, a gesture of respect that diminished neither of us. I wasn't sure what to make of the political savvy as well as the generosity in the act. So many things I had never expected from him.

"Thank you, Duke Blaine."

He turned to face the camera, regal and confident, yet another thing I found astonishing. Then he completely ruined the impression with a very un-regal greeting.

"Hello." I started to shake my head at the commonness of it. Hadn't he had enough experience by now to know how to talk like a noble?

And yet, as I cast about in my memory, I couldn't remember many instances of him playing any important official roles, of much public speaking at all. How had I not realized that he truly stayed out of the spotlight, as if he'd really never wanted any of it, the way he always said?

Just as I was hoping his slip wouldn't ruin the impression we made, I caught a glimpse of the nearby faces and froze. They looked almost worshipful. I felt a wash of shame at my blindness. This was why he appealed to the lower classes, and why they would listen to him. It was *because* he wasn't regal or proper. He was one of them and they *liked* that. So many things I'd never understood began to make sense.

"Duke Blaine is right," he said, "the same man who murdered our rightful emperor now has my children, our crown princess and Prince Owen. They're precious not just to me but to the Empire. That man has stolen our emperor, our empire, and now he has stolen the royal children as well." There was a long moment in which he seemed to struggle with emotion. It was a good idea, the appeal to the people as a bereft father. I didn't think he was acting, though.

"Duke Blaine and I are working together to make sure he doesn't succeed, that our princess is safe, and that the empire is restored to the true heir." He looked down. "At home, we call her Molly." He looked as if he were fighting tears. I heard a sniffle and realized that some among our group of spectators actually *were* crying.

"Duke Blaine asked you if we were going to stand for it. Well I'm going to tell you that we aren't. Not me, nor him, and I don't believe you will either."

He cast an almost embarrassed glance at me. "Duke Blaine and I have been at odds, often bitterly, sometimes mortally. There are times in the past when either or both of us would have killed the other and considered ourselves in the right." He faced the camera again.

"But the time for such petty squabbles is past. We cannot allow our differences to divide us now. All of us—the nobility, the high, middle, and low classes, the unclass—we face a common enemy. We can defeat him together and take back our empire.

"The Grand Duke Laudley would destroy the hard work and legacy of an emperor who did more for every one of his subjects than any who came before him. Rikhart IV looked at each individual and he saw the man, not the class. He fought to make things better for all of us and each of us. And I for one *won't* stand by while a greedy, grasping traitor takes that away from us."

His expression grew intense. "So I'm asking you to stand with us. Five days from now," his voice quieted, "on what would have been Emperor Rikhart's thirty-first birthday, I'm asking you to join us. In every town center, in every city square, on the palace lawn of every Imperial world, even the Imperial Palace itself, we will stand up together and show this traitor that he won't take our empire from us. We will reclaim our own, the royal children he now holds hostage. We will reclaim our empire. I'm asking everyone, from the highest noble to the smallest unclass."

His voice grew soft with sympathy. "I'm asking those of you who serve the empire in all the branches of the ISS to turn your weapons away from your fellow citizens, and ignore the orders of any but those who have the right to issue them. I'm asking the men and women in the palace to stand with us, to stand up on that day and take Laudley into custody so that he can answer to the entire empire for his treasons."

He bowed his head before looking up. "We are brave and strong enough to do this. We *will* do this, whether it's easy or whether it's hard. And I'm not asking you to do it alone. I will be there as well. I will gather with you and I will not hide my face. We can do this together. We *must* do this together, or together we will all lose, and our children and grandchildren will look back on these days and wonder what it must have been like when the empire was still grand and glorious, and why we didn't fight for it."

I watched him, astonished at how powerfully his words affected even me, wondering how I could have underestimated the power of what he was doing, this appeal to the populace. I couldn't deny I'd always seen them as little more than children needing our guidance and sometimes a firm hand. Yet now the sheer scope of how greatly they outnumbered us, how decisively *they* were the empire, overwhelmed and shamed me.

"We will do this. Five days from now, on what would have been an imperial holiday to celebrate the birthday of the emperor, we will stand together." He stared down the camera. "Laudley, this message is to you. If you're smart you'll give up now, or else run and hide. You've lost already. And we're coming for you."

I shivered as the display switched to the imperial seal with the imperial anthem playing strong and clear. It played through from beginning to end before the official programming popped back into place like a soap bubble had burst.

Dawes turned to me. "Now we'll see what happens."

I'm sorry about what I said last night.

I knew you didn't mean it.

I'm still sorry.

iv 44

With that done, I returned to helping them assemble blinders. A shipment of parts had found its way to us. I suspected Governor Kagawa had rerouted it and I hoped he'd taken it away from some project that would benefit the imperial government right now. He probably had.

He'd been the governor of my duchy for almost a decade, and I had learned to spot and enjoy his sense of irony. Of course, he'd needed one just to have taken the position from me in the first place. It made it all the more fun a few years back when I made him a minor noble. He nearly choked. Pete had shaken his head at me for telling him at a formal dinner and waiting until he had food in his mouth. But he'd been grinning, too.

I sighed.

"Are you all right?" Jonathan's voice was still as familiar as it had been to me years ago, when he'd seemed like an extension of myself and there was nothing hurtful between us. "I was just thinking, I sort of wish we hadn't scheduled all this for our birthday."

"Oh?"

I kept working on the tiny device in my hand, not looking up. "Yeah. It was going to be a milestone year, for us anyway." I glanced at Jonathan, only to look away again at the compassion on his face.

"It's fifteen years since he gave me those cuff links for our birthday. That was the day I realized that what had been puzzling me about him was that he really was as genuine as he seemed. He had this great sense of humor and really saw me as a person." I shrugged. "I had cuff links made for him this year. With his real initials, not the official RK. These have PDK on them."

"Peter Dawes-Killearn," Jonathan said quietly. I just nodded.

"On the island I was thinking that if I ever got them back, I'd give them to Owen." I looked up at the gray ceiling. "I won't be giving Pete anything at all this year."

"Nonsense."

I stared at Jonathan. He huffed a laugh, shaking his head at me.

"You never see these things, do you?" He pulled my hand away from the device when I tried to start working on it again, to avoid his eye. "This year you're giving him a gift that's more profound than anything you could have put in his hands. You're reclaiming his empire and giving it back to his daughter. You think that's not a good birthday present?"

I smiled, though tears prickled my eyes. "Yeah. I suppose you're right." I dropped my eyes back to my work. "Too bad he'll never know about it."

The rest of the day and through that night we assembled devices, and as quickly as we finished them, Lady Chou handed them out to volunteers, sending them off to the imperial planets that could be reached within five days. Whatever Blaine did most of that time I didn't know, and didn't try to find out. We were allies in this, even partners of a sort, but it was an uneasy alliance still. I tried to remind myself to be wary, not to forget all the things he had done to me, but it just felt like too much effort.

I was turning away from the worktable, too tired to see the

tiny pieces anymore, when Blaine approached with Jonathan shadowing him.

"I'd like to have a device too, if there is one available."

"There is. Why do you want one?" I looked him up and down. "No offense, but I just don't see you wading into a crowd of commoners wearing a Jacob Dawes suit."

He coughed in amusement. "No, I think that's stretching this new accord rather more than is possible." He sobered. "There is another role I can play, one that no one else can. But it will require stealth to get where I need to be."

Lady Chou stepped closer, giving me an incredulous look when I didn't turn him down right away. "You'd trust him?" she scoffed.

I gave Blaine a long look before I nodded. "I trust him to put Owen's welfare above everyone else's, including his own. And since we've established that Owen and Molly are a package deal, that means my daughter's safety is one of his highest priorities. Yes. I trust him."

"You realize that with one of those devices he could betray you. Profoundly. As profoundly as he's helping you now."

I held Lady Chou's gaze. "I know."

I picked up the device I had just finished and handed it to him. "You'll need to replace the image we loaded with whatever it is you need. The kids here can help you with that."

"Thank you." He frowned at me, as if puzzled. "Aren't you going to ask me about my plan?"

I hesitated. "Do you need me to know?"

He examined me for a long time. "It's like every time you open your mouth you surprise me." He grinned. "That's probably not a good thing, if we're to work together. Yes, you'll need to know what I'm doing." He laid out his plan and I nodded as he spoke, impressed and relieved. He gave me a grave nod of respect before he walked away.

I turned back to Jonathan. "Well, I've just put my biggest assets into the hands of my oldest enemy."

Jonathan had a funny smile on his face.

"What?"

"You're really getting good at this, aren't you?" he said.

I blinked. "Well that's not what I expected you to say." His smile widened. "I thought that was me being stupid."

He huffed a laugh, shaking his head. "The only thing you're ever stupid about is knowing whether or not you're being stupid."

I think I'm going to spend a few days in Mexico soon. Maybe next week. Kagawa's making all kinds of plans for his big projects. Apparently, this requires me to approve funding. I don't know why I can't do it from here but he's asked me to come.

You're not as afraid of Mexico as you used to be.

Maybe.

You can't fool me.

Do I really have money somewhere that's mine just for Mexico?

I'm going to tell Jonathan you asked that.

Please don't.

iv 45

I was heading for my bunk but I stopped, turning on my heel and re-entering the control room. Lady Chou was easy to find and it occurred to me she was always there when I looked for her. When did she sleep?

"I think I'd like to stay outside for the night, in the tunnel. With the others."

Lady Chou's eyebrows shot up. "You mean in the main tunnels, with the residents? Why?"

I appreciated very much that she hadn't called them 'the unclass,' and it said a lot about her and what she was doing here that she hadn't. "Why wouldn't I?"

Rather than waste a blinder, I disguised myself the old-fashioned way. I wasn't the first one here to go into the tunnels in disguise, and they had a collection of wigs and the appropriate clothes for the role I would play. Since I was too easily recognized, I chose a wig of long dreadlocks that fell in my face and added to that a wide strip of cloth tied like an eye patch around my head. Jonathan frowned as he helped me with my disguise but said nothing.

When I stepped out into the corridor again, Lady Chou gave me a long appraisal, finally nodding her head once. "Yes, very good. The eye patch covers quite a lot of your face. I wouldn't recognize you if I wasn't looking for you."

I grinned at Jonathan who only met my gaze grimly. "Be careful."

"Of course." I waved at him and followed Lady Chou to a marked door.

"This will take you into a deserted side tunnel. Where it connects to the main tunnels it looks like the debris piled up there is impassible, but on this side the empty crate is clearly marked. You can simply crawl through it to the other side. It shouldn't matter too much if you're seen. Just take note of which one you came out of, because it's not marked on the other side. When you come back, there's a pad by this door that looks like it's broken, but if you scan your thumb it will open."

I grinned. "So I've already been granted access among the Resistance, then?"

She gave me a puzzled look. "You've always had access among the Resistance." I sobered. Her smile always looked pinched and painful, but the one she gave me in parting looked like less of an effort to produce.

Everything was exactly as she'd explained and I was quickly out in the main tunnels, crawling out of what looked like a sealed crate when it closed behind me. One or two people cast incurious looks at me and went back to their own concerns. Lady Chou had told me to go first to one of the blanket stations and I found one not far from where I'd entered the tunnel. A pleasant looking woman, wearing the uniform of a duchy employee, met me at the counter.

"Are you new here?" she asked. I nodded, wanting to use my voice as little as possible. She smiled. "Well then, let's get you some things."

She turned aside and returned with a thick gray blanket, unadorned but soft and warm. "Everyone gets a free blanket. You can return it at any time for a clean one. If you continue down this way," she pointed further down the tunnel, "you'll find the kitchens and sanitary stations. One meal a day is free, and one shower a week. Any more can be purchased with vouchers you earn down here in the laundries or kitchens, or on various cleaning and maintenance crews. Or you can earn credits above on the work crews."

I must have looked slightly stunned because she patted my hand. "You must have been out there a long time if you've only just arrived." I nodded again, not quite sure what she meant. "Well, it's nice here, warm and dry, and you'll have everything you need. The clinics are always free, no matter how many times you need them. And credits earned above are credits good anywhere in the empire. If you take work up there, you'll automatically get a shower credit for each day you work and an additional meal provided on-site. If you want, you can take less pay in exchange for getting on the waiting list for a home above."

She gave me a sympathetic look for my confusion. "A portion of what you would otherwise have earned will go toward the down payment for when your name gets to the top of the list. It's a good plan for a man like you, if you haven't a family yet. By the time you settle down, there will be a place of your own for all of you."

I'm not sure I could have spoken then even if I'd known what to say. My throat was tight and I struggled to keep tears from my eyes. I felt a disorienting mix of pride, grief, and gratitude. It was one thing to have affected these changes from afar. It was quite another to be here, asking for help and getting it, from a woman who didn't seem to care if I was the part I played: unclass, destitute, and alone.

I nodded thanks and turned away before I could be overwhelmed by the realization that, in a way, that was actually true. I had nothing that was my own. Assuming I made it out of this with my head still attached to my shoulders, nothing separated me from homelessness and poverty now except those who were willing to help me. A lot like it was for the people down here.

I wandered down the tunnel in a fog. The tunnels had been built to bring troops and police into Abenez, and were wide enough to accommodate military vehicles. Now, the broad corridors created places to live. The parking areas had been converted to the soup kitchens, clinics, laundry, and distribution centers. The floor along the edges of the tunnels had been lined with sanitary padding, the width of two men lying shoulder to shoulder. It was here, with their meager possessions and materials salvaged from above, that the people of Abenez who had survived the great fire built their homes in their homelessness.

It wasn't long before I realized that everyone down here was elderly, or else a child with a scattering of young adults. There were more children than the younger people here could account for. As I watched them, it became clear that this was some sort of communal childcare arrangement. The few not-quite-adults and the elderly ones were watching the children as everyone else worked above. I didn't see anyone able-bodied who wasn't occupied. Occasionally some passed by but they wore badges identifying them with the laundry or the clinic.

Soon, people began to trickle into the tunnel, becoming a steady stream of workers returning from above. I watched them rejoin their families or detour to the sanitation stations or kitchen. A sweaty, dirty man joined a family near me and a boy and girl pounced on him, hugging him and chattering about their day. I looked away.

For the rest of the evening I simply sat in place and watched the huddled families, wandering lonesters, or groups of twos and threes. They had their own character, their own purposes, but none were hostile to any other.

I knew too much to believe this was just a sense of shared community. I began to recognize in a few of the pairs passing by from time to time that there was a security force down here too. But they weren't outsiders brought in to impose order on an unruly populace. They were from down here too, just performing one of the necessary jobs to keep their makeshift city running, like the laundry or the kitchen.

They were probably people who had gone to find work above and were given this assignment instead. The building work above was vital, but so was the peace and survival of the refugees in the tunnels. Perhaps more so. We could rebuild. We could always rebuild so long as we survived and banded together.

I truly was tired, and the weight of all I had seen tired me more, so I concentrated on finding a place to bed down for the night.

The improvised living areas along the edges of the tunnels were scrupulously clean. I didn't know if everyone was required to clean up after themselves or if this was the work of cleaning crews. Probably both. When I found an empty space large enough for one man, it was a place that was clean, dry, and safe. On each side of me was a family with small children. Across the tunnel were three old men, their belongings and oddments delineating separate spaces, but they sat together in the middle, joking quietly as they played a game with well-worn cards.

I settled into my solitary spot between the two families. The children on both sides watched me curiously and openly. One mother held hers back when they would have spoken to me but the other, who had older children and one little girl, smiled at me and I smiled back. The little girl, who looked no more than three years old, made her wide-eyed, careful way to the edge of their space, marked off by a sheet of plastic. She ducked behind it but peered around at me. I lay down, but she took that as a sign that I wasn't dangerous and crept around the barrier.

"You sleepy?" she asked. Her words were still muddled with a baby's inflection, but already I could hear in them the lingering accent of this place, the musical predictability of the vowels. I wanted to make her say more, to see if she rolled her r's. Molly never had. She spoke the formal and accentless language of power and prominence. I ached a little at the thought.

"I'm a little sleepy," I answered quietly so as not to scare her off but not so quiet as to discourage her. She grinned and came forward, plopping herself down by my head.

"Want to play a game?"

I propped myself up on one elbow. "What game?"

"Hide and seek."

She spoke as imperiously as a princess, and I couldn't help but smile. "It's getting late. And I don't think your madre would allow it."

"I have to ask," she said seriously, standing to go.

"Wait," I said, "how about Silly Words?"

She frowned at me. "Don't know it."

"You don't know the game?"

She scowled and crossed her arms, looking back at her brothers as if this was something they hadn't told her. I stifled a laugh. "It's a game I brought with me from far away," I said. "I bet your brothers don't know it yet."

She beamed, clapping her hands together in excitement. "Yes!"

Something clenched hard in my chest, and at the same time I felt a smile spread across my face. This was a game I'd learned from Molly's tutors.

Standard was spoken all over the empire, but our neighboring states had their own languages, and the empress would need to speak them. So we used the game to help her learn the vocabulary of other languages. I would say a random word, and she would try to answer it with something related but in another language. I was sure I could adapt it to entertain a three-year-old who knew only Standard.

I explained the rules to her and she grinned. "You first!"

I pretended to think. "Elephant."

She frowned at me. "What's that?"

I felt a moment's pang, realizing it was stupid of me to assume a child living in the tunnels under a ruined Abenez would have any idea what an elephant was. How long ago and far away this life was to me now.

"Poop," I recovered. She put her hand over her mouth, giggling.

"Eduardo," she replied, giggling harder. From the way she glanced at her family, and the brief smile her mother gave me, I guessed that was the name of one of her brothers.

I smiled. "Your turn."

"Boogers"

"Brothers."

She laughed. "Apples!"

"Feet."

She plopped down on her stomach, head propped on her hands, totally engrossed. "Smelly."

"Boogers."

She rolled over, grabbing my face as she laughed. "I like this game!"

"What's your name?"

"Marquilla."

I froze.

"Like the princess!" she said earnestly, as if I wouldn't understand. "I'm a princess, too!"

I took two deep breaths, fighting back my reaction. "I bet you are," I said, too quiet, too strained. Her mother noticed and moved toward us. "My brother's name is Jacob," the girl rattled on. I wanted to hide my face. "It's the prince. The prince of Mexico!" She spread her hands wide. The title was wrong, but Pete probably would have said the sentiment was right. Before.

"Yes," I said, as her mother gathered her up. "I know."

"Excuse us," her mother said. "Mari is too friendly sometimes. She will not learn to leave others to themselves."

"It's all right," I said, but the woman gave me a funny look, and I knew I wasn't hiding anything from her, except perhaps who I really was. She smiled kindly.

"Do you have children of your own?" she asked.

I nodded, dropping her gaze because there was too much understanding and compassion in it. "Yes," I managed. "Yes, I do. Just..."

Her hand was gentle on my shoulder. "You must miss them."

I could only nod.

"It will be lights-out soon," she said, as if I weren't losing it in front of her. "And we are all tired I'm sure."

"I'm not tired!" the girl protested. It drew a laugh from me, and when I looked up I found the so-familiar indignant look of a toddler and the fond smile of her mother.

"I'm sure you're not." Our eyes met and we both grinned, though mine was watery.

"Sleep well, sir," she said.

"Jacob," I corrected. She stopped.

"I have a son of that name as well."

"Yes, Mari told me."

She gave me a lopsided grin. "It's silly, I know," she said, "But when they were born I wanted to give them names that have done well by others. Maybe they'll be lucky names."

"I hope they will," I said.

Her look held too much sympathy. "I hope it will be for you as well," she paused, "and for them."

I knew from the way she looked away, the way her voice got distant, that she no longer meant anyone here. She meant the empress and the prince. My own daughter. And me.

"Yes," I choked out the words. "May she live forever."

The woman gave me a long look and nodded approval. "May she live forever."

Molly's just asked if we can stay for the festival while we're in Mexico.

You should. I thought you'd planned it that way.

That would put us there almost three weeks. I hate for us to be away from you that long.

I know. Me too. But you should still stay for the festival. The kids will love it.

iv 46

I woke to the sound of too many people pounding down stairs and out of doors and rushing down the hallway. It took me a moment to remember where I was. I levered myself up. Around me people cried out in shock, surprise, and fear as ISS troops rushed into the tunnels, rounding up everyone in their path.

"Let's go! Move!"

There was no pretense that this was anything but a raid, and my stomach dropped. What had I done?

"What's this about?" one of the men who had been sleeping across from me demanded of the soldier who snatched him up. "What are you doing?"

"Move, old man," the soldier barked. The man's friend dug in his heels as another tried to shove him.

"What do you want with us?"

"We want you to move!"

En masse we were herded down the tunnel and I kept my

head bowed, thinking furiously. Were they just here for me? If that was all, wouldn't it have been simpler to hold everyone in the tunnels and search here? All this moving and shoving about made it easier, not harder, for one man to avoid detection. This seemed to be about more than just me, so I bit my tongue hard when the soldier jabbed me because I wasn't moving fast enough and I said nothing.

In a clatter of noise and shouting we climbed the stairs and ladders that led us out of the tunnels. Above, it was just lightening to morning, the air fresh and new. The buildings around us were sparse and mostly ruins, but to the south I could see neat clusters of buildings rising from the valley floor.

They were breathtaking, but not because they were in any way impressive to the eye. They were the opposite, simple and functional, but they were orderly and organized, purposeful in a way that nothing in Abenez had ever been before. A slum had been destroyed, but a city was being built to replace it.

I must have stopped moving as I took it all in because in the next moment a soldier's gun slammed into my back. "Move!"

Around me children were crying, and some of the adults as well. Sounds of dismay rippled in my direction and I saw then what the others had seen.

Transports. They were simple, long and jointed, and clearly long distance vehicles.

"What's going on?" I cursed myself for the stupidity of drawing attention to myself even as I froze in horror. "Where are you taking these people?"

A guard from behind me grabbed my arm and spun me about. "These people?"

He was wearing a visor like all the other guards garbed for crowd control, but he pushed it up and out of the way. Oddly it was his sneer more than anything else that made me recognize him. Bertl. A huge, beefy man with shockingly blond hair, he'd stood out even among the palace's handpicked Imperial guard. He hadn't been on palace detail for some time, though. Not since the end of The Patriot mess. The way he'd looked at me back then made me uncomfortable and, loath as I was to voice such a juvenile complaint, I'd learned it wasn't worth it to keep my suspicions to myself. So I told Pete. He'd looked into the man's background and found nothing suspicious. Still, Pete had asked Sam to reassign him elsewhere, and I never saw him again.

Our eyes widened in a moment of shocked recognition, though his immediately narrowed as he took in my disguise, reconsidering his conclusion. I ducked my head, hoping to salvage the situation but he grabbed my hair to jerk my face back up to his.

The wig hadn't been designed to withstand that. In one neat piece, the wig and eye patch slid off into his hand. Everything went quiet, even the cries of the crowd around us seemed muffled. He chuckled, brief but clear and full of delight. He grabbed my real hair and jerked again, this time with the results he was expecting. There was no surprise on his face now, just satisfaction and a touch of amusement.

"I didn't believe we'd actually find you here," he said. "I was sure you'd gone too high and mighty to crawl around with the roaches again. But here you are."

"I don't know what you're—"

The punch in my stomach drove words and breath out of me. Blind reaction sent my own fist flying and the thud of impact reverberated in my whole arm. No return punch came. I looked up at him in confusion only to watch with horror the slow line of blood trickling from his grinning mouth.

Suddenly I was there again, I could see the slick gray prison walls and smell the stale recycled air and I knew, with every cell in my trembling body, that tomorrow I would be out there alone, days and days and days alone with nothing but the silent stars and my own panicked breaths.

Someone slammed into Bertl, knocking him to the ground, and the flashback shattered.

No one had ever helped me on Dead End.

"No!" The little girl's shriek made my heart stop and for a moment I forgot it couldn't be Molly. I whirled around to find the girl from the tunnel, Marquilla, barreling into a soldier holding my arm. With his shield he swatted away the annoyance he hadn't even seen. There was a sickening crack and the world stood still as Mari jerked like a puppet on strings, going limp and falling at his feet like a discarded doll. Her head lay at an unnatural angle.

"No!" I screamed, hearing the dim echoes of others around me, the swelling of anger.

But the struggle that followed was brief and accomplished nothing. Soldiers waded in and quickly cowed the others, isolating me and helping Bertl to his feet. I searched for Mari, hoping, wishing, but I couldn't even see her anymore. Nothing but the image in my memory of her sprawled in the dirt, discarded and broken.

A long wail sliced through the air and I knew Mari's mother had found her. It could have been so different, there were so many more of us than there were of them. But the roles were too old and the conditioning too deep. The unclass were too good at giving up.

The crowd rippled around us as it parted for a clump of soldiers guarding one man in their midst. I was forced to my knees, head jerked back again by someone's fist in my hair. They approached and the man looked down at me with an odd smile on his face.

"Good work," Naganika said. "That's him. Take him to my transport."

Whatever Naganika's game was, the guards were clearly Laudley's men. They proceeded to beat me with an enthusiasm and attention to detail that would have been impressive if it hadn't hurt so damn much. I lay on a hard cot in a clearly improvised brig on a noble's transport. Long ago Pete had added a real brig to his personal transport. Because of me, actually. Naganika should have borrowed it. I chuckled bitterly at the thought.

"Something amuses you?"

Either my preoccupation or the ringing in my ears had allowed me to miss the sound of Naganika's entry. I thought of sitting up, decided I really didn't want to, and then, with a sigh, struggled upright. I couldn't have this conversation lying down. He made no attempt to help or hinder me and seemed almost to be averting his eyes to give me some dignity. I fought a wave of confusion and pain.

"The men are well-trained," he remarked.

"Or just well-goaded," I said around a swelling lip. He shrugged as if it didn't matter. The ache of dread and the horror of being trapped once again by my own stupidity consumed me. "Is the girl dead?"

He nodded slowly. I didn't know what to think of the fact that he knew what I was talking about. Why should he care?

"So where are we going?"

He considered me as if wondering if he should answer or not. "The palace."

I nodded. "Whose side are you really on, George?"

He gave me an indulgent smile and said nothing. Not that I'd expected any different. It would have been profoundly stupid to answer that question, and he wasn't dead yet only because he wasn't stupid at all. I wondered if he was on any side, other than his own.

"Where are the others?"

He didn't pretend to misunderstand the question. He glanced at his comm. "Blaine may be at the palace already. Don't worry, we've made him at least as uncomfortable as you are." He smiled at me as if we had shared the joke. "Jonathan, however," his voice sobered but he didn't pause or hesitate, "I'm afraid he forced us to kill him."

He ignored the noisy sound of my startled gasp and made a wry face at himself. "I don't suppose that will placate Grand Duke Laudley much; he was so set on having all of you alive. But Jonathan's a wily one, and a far better fighter than the guards were prepared for. He refused to go quietly or really any way at all." He crossed his arms and shrugged. "I've reviewed the recordings and I don't see how the men could have done it differently. Jonathan was determined to escape or die trying. So he did."

Nausea roiled in my gut, grief and anger tightened my chest and my vision swam. "No," I croaked. "I don't believe you."

Naganika's expression looked like pity, but then he shrugged. "I don't suppose it matters. Your end will be the same whether you believe me or not." He shook his head sadly. "There's no one left to save you, Jacob."

"You can call me Prince Jacob." I said, "Or Your Highness." I lay back down, turning my back to him. Whether the insult bothered him or not, I can't say. His silent exit was almost polite.

By that point in my life I had been a criminal and prisoner and far, far worse. But of all the situations I could never have expected to find myself in, being a fugitive on the run was a surprise, and a whole new set of fears.

iv*47*

I heard the clatter in the hallways and I did not need the looks on the faces of the others in the room to confirm that this wasn't a good sign. I glanced around quickly for anything useful but I only found a couple of blinders sitting on the table to the right. I snatched them up.

People began to scramble. Some seemed to have a purpose but most were just panicking. It was a poorly organized resistance if they had no contingency plan in the event of a breach. I didn't wait to find out.

I pried up the loose end of a vent—not as secure as it had been made to appear. My face burned with shame that I should know these criminal tricks, and at the same time I was dizzy with relief.

Dead End had similar bolt-holes, if perhaps not for the same reason. There was nowhere to escape to on that barren asteroid, but there were secret ways around the facility that some inmates knew. The ones I knew I'd learned from Kafe. She didn't show me anything that went anywhere useful, but it had amused her to act as my tutor and make me that much more indebted to her.

I crawled through ducts, mostly guessing at the junctures, but sometimes it seemed there was less dust in one direction, or faint noises. Those didn't worry me. It was the tramp and clatter of the troops I was avoiding.

At last I came to another vent and peered out of it. Luck or circumstance had led me to a hanger where Lady Chou was preparing a transport for departure.

I let myself out of the vent as quietly as possible, but I had only cracked it open when her head jerked up and she grabbed a weapon holstered at her side, aiming it at me.

"Who is it?"

I considered that and finally offered the lie. "A friend."

She held steady. "Come out slowly." I did, easing my way into the room, and though my skin crawled to put my back to her, I lowered the vent carefully closed. I turned to find her staring at me in mingled disbelief and disgust. "You." It was neither a question nor an answer. She scoffed. "I should have known that you'd find a way to run."

I ignored the implied insult, nodding at the transport instead. "I assume that can get us safely away."

She glanced at it and back to me. "It's likely to get *me* safely away. You are another matter entirely."

I lifted my hands. "Are we not on the same side?"

She made a rude noise. "I don't side with traitors to the *true* throne."

I nodded acceptance to that. "Good. Because neither do I anymore. I hope you're planning on taking that transport somewhere in the vicinity of Imperial City, because I need to get to the palace."

She laughed. "You expect me to return you to your friends at the palace?"

I stiffened. "I doubt very much that I have friends at the palace anymore, and if I do, I don't expect them to be in any position to help me. I am not going to betray the Resistance, Lady Chou, if that's what you think. I am here, with you. I think my allegiances are clear."

"Hardly."

"Will you at least help me get out of here?"

She narrowed her eyes. "I don't trust you."

"I don't need you to trust me, I only need transportation." Her mouth quirked on one side, as if she smiled unintentionally. I pressed on. "If my purpose were simply to return to the palace and Laudley, I could have more easily presented myself to the soldiers back there and their captain. That would have gotten me to the palace one way or the other I'm sure."

I stepped closer. "I'm here, with you, because we both know what Laudley intends for me and I am not stupid enough to put myself in his power again. But more important than that, the children are at the palace."

She sighed, but it was an angry, uncertain noise. I reached into my pocket and she stiffened. I removed my hand slowly.

"Here," I said quietly, "a pledge of good faith." I extended my hand and she moved only close enough to see what I offered, without lowering her gun. When she saw the blinder her eyes widened. She held out one hand, allowing me to drop the device into it.

"Now," I said, "I've just given away my best advantage, by giving you back yours. Will you at least give me transportation? That's all I ask."

She hesitated then huffed out an angry breath. "Get in the damn transport."

She made me a seat in the cargo area, securing the locks between us. I could have gotten out, but I couldn't get to the controls. I had to admit it was smart of her. Oddly it relieved me. She wasn't stupid. That was good. She was less likely to get us caught.

I did at least have two thin windows. We moved from lit and maintained passages into dark and sooty places, and I wondered if anyone had used these tunnels in the years since the fire. Of all the things I'd been blamed for when I'd been convicted of being The Patriot, this destruction had really been mine. Guilt shuddered through me, and the pang of regret.

Abenez was large, but it wasn't large enough to account for how long we were in the tunnels. I began to fear we were lost. I could only hope that it was because she was forced to use a longer route to avoid detection.

When we emerged onto the surface again it was full night. The thin slits of windows that showed little more than night sky were more unnerving than comforting. It reminded me of Dead End and I shivered.

Lady Chou's voice came over an intercom. "Food and blankets are in containers against the right wall. You should eat, and get some sleep while you can."

"And you?"

"Someone has to drive this thing."

I had no rebuttal for that. I'd never driven in my life.

"It's not the fastest transport," she added. "So make yourself comfortable. We won't be there tonight."

I sighed and started to look for the supplies.

It truly wasn't a fast transport. A decent one would have gotten us to the palace twice and back again in the time we spent in that thing. I thought of asking her if we couldn't find a way to stop somewhere and swap it out for a faster one, but I didn't think she wanted this trip to be any longer than necessary either.

Eventually she opened a small window between the cargo area and the cockpit. "Pass me some of that food, will you?"

I pulled out a packet and handed it to her. She didn't look at me. I decided I didn't care. I settled back and closed my eyes. Whatever Lady Chou might think, I wasn't just running away. I was running *to*—to the palace, and Owen. My part of the plan hadn't fallen apart yet.

"Do you know what happened to Jonathan or Dawes?" I asked, late into the night. She cast me a funny look.

"I didn't see any more than you did."

"No communications?"

Her mouth tightened and I could see that she didn't want to answer. Finally she sighed. "Nothing."

You've made me happy, Pete, more than I deserved. Thank you for that. Thank you for everything. Please believe that I deeply regret what I've done to you, how I acted, and that I ended our relationship in such a horrible way. I think even now that you wouldn't want for us to be over. You're ridiculous like that.

I love you. I never stopped loving you. I hope you'll forgive me. Actually, I know you'll forgive me. But move on before long, OK? I want that for you. You deserve it.

Goodbye,

Jake

iv 48

When I came to, I was strapped to a table in the middle of a large, open room. It looked like I was in the palace prison, maybe in an unused guardroom that had been cleaned out and repurposed. Other than empty benches along the wall, there was little in this room that wasn't on wheels or easily movable. On one side of me, someone in a nurse's uniform was moving around methodically, but I didn't register much more than that.

Standing on the other side of the gurney was Laudley. He was wearing the Imperial seal on his right hand. If it had been any closer to me I'd have tried to bite him.

Naganika stood behind him, official as ever, still and impassive. If he was looking at anything, it was the man working quietly behind me. He might have been looking at nothing at all. It was hard to tell if he even knew anyone was in the room with him.

Laudley smiled down at me, a distinctly uncomforting sneer. "Hello, Jacob."

My voice was rusty. "I haven't given you permission to call me that."

I thought I saw the briefest flicker of a smile on Naganika's face but Laudley motioned to someone I hadn't seen and I caught only a glimpse of a guard's uniform before a huge fist slammed into my gut. I was strapped down and couldn't curl up around the pain. I lay there, gasping like a fish on the beach. "Odd angle for that," I croaked.

Laudley looked confused for only a moment before he made a sound of disgust. He looked at the man behind me. "I've had enough of his smart mouth to last a lifetime. You have your orders."

The man moved more purposefully, placing receptors on my neck and the insides of my wrists. Laudley sneered down at me.

"I have your children. I have the throne. I have almost everything I want, and now I'm going to get the final prize." He looked as if he wanted to lick his lips in anticipation. "I don't suppose you'd like to publicly confess to the murder of Rikhart IV now? I assure you, if you have to be persuaded," he gestured around the room, "it will be an unpleasant experience."

I managed a strangled sound of amusement. "Confess to killing Pete? No. Not now, not later. Not ever."

He grinned. "Oh, I doubt it will take very long to convince you. And I'm glad you aren't giving in right away. I've been looking forward to this part."

He nodded to the technician.

I thought I'd known pain before. I'd been in fights and taken beatings. I'd been flogged. When I was shot at the IIC, the projectile had been coated with a nasty chemical that spread rapidly through my body and made me feel as if I were on fire, inside and out, my body charring to ash.

This wasn't like that. There was no place I hurt. I didn't feel pain, I *was* pain. I had no body, no mind. I couldn't move, couldn't scream, couldn't hear or see. There was only the concept of Jacob Dawes and the white-hot pain that defined him. No beginning, no end. I had never been anything but this blind agony and never would be again.

I slammed back into my body, trembling so hard my teeth chattered together. Something, blood or drool or both leaked from the corner of my mouth. I twitched and jerked everywhere, though there was no lingering pain except where I'd bit my tongue. In my head was a shadow of agony. Not the sensation but the threat, the knowledge that this pain existed and had found me, could find me again, would find me again. Was a part of me now, always there, waiting.

Laudley wavered and shuddered in my vision. His smile was a white and pink slash in a pale face.

"Yes. I will enjoy this part very much."

I lost perception of time and place for a while. Laudley and Naganika left, and I suppose guards remained, though I couldn't see them. Another technician came to join the first. They were wearing sanitation masks, and I couldn't see their faces. They moved competently around me as if I were only a thing to be dealt with, a cancer to excise and discard with no regrets.

Then a woman entered the room. She wasn't covered up in the impersonal garb of the technicians. She wore a blood-red suit with matching lipstick that perfectly offset the dusky tone of her skin.

"Hello, Your Highness." Her voice was thick and fuzzy, deeper than I expected, smooth and lovely.

"Who are you?" I croaked.

"I'm Anna," she replied, and somehow I knew it wasn't her name. She smiled at me, like a mother to her child. "We're going to work together to get your memories straight so that all of this unpleasantness can be worked out. It will be much easier if you just relax and cooperate. I'd rather we did this the easy way, so no one has to suffer."

I made a rude noise. "Has that ever worked for you before?"

Her smile was completely reassuring, and completely unconvincing.

"It will eventually."

Most of what happened after that is lost somewhere in a haze of pain, confusion, and despair. She asked me how Pete had died, but I didn't want to answer and she patted my hand and said that was fine because she'd help me. Then she started talking in her honey-smooth voice, explaining to me some ridiculous scenario in which I had arranged Pete's assassination.

"He wouldn't take care of the unclass," she said, not making it a question. "When you asked him to eliminate the unclass designation he laughed at you," her voice was sympathetic, sad. "He said that was never going to happen. Of course you were angry, Jacob. If you were going to protect your little girl, you had to do something, didn't you?"

"No," I croaked. The face in front of me wavered and fuzzed. Pete. No. Maybe.

"She's half-unclass too, and you were so afraid for her. You knew he had to die, even though you loved him. Any father would have done the same."

"No. I didn't, Pete. You have to believe me."

I became pain.

I don't know how long it was before I became aware of the voice again. "Oh, Jacob, I'm so sorry. Help me, and we'll get this over with."

"I'm trying," I gulped. "I'm telling you the truth, Pete, I swear. I wouldn't have hurt you. Never." A squeaked sob choked me. "I love you. Please. You have to believe me."

"No, Jacob. Think. You killed him."

"I didn't! I didn't, Pete. I didn't."

"Again."

Jacob Dawes fell away.

"Oh Jake," the voice said, and maybe it was Jonathan. "All these lies. Wouldn't Pete be so disappointed?"

"No." There was hardly any voice left. "Stubborn," I managed.

"Stubborn. That's what he'd say." I could hear in his voice, laced with amusement and affection. *Stubbornest man I know.*

I fell into the pain with a smile on my face.

I woke in a cell. I wasn't in pain, not exactly. I trembled all over. On the small table bolted to the floor by my bed was a cup of water. I spilled most of it just trying to lift it to my mouth. There was food, and it didn't even look horrible, but it felt like too much effort.

Sometimes I slept, and sometimes the door opened and they dragged me out of my cell and into that room. I never knew how long I was in there, or how long before they brought me back. There was only pain, confusion, those horrible words, and the desperation to make Pete believe I hadn't done it.

Owen had another bad dream last night?

I thought you were asleep.

I was. Until you got up.

You should have slept. You haven't been getting enough
sleep lately.

And whose fault is that?

You didn't enjoy it?

Now there's a stupid question.

iv 49

I woke to the quiet sounds of someone moving around
my room and for a while I lay there, listening, wondering
why it didn't sound quite right and if Pete had gotten up
early for some reason. I opened my eyes to find the gray
ceiling of the palace prison. I closed them again.

"Your Highness?"

I was too weak to startle. I opened my eyes again and when
I turned my head I saw Sam. He was kneeling by my bed, and I
wondered why he didn't just get a chair. There was something
odd about his face, his expression. His eyes were too bright.
His face trembled, and for a moment I thought they must
have been torturing him as well. I blinked at him.

"Please, Your Highness," he said, leaning closer, moving his hand as if to take mine but he stopped. "Please. Just say whatever they want. Please."

I stared at him for a long time. "Why?"

"Because they've already won. They're going to kill you either way. Why should you suffer?"

I managed more of a wiggle than a shake of my head. "No."

"Why? Why does it matter now? Is it the children?" He looked around. He knew the room was monitored as much as I did so I wondered who the performance was for. He put his head in his hands as if he would cry, but with his face covered he continued in a harsh whisper. "We'll make sure they know the truth. We won't let them believe that about you. We'll tell them all the good things." He raised his face. "They're too young to understand."

I shook my head. "Pete."

"He's not here anymore to know the difference!"

I sighed. It was surprisingly easy, as if I wanted nothing more than to blow out all my breath and let it go.

"I know. That's why."

I spent many years at the secret and clandestine work of treason, but I'd always been the puppet master. I never expected to be the puppet.

iv50

It was late evening the next day before we came in sight of Imperial City. We approached it from a vantage I'd never seen before. The sight of the city wasn't the magnificent towers and skyscrapers I associated with it. They were there but in the background, smudged with the drabness of the lesser buildings and the necessary but hidden functions of the city.

Imperial City didn't have a slum, but there was some unclass housing on the fringes. I was sure Lady Chou would take us there, but we passed through and into the middle class section of the city. She didn't stop until she was well into it, but still not near the high class area. We pulled into the garage of what I could only assume was a standard home for the middle class. The door shut behind us, followed by two thunks of bolts sliding into place. I didn't think that was standard for this place.

She led us into the house through a door that was also locked. She entered a code and swiped her thumb but told me to allow it to read my scanner instead. "You don't have access," she said, "but with me here, and proof that you're bound to us, it'll pass you through. Don't leave the house without me, though, because you won't be able to get back in."

"Lady Chou—"

She rounded on me. "I don't trust you. I'll help you so long as I think you're useful and not going to betray us. But you'll get no considerations from me."

She swung around, gesturing to what looked like a kitchen. "There's food in the fridge though I doubt you have any clue how to use a stove so don't try to cook anything. There's a vid with limited access in the office and you can take any bedroom upstairs that I'm not in. Right now I need sleep. Just so you know, the windows are treated and soundproofed. No one outside can hear or see you, so don't try anything."

"Does limited access mean I can get information, or contact anyone?" I asked sardonically, sure of the answer I would get.

"No. You can watch the official channels," she said with a look of amusement. "They're stunningly uninformative, but, you never know, you might learn something from what they don't say."

With that she turned her back on me and went upstairs.

She hadn't been exaggerating the limits on my access. I could watch the regular programming and news channels, but I could only do a search of data that had already been dumped into the house's main database. I had no ability to access any messages sent to me and I couldn't send messages out. I found listings of several restaurants in the area that delivered but I couldn't call any of them.

I wandered into the kitchen to find what food I could eat. There were cold cuts and cheese in the fridge, and some crackers and dried fruits in the pantry. I ate. And then, with no other options, I found an adequate bedroom and slept.

I woke to the sound of someone moving around downstairs and the smell of coffee. I entered the kitchen to find Lady Chou at the stove, cooking something that smelled much like bacon and eggs. She was wearing the clothes from the day before but her hair was mussed from sleep. I nearly laughed aloud at the common domesticity of the scene. As if we were anything like that in any stretch of the imagination.

She turned when I entered and gestured curtly to a pot on the counter. "There's coffee." I nodded thanks and, after trial and error, found a mug for it. I would have preferred sugar too, but it wasn't immediately obvious and I didn't want to make a fool of myself hunting around for it in a place I clearly knew nothing about.

"How do you like your eggs?" she said, almost as if it pained her.

"Over easy, please." She jerked and gave me an odd look. Was it because I'd said please? "I'm not really the boor you think I am."

She snorted. "What I have observed might not be what you'd think, Duke Blaine."

I wondered if I should consider it a good sign that she gave me any title at all, or if it was a bad sign because she chose one I didn't really have anymore, certainly not the last one I'd been given. I almost laughed at myself. I was anything but the emperor now.

"Is there any news since last night?"

She stiffened. She was silent so long I began to think she wouldn't answer. "Prince Jacob has been captured. He's being held in the palace prison. There are rumors about Jonathan, but nothing confirmed."

"The rumors?"

"That he's dead."

My heart dropped. This was going to be so much harder without Dawes playing the hero and the diversion, and Jonathan managing everything, especially Dawes. I refused to consider that I might dislike that news for any other reason.

We spent the day in the house. Lady Chou sat at the vid, reading and cursing. She sent and received communications, but didn't choose to share them with me. I grew increasingly frustrated.

"What about Owen?" I demanded.

"Owen is safe," she snapped. "Owen has always been safe. He should be the least of your worries right now. You can do nothing for him so long as Laudley holds the empire."

"Owen will never be the least of my concerns."

She gave me an odd look, as if seeing me for the first time. She shrugged and went back to the console.

I switched on a vid in the main family room and tried to settle myself long enough to watch the news channel. What I found instead was a documentary of the life of the Grand Duke Laudley that had superseded programming on every channel.

He was painted in glowing terms. His accomplishments on his home planet were embellished or made up, his dealings with the royal family were reduced to mere misunderstandings and lack of regular contact sufficient to nurture deep friendships rather than outright antagonism. His place in Owen's life after my "execution," and his relationship with the Imperial Family was painted as all but idyllic, and affectionate, with the glaring exception of Prince Jacob.

For the most part they ignored Dawes' accusations against Laudley in the illicit broadcast, instead simply painting grand pictures of the exact opposite. Those that were more difficult to counteract indirectly were mentioned and refuted with obfuscations and outright lies. The program concluded with a scene of Laudley, Owen, and Molly playing together, supposedly only the day before. It was beautifully done, and completely fabricated.

Most viewers probably wouldn't see the subtle things that were off, the way they never quite interacted directly. There were certainly no hugs or affectionate touches. Someone had put this together out of stock footage and some creative additions, but it would look very convincing to anyone who didn't know better.

When it was over, I sat staring at the moving images on the vid, unseeing. Lady Chou entered the room.

"Was any of that true?"

I shook my head, not looking at her. "There were bits of truth scattered in there, most of it out of context so that it looked like something it wasn't. Some of what he did for his own duchy on Torrea is true, though his motives were rarely as virtuous as they ascribed to him. The benefits to the common classes were side effects, not motivations."

I saw her nod once out of the corner of my eye. I sighed. "People will believe it."

"People will believe a lot of things," she said. "In general they believe the one who yells loudest and most often, but also the one with the story they want to believe."

"And which do you think that is?"

Her mouth thinned and she shook her head. "That depends."

"On?"

"On whether we can rescue Prince Jacob or not."

As if in answer to her, a broadcast alert sounded. We turned in unison to the vid as the imperial seal appeared. I tensed.

Citizens of the empire, Naganika said, his image replacing the seal. *I am happy to bring you the news of the capture of the traitor, the former Prince Jacob. His treasonous and pernicious lies will no longer assault our loyal citizens.*

His expression was an admirable semblance of sadness. *His supposed 'liberation' two days from now, when he would have called together other traitors to attempt to bring down the empire from within, will not succeed. No one will stand with him because we stand with the empire.*

Those loyal members of the ISS who risked their lives to bring him to justice deserve our deepest gratitude. Two days from now, when you might otherwise have gathered in your homes to make clear your intention to separate yourselves from any who would plot treason, we will instead gather in every city, the loyal citizens of the Empire, and watch as Prince Jacob is brought to trial and made to answer for crimes of sedition and an attempted coup, and also the murder of the emperor, a crime he has already confessed to.

He bowed his head as if mourning anew the tragedy. I scoffed in disgust. Lady Chou gave me a funny look.

Long live the empire!

I cast her a meaningful glance. "As if that sentence doesn't say everything."

She raised a brow. "He has to say what Laudley will approve, or he loses his access and influence."

I couldn't help but laugh. "You still think he's on your side?"

"*My* side? Not ours?" She sneered. "Of course. He plays a dangerous game, but he has always helped us."

I shook my head in disgust. "You don't know the half of it. If he has a side, it's his own. He's not loyal to anyone. Certainly not the Resistance."

She scowled. "You're wrong—"

"I was the emperor! You think I didn't see and hear things you couldn't come near in your wildest dreams? He's not on your side, Lady Chou. He'd betray you in a heartbeat. How do you think they got to Dawes?"

"There are always risks in an underground operation. Someone betrayed us, but it wasn't him." Her voice crackled with anger but less certainty.

I looked away, disgusted with her naivete. "You're wrong. He's played you, probably for a long time. He's played all of us." I looked at the vid that now showed some scene from an old movie. "If anyone is winning now, it's him." Sudden hope lit in my chest. I rounded on her. "Did he know about my plans?"

She frowned. "What plans? Other than dragging me down and trying to sell me your lies?"

I grinned. "You don't know. I only told Jonathan and Dawes." I laughed. "It's still safe." I whirled around, dashing to the vid. "Get me some access, woman, I have things to do."

You have no idea how much I miss you.

Yes, I do.

iv.51

P ain. Sleep. More pain.

I was lying on the bed in my cell, just slipping away from a sleep I didn't want to leave when a guardsman entered the room. He carried a tray of food and set it on the small table.

"How long have I been here?" I managed. He stopped, not looking at me but not leaving either.

"Three days," he said. I closed my eyes tight. And then, so quiet I wasn't even sure I heard it he said, "Your Highness." The door shut behind him.

I turned my face to the wall. There was something I was trying not to think about. "I'm sorry, Pete," I sobbed. I couldn't even remember what for. "I'm so sorry."

The door opened, light from the hallway flooding the room. I blinked into the brightness, blocking it with my hand up in front of my face. It was Pete standing in the doorway. He stormed into the room.

I sat up, sucking in a breath, the whole room wobbling around me before I could focus again. And when I did, I found Naganika standing there, looking down at me. I wasn't sure what look was on his face. Was that pity? Disgust? For the strangest moment I thought perhaps it was pride, or even regret.

I'd thought it was Pete. I wanted Pete.

"Children are so adaptable," Naganika said, as if we'd been having a conversation. I just blinked at him.

"Molly's already coming around. She smiled at Laudley this morning, though she's still a bit shy around him. Owen is helping her. He's just happy to have his grandpa back and to be home and safe. It's amazing how little it takes and they just do everything you ask." His mouth twisted in a funny smile. I watched him, stunned. When I didn't react, he shrugged as if unsurprised and left the cell, closing the door behind him.

I lay on the bed, staring up at the ceiling, and started laughing. I covered my face with my hands and laughed into palms that were still wet from sweat and tears. Did he have any idea what a gift he'd just given me?

He was lying. My Molly, who could throw a two day tantrum over a dress? Owen, who was fiercely protective of his family and so careful with his trust? No, they weren't won over so easily. I had no idea why he'd said it, why he'd thought I would believe it.

The door opened again and the guards hauled me off the bed and down the hall. I closed my eyes. My children hadn't given in.

So neither did I.

It might have been a day or an hour later. I came out of the pain and lay for some time, disoriented and confused. I wasn't in my cell, but Anna wasn't talking to me in her velvety-vicious voice. The technicians weren't unstrapping me, either, or removing receptors while guards waited to take me back to my cell. I didn't bother trying to sit up—I could barely breathe after a session—but by turning my head just slightly I could see that the door to the corridor was open. Just outside, Naganika stood, angled away from me, talking to someone. His voice carried into the room.

"It could be any day now."

"Day?" a voice demanded. It sounded like Laudley, or maybe I just thought it did. It was so hard to tell.

"Or hour. They thought they were close this morning, and then he regressed."

"Why is it taking so long?"

"Because a real noble would have broken by now, but he's an unclass and too stupid to know what he's supposed to do?" Naganika's voice was cut off by the sound of an openhanded blow. He rocked backward for a moment, silent until he steadied himself. "Forgive me, Your Excellence. My sarcasm was out of place."

"You are out of time," Laudley snarled. "It is already past midnight. I want him at my feet and begging to confess."

"I know, Your Excellence. We're doing our best. We may have to consider giving up on getting a confession and use a more smoke-and-mirrors approach."

"Which everyone now knows is how Rikhart hid the fact that Blaine wasn't executed. There has to be something public. Dawes has called them all out to be part of something. I intend to give it to them." Suddenly, as if it just occurred to him, he protested, "Why are we having this conversation here?"

Naganika's head turned and before I could look away, he met my gaze squarely and held it. He turned back to Laudley. "He can't hear us."

I lay there, weak and stunned.

"Get back to work, Anna," Laudley said. "Or perhaps we will see if some personal experience with the machine will teach you how to use it more effectively."

Her reply was stiff but clear. "Yes, Your Excellence."

There were sounds of movement and quiet talking and I lay there with my eyes closed, wishing I could just disappear.

"Prince Jacob?" I didn't want my eyes to open and see Naganika, but for some reason, they did anyway. "There's an easy way to end all this," he said, soft and kind. I'd have punched him if I could have moved. "Laudley's given them a deadline but that still means they can zap you with that thing five more times. Is all this struggle really worth that?"

I blinked. He shook his head sadly, turning to glance at Anna as she entered the room. "Oh well," he said to himself as he walked out. "I tried."

I just stared at the empty space where he'd been. Five times.

I only had to hold out five more times. I started to cry and Anna smiled at me, a look of fake compassion meant to hide her relief.

"You see, Jacob. It's too hard. We don't have to do this anymore. Don't worry, we'll stop now. Why don't you just tell me the story and we'll leave this room right away and never come back."

Only five more times. I smiled at her.

"Go to hell."

I have come to conclude that I'm a better actor than I realized. Also that I hate acting more than I ever imagined.

iv52

I concentrated on my tablet and on not meeting the eyes of my fellow passengers without appearing unfriendly or out of place. The servant I was impersonating had been at the palace long enough to be trusted, but not so long that he was familiar to everyone. Still, while the blinder could mimic his looks, even his fingerprints and retinas if they were on file, they couldn't mimic his mannerisms.

His name was Niel and he was a member of the Resistance. He'd been away from the palace since shortly after the emperor's death, supposedly spending time with family off-planet in the wake of the tragedy. Where he really was I didn't know, but I had studied all the data on him and watched all the available recordings on which he appeared and now I had to play the part as well as I could.

In only a few hours it would be daylight, and through some coordination by the Resistance all over the empire, the gatherings were to begin at dawn in Imperial City.

I wished I could believe I wasn't afraid. I was, and the more I thought about it, the more I realized that wasn't just understandable, it was smart. I was no stranger to the covert and illegal, but my part had always been played out behind the scenes.

It's one thing to practice treason in the dark and present an innocent face in the light; it's quite another to put on a disguise and walk into the lion's den.

My protections were flimsy and few. If the device I wore and the part I tried to play were exposed, I was completely powerless. I didn't even have Dawes' curiously powerful shield of popular opinion. My safety had always rested on power and wealth and position, born to, strengthened, and perpetuated by the status quo. Laudley had destroyed that, not only for me but for all of us. He'd taken our splendor and separateness and made it something cheap and gaudy; exposed it for the transparent, baseless lie it was.

I felt like a traitor even thinking that, but when I examined the emotion further, it tasted suspiciously like wounded pride.

The transport came to a stop and the other servants returning to the palace began to disembark. I hung back. I'd considered hiding myself in the middle of all of them, hoping the crowd would conceal me, but we'd all have to be singled out for scans before we made it through the door and I decided it was safer to have as few people around to watch me as possible. This wasn't my area of expertise. At least, I thought wryly, I had the years of experience on Dead End to draw from. Duke Blaine the noble wouldn't have had the first clue how to do something like this.

I tried to hide how carefully I watched as the others were checked and cleared. It seemed no more than a quick scan of hand and retinas and more or less friendly banter with the guards passing them in. I wondered if the undercurrent of tension was just my imagination. I wasn't used to noticing the servants, or even seeing them. But I didn't imagine they'd always been this keyed up when they were serving me. The nervous tension in the air was like a noxious smell.

I stepped up to the empty scanner.

"Back early, Niel?" the guard said.

I shrugged, keeping my eye on the pad where my hand lay, watching it flash green. "As if I'd be anywhere but here today," I replied, hoping to sound casual.

He laughed but there was little humor in it. "I don't think there's any good place in the empire to be today." He glanced at the results of my retina scan and nodded me through.

On the other side I took a deep breath, dizzy with relief, and stopped to orient myself. I knew the nobles' area of the palace well, but not the servants' passages. I tried to reconcile the map Lady Chou had given me with my own recollections and finally took the passage to the left, hoping I was right.

I began to pass identical doors, each labeled in the servants' code, so that anyone here without authorization would have to guess where each door led. But I'd been given this information too.

I only backtracked once, and tried to look as if I had simply gotten distracted, if there were any cameras on me, before I found the right door.

I entered the playroom connecting Owen's room to Princess Marquilla's, more nervous than I could remember being before. About anything at all.

The children turned at the sound of the door. Owen subtly moved Princess Marquilla behind him. She clutched his hand and glared at me hard enough to bruise.

"We'd like to leave the room now," Owen said, steady and clear and with a tinge of weariness, as if this were a script that had been repeated again and again.

"Of course, Prince Owen," keeping my voice neutral with effort.

His eyes widened as if the request had been purely for form, as if he hadn't even considered I'd say yes. He recovered with a maturity and aplomb that made me long to go to him. He looked so like Hera. He nodded, the prince expressing approval and the proper amount of gratitude to a servant.

"Please take us to see Prince Jacob," he said.

I stifled any reaction, but I was taken aback that he'd even known Dawes was in the palace. I cut a quick glance at the servants and guards in the room. Which one was it? I was certain it was no part of Laudley's plan that the children should know Dawes was there while his head was still connected to his shoulders. I bowed the proper deference.

"Right away, Your Highness."

His eyes went even wider, his hand clenching around Princess Marquilla's.

"Thank you," he said, his voice hoarse, and finally I saw the boy behind the mask of calm and maturity. If I hadn't known what reaction I was likely to get, I would have dropped my disguise right there, taken him in my arms.

My son.

How had I ever believed anything in the universe was more important than this?

The other servants were glancing among themselves, clearly confused by this sudden change of direction.

"Niel—"

It was Sabria. The informants hadn't been clear on whether Laudley had given her the position with Owen again. If she was here, Laudley must not know, or care, that she was the one who knew I went to the safehouse, and who was going to trigger the return mechanism for me. I approached and stood before her, watching her intensely, begging her to understand.

"Hello, Sabria," I said, letting my assumed voice slip a little. "I meant to send you a message while I was away, but someone unexpected came to visit and I wasn't able to."

She frowned, her eyes searching my face. "I wasn't expecting to see you here now."

"Yes," I nodded. "I know."

After a long moment of silence, our eyes locked, she gave me the slightest nod. "Our orders were to keep the children here for the day," she said.

"I have new orders."

"Very well."

The servants began to prepare the children. One servant moved to straighten Princess Marquilla's hair. She batted the servant's hand away and glared at her. The woman backed off, giving me a look of exasperation and exhaustion. Part of me wanted to smile.

The princess had all the determination of one father and all the fiery spirit of the other. It was a good combination, for this young woman in particular. She'd need it.

Without prompting, Owen smoothed his hands down his jacket, making no protest when a servant ran a brush quickly through his hair. He took Princess Marquilla's hand and faced me. "We're ready."

Thank you for marrying me.

You already said that.

I mean it twice.

You're such a sap. I love you.

iv53

When the fifth jolt ceased as suddenly as they all had, I began to laugh. It quickly turned into sobs of relief.

"You were supposed to clean him up." Sam's voice dragged my head up and I found him standing there, at the head of his guard, looking down at me in disgust.

"There was no time," Anna snapped, hard and bitter. "We had to work until the very end."

"So he's not ready?"

She looked pale. "No."

Sam met my eye, still examining me as if I were an unknown specimen. "Well, the Grand Duke won't be happy, but we've a plan for it anyway."

He held out his hand and one of the guards dropped something into it. "If he's not going to say what they want him to, he's not saying anything." He stepped close, placing a tiny, skin-colored patch, no bigger than a fingernail, on my jaw behind my ear. He held up a remote device for me to see. When he activated it, a low tingling began to itch under my skin. I opened my mouth to protest but my mouth didn't open.

He jerked his head at two of his men. "Get him ready."

They fitted the restraints on my arms and legs. Sam told two guards to carry me, but when he saw I could walk he just shrugged and led the way. We passed out of the prison and into the palace corridors. A moment's deja vu caught my memory and I chuckled. Sam frowned at me, pulling the remote from his pocket and flicking it. The tingling in my face stopped and I opened my jaw in relief.

"Did you have something to say, Your Highness?"

I laughed again. "Yeah. I was just thinking that you and I have done this before, Sam." He looked away.

"I serve my emperor."

"Yes. I respect that about you."

He gave me a sideways look, as if not sure how to take that. "Thank you," I said. He looked away before I did, and activated the device again.

They brought me in by way of the front doors, parading me down the length of the throne room. Laudley sat in a chair beside the throne, his expression haughty and gloating. I looked around at all of the assembled spectators as we passed. Some watched, some didn't. None met my eye. They brought me to a stop in front of Laudley and shoved me to my knees.

He eyed me, a smile twitching at his mouth and shining in his eyes. I watched as he tried to sober his expression.

"Ahh, Jacob," he said. "I wish I could say it is a pleasure to see you again. But I am afraid it is profoundly distressing. I have dreaded the day I would have to look into the face of a man I trusted, who took good care of my grandson, and see the face of a murderer." He sighed. "A man who would murder his emperor, his own husband."

He shook his head. "I must say, it is impressive that you managed to avoid the imperial security forces so long. You must have been building up this network of informers, traitors, and bolt holes for some time. Tell me, Jacob, how long had you been planning to kill the emperor?"

I would have dearly loved to have been able to speak. At the same time, I was almost grateful to Sam for the blocker. I had a bad record when it came to situations like this. I stared him down, not flinching. He looked away and spread his arms wide.

"You planned quite an event to celebrate the birthday of the emperor you murdered. All over the empire! And, while I thought Lord Naganika understood the instructions to direct the people to celebrate in their homes today," he cast a withering glare at Naganika, "because I would hate for loyal citizens to be caught up in any unrest you have planned, this might well work out best for everyone.

"The traitors will be identified, bringing themselves willingly to where our forces wait for them, but also serving as proof for the loyal. They will see with their very eyes that the empire will always protect them and never countenance such treason."

He nodded to Naganika. "Shall we watch?"

Naganika gestured to a man standing nearby and projection vids began to appear all around the room. On each one was a view of a different city center, some sparsely populated with a nervous crowd, some packed and overflowing, the air vibrant and restless. Surrounding each of them was a wall of armed ISS troops. My face stiffened. Of course, I'd prepared myself for that to happen, but I was supposed to be there. Pete talked about the power of symbols.

Some symbol I made now.

Laudley grinned at me like a predator. "Now, let us see what we can do."

His image appeared in the bottom corner of every screen, and in each city, a projection of him came alive on each side of the crowd.

"Citizens of the empire," he said. "Do not be afraid. The soldiers are there for your protection. The traitor prince tried to fool you, but rest assured, I understand that in this time of tragedy and crisis it was easy to misunderstand and become confused. Those of you who peacefully surrender now will be granted forgiveness and amnesty from your imperial ruler. You will allowed to go home."

The people in the crowds began to look around at each other. No one moved.

"Your cause is futile," he continued, and the view expanded to include me on my knees before him, shackled and silenced. I glared at him, but it was a powerless gesture. "The day is already lost."

In what looked like Mexico City there was a stir near the steps of the governor's residence, gasps and cries as the people pulled back to allow someone to emerge from the crowd and climb to the top step. It was me.

"Citizens of the empire!" he shouted. I knew that voice and shivered hard all over. "I am not Prince Jacob." With a shimmer, the image of me disappeared and Jonathan stood in my place. I wanted to cry with relief and at the same time yell at him for turning his shield off.

"Citizens of the empire," he repeated, his voice quieter but pitched to carry over the watching crowd. Around the throne room, the vids blinked and Jonathan filled them all. Laudley froze.

"What is happening?"

Naganika looked pale. "I don't know, Your Grace."

"Find out!"

Naganika left the room, gesturing for several other men to follow him.

"I am not Prince Jacob," Jonathan said again. "Though I am honored he sent me here to speak on his behalf." There were hundreds of ISS within range of him but no one moved.

"He would have been here today, but," he gestured to the screens that still showed the image of Laudley and me, "he cannot. The Grand Duke Laudley murdered our emperor, kidnapped the royal children, and now he has taken and tortured Prince Jacob, with the goal of forcing him to confess falsely to the murder of the emperor and husband he loved."

In the opposite corner of each screen, images of the other cities appeared again. They watched on their own vids as the tableau played out. In one of them, another me ascended the steps of the mayor's mansion.

"I am not Prince Jacob," he said, deactivating the blinder that had projected my image. "We all are."

"I am not Prince Jacob." In another city, a woman appeared. "We all are."

"I am not Prince Jacob." Like the chorus of a children's song sung in the round, the declarations sounded and echoed across the vids, in city after city. I was fighting tears. I glanced at Laudley. His face was red.

"Stop them!" he shouted.

In a city I didn't recognize, a soldier stepped forward and began to fire into the crowd. People shrieked and screamed and began to scatter, but another soldier tackled him from behind, wrenching the gun out of his hands. He pointed the gun at the man on the ground. I couldn't hear what he said, but the guard who had started the shooting didn't try to get up.

It was only one such scene. In some places the soldiers began shooting into the crowd and the people scattered. I saw at least one "Prince Jacob" crumple to the ground. In other cities, the people rushed the soldiers, disarming them before a shot could be fired.

In some, the ISS forces raised their hands, surrendering their guns to the first citizen in range. It was chaos, and at times I wasn't sure who was winning. I kept my eyes locked on Jonathan. Stupid, brave, beloved Jonathan who had turned his shield off and was standing above the crowd, a perfect target.

Jonathan, who stared straight at me and said, "Don't worry, Prince Jacob, we're coming for you."

Do you think she'll be born at night or in the morning?

Or in the afternoon?

That, too.

Does it matter?

Do you think we can do this?

Bit late to be asking that now.

iv54

Somewhere in the back of my attention I realized Laudley was screaming.

"Turn them off. Turn them off!" White faced palace officials were scrambling, looking befuddled and afraid. The vids didn't change.

Gasps began to ripple through the room and I turned my head to see Owen and Molly running toward me. Molly threw her arms around me so hard that only the steadying hand of the guard kept me upright.

"Daddy!" She cried hot tears into my neck. My arms were still shackled in front of me, trapped between us, but I bent my head over hers, cheek against cheek, and breathed in the scent of my little girl. She squeezed harder until I almost couldn't breathe. Then, with a jerk, she pulled away from me and rushed Laudley.

He sat unmoving, wide eyed, as people scrambled to get out of the way of their princess, a darting, determined midget. She slammed into him, pounding her fists on his knees, tears streaming down her face.

"You're a bad man and I hate you!" she screamed, flailing at him like a furious tornado. "Let my daddy go!"

Laudley was watching her, thin lipped, his expression dark. She punched his leg one last time before she rushed back to me, throwing her arms around my neck, burying her face in my shoulder.

"I'm sorry, Daddy. I'm sorry," she gasped around a huge sniffle. "Papa would have fixed it but I don't know how. I don't know how!"

I looked up at Sam. His expression was hard as stone. His hand went to his pocket and he produced the remote for the silencing device. He held it up for me to see and then dropped it. With a tinkling like chimes it hit the marble floor and he stepped on it, his heavy boot muffling the crunch. The tingling in my jaw stopped suddenly and my mouth nearly dropped open. I levered myself to my feet and turned to a guard behind me, holding out my hands.

"Dhal, will you unlock these please?"

Without a moment's hesitation, the guard activated the release and the restraints fell away. He knelt to remove the leg shackles as well.

"Thank you," I said.

Still kneeling before me, Dhal said, "It's my honor, Your Highness. Long live the empress."

I searched for Owen. He was standing a little off to the side, behind Molly, pale, his lips pinched together. I rushed the few steps between us and gathered him in my arms, pulling Molly in too.

"Owen," I breathed into his hair. He was trembling. "I told you I'd come for you." He threw his arms around me, head-butting me in the stomach he hugged me so hard. I just squeezed back. "I'll always come for you."

"What are they doing here!" Laudley's voice was a pale echo in the background that didn't intrude on my moment. "I ordered them kept away!"

A servant came to stand before me. "I'm glad you made it, Dawes."

I grinned, searching his face and knowing it for what it was.

"Thank you. I suppose I have you to thank for bringing the children?" He smiled, and the image dissolved, revealing Blaine standing before me.

My triumphal return to the palace was far less triumphal and much more a return than I ever expected.

iv**55**

Gasps and startled cries filled the room. I found Laudley, his expression hard and murderous.

"Enough," I said, clear and steady. "It's over, Laudley."

Laudley laughed. "And yet look where I sit, Blaine, and where you stand." He jerked a nod at the guards. "Take him."

No one moved. Dawes glanced back at the guard captain, who met his gaze and held it. Something passed between them that I didn't understand.

"Thank you," Dawes said to him.

The guard captain bowed his head. "Your Highness."

I approached Laudley, registering the way Dawes stepped up beside me, the princess clutching his hand with both of hers. Owen stood on the other side of her, farthest from me, and I refused to be distracted by what that might mean.

"You've lost, Laudley," I said, gesturing to the crowd of assembled nobles and other observers. "They've all seen. They understand now that you've been lying to them. I don't think any one of them will be surprised when I produce the proof that you orchestrated the murder of the emperor. They see now what the children already knew, that you're, to quote the princess, a 'bad man.'"

He scoffed. "Children."

"You can speak so disrespectfully of your future sovereign," I said, shaking my head. "Because you never intended for her to rule. How easily you give yourself away. I thought you were a better schemer than that. I suppose it's difficult watching it fall apart around you." For a moment I actually pitied him. "You killed an emperor for nothing. There's no way to manipulate your way into a throne anymore. You won't even be able to manipulate yourself out of a beheading now."

"Arrest him," Dawes said, his voice cold and quiet, but I doubt a person in the room missed it. The guards didn't hesitate, advancing on Laudley.

"Stop!" Laudley commanded, but he was ignored. They surrounded him, a man on each side taking an arm to haul him upright. "Unhand me!" There was a scuffle and suddenly I caught a clear glimpse of Laudley, a gun in his hand, pointed directly at Dawes.

"No!" The shout was loud in my ears. Everything happened as if time had frozen, and then kicked into overdrive. A blur passed in front of me just as the zing of an energy weapon registered. I looked down to find the guard captain lying at Dawes' feet, a hole charred in his uniform just above his heart. His eyes were locked on the prince.

Dawes fell to his knees beside him, gathering him close like a child. "Sam!"

Sam's reply was soft and strained. "Finally," he said.

"What are you talking about?" Dawes demanded, his voice cracking.

"It was always supposed to be me. All those times I failed." His breaths were harsh and stuttering. "I finally got it right." He groaned but held Dawes' gaze. "He would have approved, I think."

"Stop that. He never blamed you. Not for any of it."

"I know. He should have, though." His smile was just a flicker before he spasmed, his eyes rolling back. He went limp and still.

Dawes shook him. "Damn you!" he yelled, his voice cracking. "You can't die."

Princess Marquilla stood beside him, petting his hair again and again. "It's OK, Daddy. He was very brave."

Dawes looked up at Laudley, murderous hatred contorting his face. "Take him to the prison!"

Laudley struggled against the guards. "Do you really think this is over? You cannot win. Unclass scum and a tarnished noble who spent too long among them. Your dirty friends in the streets might make for a pretty show, but the power in the empire is here, and you two together are less than nothing. Do you think anyone with a history and bloodline and any pride will stand behind you?"

"I think," I said, "Grand Duke Laudley, that in matters of high treason the word of the empress is final. And she's made clear her opinion of you."

His face contorted in rage. "Fool!"

But if he said anything more, it was lost in the echoes as he was hauled from the room. I looked down at Dawes, still cradling the body of the guard captain, both children plastered to him. I didn't want to see but I forced myself not to turn away.

"We've won, Dawes. You and me together. Isn't life strange?"

I spent a lot of time alone in the days following Laudley's downfall. The world had been remade, and I with it. I needed to figure out what sort of man I was to be now.

iv.56

I quietly took a room in the Family Wing. I was offered a better one, but I asked for the one farthest from the emperor's rooms and was given it.

I didn't know what to do with myself. I was...alone. I didn't know what else I was or wasn't. I had no place, no purpose.

My son was with Dawes. That was his own choice. I hadn't asked him to do otherwise; I couldn't bear the fear in his eyes when he looked at me. I spent days cloistered with my loneliness and my fears. Then the message arrived.

I arrived an hour early for my appointment to meet my son. I stood on the beach watching the roll of the waves, wishing my nervousness could be so easily washed away. I began to set up my things and sat down to wait.

I'd allowed no servant to come with me, but I found the simple acts of unpacking my paints and brushes, and setting up the tripod and canvas soothing in their familiarity. I distracted myself with the soft scrape of brush on canvas, the kaleidoscope of colors on the palate, the sharp smell of the paints contrasting the salt-and-mineral smell of the sea.

Some sound or sensation alerted me to their presence and I turned to find Dawes and Owen standing nearby, watching me. Owen was holding Dawes' hand, not trailing behind him, exactly, but keeping Dawes between himself and me. I stood, locking my knees.

"Hello, Owen." The words came out in no more than a whisper. He was pale, watching me with his eyes wide, but his cheeks pinked, as if he understood how hard this was for me as well.

"We can come later if this is a bad time," Dawes said.

The words were ostensibly for me, but the way he angled his body and turned his head toward Owen made it clear he was giving the boy a way out if the reality of confronting the beast was more terrifying than he'd bargained for. My heart squeezed painfully.

"Is this a bad time, Owen?" I asked.

He shook his head without taking his eyes off me. Dawes examined me, his expression asking some question I didn't understand.

The words came tumbling out of me, as if I couldn't help myself. "You look so much like your mother. Has anyone ever told you that?"

He nodded, his hand tightening on Dawes'. I wiped my sweaty hands on my pants. Owen stepped closer and I froze, waiting, but he wasn't looking exactly at me.

"It's the shells."

I sat down again in front of my painting, giving us both something else to focus on and some relief from the awkwardness for a moment.

"Yes. It's not a faithful rendering, though."

I'd been painting the tiny bivalves at the edge of the water that submerged ahead of each wave, surfacing again when it passed only to burrow into the sand again before the next one. They were mostly blues and purples and faint yellows, but I'd painted them differently. Deep reds and vibrant oranges, bright yellows, crisp greens, shaded just right to contrast the rich blue of the water and the dark, damp sand.

"I like it better this way," he said. I opened my mouth to apologize but then I realized he was turned toward the painting, not the shells burrowing back into the sand beneath his bare toes.

"Thank you," I answered. "Do you like to draw?"

I saw him nod out of the corner of my eye. "Yes. And paint too."

"I hear you play music as well."

I believe he nodded again but I wouldn't allow myself to turn and look at him, for fear of frightening him away.

"Your mother played the piano."

He went very still. "Daddy told me."

My heart dropped at the name but I knew I was being foolish, thinking that would ever change.

"Sometimes, when I would paint," I said, "your mother would sit nearby playing the piano. They're some of the best memories I have."

"She played well?" he whispered.

"She played very well."

I turned and extended the palate and brush to him. "Would you like to try?"

He shook his head. "But can I watch?"

I released a long breath, what felt like the first I'd taken since he'd arrived.

"Yes, of course. I'd be very happy if you would."

I think I've decided what I'm going to wear to Owen's costume party.

Oh?

Yeah, I'm going to go as the Prince Consort.

Funny.

What? I'm good at playing that character.

iv.57

It was all very messy, in the end. I was used to the brutally efficient operation of the imperial government machine, but Laudley had been right about one thing: there were a lot of frightened and disillusioned nobles who saw me as a threat to their way of life. There weren't enough of them to stop the inevitable, but enough to make it a long few months. Laudley's wasn't the only head that rolled.

There were long weeks of negotiations, none of which mattered to me so much as the late night talks with Jonathan, sipping fine whiskey in the library, talking until the sun came up. I moved back into the emperor's rooms for a time. They asked me to. A powerful symbol, they said, with my daughter and almost-empress just down the hall. It was lonely without Pete.

The end result of all our public shows and private wrangling was that Molly was crowned empress, at the ripe old age of five, and engaged to be married to Owen. Blaine served as her regent.

Owen officially returned to being Blaine's son but he kept his old bedroom. He and Molly still shared a playroom. I wondered how long that would be allowed to last. Naganika returned to his home planet of Carolis. I never could decide which side he truly supported, but he'd done enough for our efforts to escape the block. He wasn't exiled formally, but he was largely ignored, which is its own exile, I suppose.

Blaine and I coexisted, though I don't think he was ever a friend. That was Jonathan. He kept his servant's room off of mine. I argued myself hoarse trying to convince and eventually force him to take a room of his own. I even made him a minor noble. He just ignored me. We had never been better friends.

Molly grew up under my inexpert parenting. I spent those years in fear of getting it wrong. I didn't know how to raise an empress. That was Pete's job. Jonathan suggested I simply raise a daughter instead.

When Blaine stepped aside for eighteen-year-old Molly to assume the throne alone, I cried, and I wasn't sure if it was joy or despair. Pete would have been proud of her. She was so beautiful and strong.

After that I slowly transitioned back to the IIC. Jonathan came with me. I'd been many things in my life. Impoverished and hungry in the slums, a scientist at the empire's own center for study and research, a convicted traitor and prisoner in a hard labor camp. I was also husband to an emperor and father to an empress.

But a scientist, and the IIC—this is what I always was, and where I always belonged.

Pete would have understood.

Transcript of the speech given by Empress Marquilla I at the funeral breakfast for Prince Jacob Dawes-Killearn.

$_{iv}E$

We're gathered here to remember my father, Prince Jacob Dawes-Killearn. And yet, first I'm going to share with you a story of my other father, Emperor Rikhart IV. I know Daddy wouldn't mind. In fact, if he were here, he'd tell me to stop after that.

Audience laughs.

Daddy never did learn to like the spotlight.

I have few memories of the emperor, my Papa, and many of them are no doubt created by stories I was told of him. But there is one I'm sure is my own. I was probably four and I had a bad dream, something about monsters. Papa took me—both of us in our nightclothes—to the throne room. He left most of the lights off and if there were even guards with us I couldn't see them. In my memory we're alone. He sat down on the throne, and put me on his lap, and proceeded to hold court. He called all the monsters to answer for their crimes and then banished them from the Empire forever.

As I contemplated the story I wanted to share, of the father I've recently lost, I was reminded of that night. You see, the first and only memory I considered sharing with you today also happened on a sleepless night.

I was sixteen or so. I must have been worrying about some problem or another too much to sleep. Daddy knew somehow, and he came to my room and invited me to walk the halls with him.

We walked for hours. He took me to parts of the palace I didn't even know existed. He had spent many years wandering the palace this way and he showed me places that he associated with one memory or another. "This is where I used to come when I first moved in with Pete." "This is the room I often sat in during the riots on Carolis."

As we walked, he told me stories of his life, stories I'd never heard before. He told me of his mother, his father, his sister, moments of his life in Abenez or at the IIC. The trivial, unimportant bits of life that we so easily discard. I'd only ever known him as a prince, an emperor's consort, the empress' father; and Daddy rarely talked of his past. But that night he relived his life for me. His triumphs and losses, his fears and joys. It was as if his whole life could be mapped out on a schematic of the palace. Sometimes his stories made me cry, sometimes we both cried, but there were beautiful moments too.

It occurred to me later that was one of the reasons my fathers were drawn to each other. Daddy was the one who could find all the monsters in the dark, and it was Papa who could vanquish them. But Daddy also found all the magical things in the hidden places where the emperor never would have gone without him.

I have often been called The People's Empress. If I have been so, it is because of my Daddy, perhaps even because of that night. *He* is why there are people of every class in this room, why every year we remember the day the people rose up and took back the empire as a triumph and not a rebellion, and why the lives of the lower classes in the empire have been substantially improved in ways we can measure and ways we never could.

The empire has truly lost something great, now that both of my fathers are dead. But if I live up to what they expected of me, then I will have succeeded as a person and as your empress. May they never be forgotten.

www.ingramcontent.com/pod-product-compliance
Lightning Source LLC
Chambersburg PA
CBHW022004010726
47494CB00003B/882